KU-503-359

SECRET LESSONS
WITH THE RAKE

Julia Justiss

MILLS &
BOON

Published in Great Britain 2017
by Mills & Boon, an imprint of HarperCollins*Publishers*
1 London Bridge Street, London, SE1 9GF

© 2017 Janet Justiss

ISBN: 978-0-263-92604-0

Our policy is to use papers that are natural, renewable and recyclable products and made from wood grown in sustainable forests. The logging and manufacturing processes conform to the legal environmental regulations of the country of origin.

Printed and bound in Spain
by CPI, Barcelona

Hadley's Hellions

*Four friends united by power, privilege
and the daring pursuit of passion!*

From being disreputable rogues at Oxford
to becoming masters of the political game,
Giles Hadley, David Tanner Smith,
Christopher Lattimar and Benedict Tawny
live by their own set of *unconventional* rules.

But as the struggle for power heats up so too
do the lives of these daring friends. They
face unexpected challenges to their long-held
beliefs and rigid self-control when they meet
four gorgeous independent women
with defiant streaks of their own…

Read Giles Hadley's story in
Forbidden Nights with the Viscount

Read David Tanner Smith's story in
Stolen Encounters with the Duchess

Read Benedict Tawny's story in
Convenient Proposal to the Lady

Available now!

This is the final book in **Hadley's Hellions**,
Christopher Lattimar's story:
Secret Lessons with the Rake

526 220 49 0

Author Note

It's difficult for the modern reader to understand how limited the world was for a 'gently born' nineteenth-century girl. Her sole occupational choice was marriage, her behaviour was held to an exacting standard, and any serious lapse of conduct meant permanent exile from her class and her family.

Cast into the demi-monde, my heroine must survive in a world for which she's had no preparation. Ellie Parmenter is particularly grateful for the friendship of a scandalous matron of her own class—and for her son, who treats Ellie like the lady she was when she was born. When the opportunity arises to repay that kindness by teaching Christopher Lattimer how to court a girl with the wealth and connections to advance his Parliamentary career she welcomes it—even though success will mean terminating her association with the man who's become so dear to her.

Christopher realises it's time to end his wandering ways and take a wife, as all his friends have. But after an adulthood spent among the demi-monde he knows nothing about how to behave around a proper young virgin. Though he'd rather woo the lovely and now available Ellie, an affair with a famous courtesan might harm his career—and marrying her is impossible.

But love has a way of breaking all the rules…

I hope you'll enjoy Christopher and Ellie's story.

Julia Justiss wrote her ideas for Nancy Drew stories in her third-grade notebook, and has been writing ever since. After publishing poetry in college she turned to novels. Her Regency historical romances have won or been placed in contests by the Romance Writers of America, *RT Book Reviews*, National Readers' Choice and the Daphne du Maurier Award. She lives with her husband in Texas. For news and contests visit juliajustiss.com.

Who else could I dedicate my 'son and dog' story to but Eve Gaddy? Brainstorming and critique partner, conference travelling buddy and friend who has shared so much of this up-and-down writer's journey with me. You're the best.

Prologue

London—March 26th, 1832

Laughing and energised, Christopher Latti-mar, Member of Parliament for Wiltshire, led his friends into the small private room at the Quill and Gavel, a tavern on a quiet street near the Houses of Parliament. 'Time to celebrate our achievement. I'd say it's a night for wine, women and song!'

'Or at least wine and women,' Ben Tawny agreed with a grin.

'Two of my favourite things,' Christopher said.

'As we well know,' Ben replied.

'You should,' Christopher tossed back. 'Since until recently, you outdid me in enjoying both.'

'Enough, you two,' Giles Hadley, Viscount Lyndlington, said with a mock frown. 'Ah, here's Ransen with some ale. Though, given the momentousness of the achievement, Ben, you might have ordered champagne.'

'Too French!' Ben replied. 'To celebrate the first change in four hundred years in the way Parliamentary representatives are chosen, we needed good English ale.'

'We're not there yet,' David Tanner Smith cautioned as he deposited his tall frame into a chair. 'The Third Reform Bill only passed the House today. We've still got to get it through the Lords.'

'After all the riots and dissention when the Second Bill failed last autumn, the Lords wouldn't dare oppose it now,' Giles said. 'The country won't stand for any further delay!'

'We'll see,' Davie replied. 'Still, getting it passed in the House *was* a momentous achievement.' Grabbing a mug from the tray the innkeeper left for them, he lifted it high. 'To Lord Grey's leadership!'

'And to yours,' Ben said, raising his mug to Davie. 'We provided the agitation, but you honed the bill's provisions.'

'I think we should drink to us all,' Christopher said. 'Who would have imagined ten years ago that four Oxford misfits would band together, win seats in Parliament, and help bring about the biggest change in British government since the

Middle Ages?' He raised his mug. 'To my dear colleagues and best friends. To the Hellions!'

'To the Hellions,' the others echoed, and downed a long draught.

'Shall we talk strategy?' Davie proposed. 'Draw up a list of which peers are most likely to be persuaded, and decide the best arguments to sway them?'

'We shall—but not tonight,' Giles said. 'Let's just enjoy this first victory. Speaking of which…' he paused to drain his mug and set it on the table '… I'm afraid I must abandon the celebration. Maggie's increasing, as you know, and hasn't been feeling well. I should get back to her. Don't let me break up the party, though! Have several more rounds, and tell Ransen to put it on my tab.'

'Thanks for the offer, but I should go, too,' David said. 'I can't wait to share the news with Faith.'

'She'll be so proud of you,' Christopher said, admiration for his quiet, determined, brilliant friend filling him. 'Through skill and planning, the Dowager Duchess's commoner husband has brought a recalcitrant aristocracy to heel.'

Davie waved a deprecating hand. 'A joint achievement—for all of us.' Setting down his own mug, he said, 'Goodnight, gentlemen! And thank you—for your hard work, and most especially, for your friendship all these years.'

'That goes for all of us,' Ben said. Raising his mug to the company, he said, 'To the Hellions.'

Giles and Davie clapped Ben on the shoulder as they walked out. After finishing his own mug, Ben added it to the tray. 'I'm off as well.'

'Isn't Alyssa away on one of her sketching expeditions?' Christopher asked. 'You could come out with me. Just a few rounds of ale, for old time's sake.'

Ben raised his eyebrows. 'A few rounds of ale? What about the "woman" part of the celebration? I understand you recently parted company with the Divine Clarissa. Have you replaced her yet?'

'Not yet. There are several matrons of great appetite and small morals who have made their interest quite clear.'

'And Mrs Anderson recently left the Duke of Portland's protection. I seem to remember her casting lures in your direction, even while she was with Portland.'

'Can't help being irresistible,' Christopher said, and ducked his friend's punch. 'Oh, they are all lovely enough. But none of them…quite tempt me.'

The image of a courtesan who had always *more* than tempted him came to mind. How fast he'd jump to follow, were Ellie Parmenter to crook a finger in his direction!

Shaking his thoughts free, he said, 'How about spending the rest of the evening at Madame Aurelie's? Good wine, lovely women to pour it, and a few hands of cards. Almost as respectable as a gentleman's club. I don't think Alyssa would object.'

Ben gave him a wry grin. 'She probably wouldn't. But going to a gaming hell run by a famous former courtesan, with ladies discreetly available for select customers who can afford their high fees, isn't the sort of behaviour I want to indulge in.'

Before Christopher could remind him how often he'd indulged in it in the past, his friend quickly added, 'I know I could accompany you, share a bottle of wine, a round of cards, and nothing more than conversation with ladies who are as witty as they are beautiful. But…it just doesn't appeal any more. Sorry. Don't let me spoil your pleasure, though! In fact, in honour of our frequent revels in the past, drink twice the wine and beguile twice the ladies, for me.'

He gave Christopher's hand a pat. 'Enjoy yourself—as if I need to tell you that! I'll take the tray down.' Picking it up, he gave Christopher a wink and headed out the door.

Though Madame Aurelie and her charming company beckoned, as Christopher watched his friend leave, he couldn't stifle a little sinking feeling in his gut…that surely wasn't *loneliness*.

Chapter One

Two weeks later

Afternoon sun, diffused to a soft glow by the sheer curtains at the window, cast a flattering light over the face and figure of the voluptuous blonde in the diaphanous dressing gown. As Christopher crossed the sitting room to the couch on which she reclined, the lady stretched out an arm, a diamond bracelet dangling from her fingers. 'Christopher, darling, what a pleasant surprise! Fasten this for me, won't you? The clasp is troublesome.'

With an indulgent smile, Christopher bent to perform that task, tweaking one blonde curl after he finished. 'Troublesome, like its owner?' he teased.

China-blue eyes widening in reproach, she pursed full pink lips in a pout. 'That's no way to talk to your mama.'

'Maybe not. But the usual rules of filial behaviour don't apply when your mother is a Beauty who still twists men around her little finger and looks more like a sister than a parent.'

A fact that, depending on the day, inspired him alternately with pride, amusement or chagrin.

'Where did you get that new bauble? Henderson?' he asked, naming the most assiduous of her current admirers.

She waved a hand. 'Yes. Henderson positively begged to be allowed to send me a small token of his esteem, so I at last relented. The bracelet is lovely,' she observed, lifting her arm to admire its sparkle. 'However, I think I must dismiss him. He's becoming quite tiresomely possessive, and you know I can't tolerate that.'

If she did send him packing, it wouldn't be because Christopher's father—or rather, the man who legally filled that role—objected. Lord Vraux and his Lady had gone their separate ways for years, and everyone knew it. Just as they all whispered about the identity of Christopher's real father and that of his sisters, his elder brother Gregory being the only one of the 'Vraux Miscellany' believed to be his lordship's legitimate offspring.

'Have you already someone in mind to replace him?' he asked as he took the seat beside her. 'Chernworth would happily claim his place. Then there's that new puppy—Lord Rogers?—following you about, writing execrable verse in your honour.'

'He's just a boy,' his mother said, shaking her head dismissively. 'Chernworth's amusing enough, but Kennington has become quite sharp of late. Really, I'm thinking of giving them all up. Retiring to the country, perhaps.'

'Retiring to the country?' he echoed. 'You can't be serious! Without the shops, theatres and entertainments of London, you'd expire of boredom in a week. And so would Society, without you to sparkle on its stage.'

'Without me to scandalise and fuel its gossip, you mean,' she retorted good-naturedly. 'Still, it might be better to leave that stage while I'm still sought after. Before my beauty fades, and the admirers drift away.'

His charming, effervescent mother looked almost…sad. Surprised, Christopher said, 'What brought on this green melancholy?'

Picking up a mirror from the table beside her, she inspected her face. 'See, that wrinkle there?' she pointed. 'Kennington teased me about it last night.'

Christopher bent to peer at his mother. 'That?

It's barely noticeable. Kennington's an ass. You've more than a few good years left before you're in your dotage! Besides, the girls still need to be settled.'

'You'd have me attend those dreadful parties full of insipid virgins and their matchmaking mamas?' His mother shuddered. 'In any event, I wouldn't be much help in getting your sisters respectably married. You know all those society beldames detest me.'

He couldn't dispute that claim. Lady Vraux was much admired—by the masculine members of the *ton*. Jealous of her beauty, charm and the mesmerising effect she had on men, society's women were less appreciative. Though her birth and position guaranteed his mama invitations to most society entertainments—as well as to others far less respectable—her successful flaunting of the standards of proper feminine behaviour had won her few female friends.

She shrugged an elegant shoulder. 'If those women devoted a fraction of the time they spend criticising me to enticing their men, they wouldn't have to worry about my charms. In any event, I'll probably call upon your Aunt Augusta to ferry the girls about when the time comes.'

'Gussie would excel at it,' Christopher agreed. 'She thrives on keeping track of who's pursuing whom and who's the biggest prize on the Marriage Mart.' He paused. 'Maybe I ought to enlist her help. I've been thinking…' He hesitated, not sure, given her probable reaction, he wanted to divulge his intent. 'Perhaps it's time I found a wife.'

Shocked silence reigned for a moment before his mother burst out laughing. 'You, married?' she said when she'd recovered herself. 'What nonsense!'

'No, Mama, I'm serious,' he protested.

She fixed him with a penetrating look. 'You're just lonely, with all your closest friends wed now. Which is hardly a good reason to get yourself leg-shackled. But then, you're well aware of my opinion on marriage.'

'I miss my friends, it's true,' Christopher admitted. Especially Ben Tawny, who'd been his carousing partner on many occasions—until he met and married his lady. 'Despite your view of the institution, all the Hellions have found wives who make marriage look quite attractive.'

His mother waved a dismissive hand. 'But they are all virtually newlyweds, aren't they? If they *remain* happy, they will be luckier than most.'

Luckier than she'd been, Christopher knew. His beautiful mother had been married off by her financially hard-pressed father to the highest bidder—Lord Vraux. A connoisseur of all things lovely, the years-older baron had been mad to add to his collection the most dazzling girl of her debut Season. Cold, withdrawn, and remote, he had never been able to give his passionate, outgoing, demonstrative wife the affection or companionship she craved.

Whatever the beldames thought of her morals, none could dispute that she'd been a devoted mother. Especially to Christopher, son of the man rumour said had been the love of her life.

'You are serious, then?' his mother demanded, after studying him as he'd sat silent, lost in thought. 'Have you a candidate in mind?'

'No. Which is why I need Aunt Augusta. I'm hardly a romantic, Mama. I'm not expecting to discover a woman who inspires me to write bad verse, like Lord Rogers.'

Even if his friends did seem to have found such joy, he thought, the loneliness that had dogged him of late deepened by a wistful envy.

'All I require is a respectable young lady of good birth who can manage my household and give me heirs. Not a chit right from the schoolroom, of course; even a young widow would do. Although that's not absolutely required, someone with an interest in politics would be a plus. As I've always avoided parties where respectable virgins gather, besides my sisters, I don't know any. Hence my need for Aunt Gussie.'

'A respectable young lady of good birth to manage your household and give you heirs? Sounds like a devilishly cold arrangement.'

'Come now, Mama, you can't claim to have been rapturously in love with every one of your... admirers!'

'I was when the liaison began,' she shot back.

'A prudent match doesn't have to be cold,' he argued, not surprised she resisted the idea, after having been disposed of herself in a completely dispassionate manner. 'I know better than to wed someone to whom I am indifferent, or who feels nothing for me. There's no reason I couldn't share a mutual respect and affection with a more...traditional woman.'

'"Mutual respect" with a "traditional" woman?' She shook her head. 'Christopher, darling, you're much too like me for such a match to ever work! After a decade of liaisons with the most beautiful, witty and seductive of females, a dutiful, respectable virgin would bore you to flinders. And what of passion?'

'Just because a female is respectable doesn't mean she must lack passion.'

She sniffed. 'If that were true, I'd have far fewer married admirers.'

Giving up on that tack, Christopher continued, 'I've reached the age where the idea of returning home to tranquillity and peace in the arms of a friend sounds more attractive than a night of drinking and debauchery in the bed of a courtesan.'

He wouldn't admit to her—or even to himself—that the idea of possessing an eminently respectable wife did sound a bit dull. Or how much the loss of the camaraderie of the three now-married men who'd been closer than family to him for a decade was driving this newfound resolve to take a wife. Once he, too, married, their intimate circle would again be complete.

But above all, he couldn't confess he felt compelled to wed that eminently respectable female so his own children would never have to wonder who their father was, endure the sniggers and whispers of their peers about their mother—or bear the cold disinterest of the man who was legally their father.

Such a confession would sound too much like an indictment. And despite all the turmoil, slights and indignities he'd endured growing up, he truly did love his volatile mother.

The disapproving expression on her face told

him she wasn't convinced. Before he could think of another argument to persuade her, a knock sounded at the door, followed by the entrance of a tall, dark-haired woman.

Seeing him sitting beside his mother, the lady halted, her smile fading. 'I'm sorry, Felicia! I don't mean to intrude. Billings told me you were free.'

'Ellie!' Lady Vraux cried, jumping up from the couch in a swirl of silken draperies to go meet the newcomer. 'Of course, you're not interrupting—I got your note, and was expecting you! How are you, my dear? I haven't seen you this age!'

Gladness warming him, Christopher stood and drank in the pleasure of watching the quiet elegance that was Ellie Parmenter walk across the room. Though it must be ten years now since they'd met, each time he saw her he felt the same sense of awe—and sharp pull of sensual attraction—he'd felt the first time he'd beheld her in his mother's drawing room, when he'd returned from Oxford on a term break. Her figure lush and well formed, her movements grace personified, her pale face perfection beneath a curly mass of dark hair, she had huge violet eyes with an air of mystery about them that he'd immediately lost himself in. The young collegian had been first mesmerised, then dismayed and disappointed to discover that this beauty a few years younger than himself was in keeping to a dissolute, much older peer.

Though neither she nor his mama had ever volunteered the details, he knew there'd been something havey-cavey about the way she'd come to be Summerville's mistress. He'd been happy for her when the man died last autumn, freeing her from that relationship.

Had he not been entangled at the time with the Divine Clarissa, he might have pursued her himself.

'I'm quite well,' Ellie was saying as she returned his mother's embrace. 'I can wait in the drawing room until you finish your chat with Christopher.'

'Nonsense! I'm sure he'd be interested in hearing your news, too. Wouldn't you, my dear?'

'I would indeed. Although, since I'm the one who turned up unexpectedly, if you ladies would prefer to have a comfortable coze, *I* could leave.'

'No, please, stay, Christopher,' Ellie said, echoing his mother's request.

That matter disposed of, his mother rang for tea and, arm in arm with her visitor, proceeded to the sofa. He waved Ellie to the seat he'd just vacated and she took it, her dark beauty a perfect foil to his mother's blonde loveliness.

'So, what *have* you been doing to occupy yourself since Summerville's demise, when you left the social scene?' his mother demanded. 'Not mourning, surely. More like celebrating, I'd expect.'

'I was…ready to move on,' Ellie allowed, her expression unreadable.

'Summerville did leave you that charming little house, as well as an annuity, didn't he?' his mother asked. 'Why don't you set yourself up with a snug little gaming establishment, like Madame Aurelie? I know you have friends in the demi-monde who would be happy to work for you. The gentlemen would certainly flock there, wouldn't they, Christopher?'

A gaming hell with Ellie as its mistress? There was no doubt. 'Absolutely. You'd be a smashing success.'

'Set that up, and you'd never have to worry about running out of money,' his mother said. 'As an independent woman, you'd retain control of your own funds and your own establishment—giving you more freedom and security than a married woman ever has.'

'If not the respect of Society,' Ellie murmured.

'No great loss, that,' Lady Vraux said with a

shrug. 'I would choose independence and control over my fortune any day! But since I take it that option doesn't appeal, what do you intend to do? Not start that school for wayward females you mentioned when we last met, I hope!'

'Actually, I have started it,' Ellie said, giving his mother an apologetic smile. 'I'd been thinking of doing something like that for years, particularly for girls born at fancy houses who don't want to follow their mothers into the trade. It's true that courtesans at the highest levels have the independence you so admire, but few females achieve that. Most girls caught up in the life can never leave it, either because they have no other way to support themselves, or because the madam or pimp controlling them won't permit it. Which is why I was so grateful for Lord Witlow's assistance in the matter of the girl who trapped Ben Tawny at the Quill and Gavel,' she said, looking over at Christopher.

'It's Ben and the rest of us Hellions who owe *you* thanks,' Christopher responded. 'Without your sleuthing efforts and your knowledge of the demi-monde, we'd never have found her, and Ben might have been facing the ruin of his Parliamentary career. We've worked too hard for too long to lose one of our key members now, when

She shook her head. 'No need to apologise. *I've* wondered for years what it would be like to kiss a man who…truly cared about me. But I shall not let it happen again.'

Ignoring the voice that wanted to ask if she'd *liked* kissing him, he said instead, 'No, we shall both guard against a repetition.' Though he couldn't make himself believe it, he added, 'The kiss we both wondered about is over and done. In the past now. We'll do better in future.'

Liar, a scornful voice whispered. That touch and kiss only whetted his desire for more, pulling him ever more deeply under her spell. How was he to reconcile that realisation with his determination to marry?

'Yes, we'll do better,' she affirmed. 'However, while we both work on…retraining our instinctive reactions, perhaps we should continue the lesson in a more public place. I'd planned this for another day, but do you have time for an outing now?'

It would be wise to go out and defuse some of the sensual tension still simmering in the air. 'An outing? Where?'

'Quite likely, you will meet your young lady first at a ball. If you dance with her, you may signal your interest by sending her flowers the next day. But which flowers do you choose?'

He shrugged. 'The most expensive variety available, I suppose. Although I haven't sent flowers very often. My...ladies preferred a more lasting expression of interest—like jewels.'

Laughing, she shook her head. 'Goodness, no! A gentleman never gives jewellery of any sort to a respectable single lady.'

He gave an exaggerated sigh. 'Very well. No kissing. No touching. No jewellery. Despite its other drawbacks, it appears courting the Virtuous Virgin will be easier on my purse.'

Ellie smiled, her lovely eyes sparkling. 'True enough—*before* the wedding. After it, the bills for jewels, carriages, horses, gowns, bonnets, reticules, slippers, stockings, and undergarments could be extensive!'

'We can dispense with the undergarments,' he flashed back without thinking—and froze, as her startled gaze whipped to his face. She opened her mouth—probably to reprove him—but managed only a parting of her lips. As she flicked her tongue over them, desire stabbed deeper, the image created by his careless words smoking in his brain.

The two of them, outer garments tossed away, standing a touch apart, gazing at each other clothed only in a gilding of candlelight.

She must be feeling it, too, for her gaze ex-the reforms we've struggled to advance are so close to being implemented.'

'Yes, I read that your Third Reform Bill passed the Commons. Congratulations!'

Christopher nodded his thanks. 'Now we just have to get it through the Lords. Though a few peers, like Lady Maggie's father, are reasonable, a great many recalcitrants will try to drag their heels. Another reason we're grateful that, with your help, we've still got Ben with us in the fight.'

'I'm so thankful for your mama and all her kindness over the years. I was only too happy to do what I could.' She gave him that sweet smile that always made his heart lift. 'Most women of her class ignore me like an unpleasant odour. No one but Felicia has ever condescended, not just to acknowledge me, but to offer friendship. Still, had Lord Witlow not stepped in to guarantee the girl's safety, she would have been too afraid of retribution for me to persuade her to come forward. Once he'd been made aware of the situation—and what I hoped to do for other girls—his lordship not only took steps to protect Jane, he invested in the project, allowing me to begin the school at once. I shall be indebted for ever.'

'*We* are all indebted that the two of you

worked in concert to clear Ben's name,' Christopher said.

A knock at the door, followed by the entry of the butler with the tea tray, brought a momentary halt to the conversation. Once they were settled with cups in hand, Ellie yielding to his mother's request that she pour for them, Christopher turned back to her.

Curious about her unusual endeavour, Christopher asked, 'How do you find the girls for your school?'

'Are you sure you want to know more? I can become quite enthused when talking about my project,' she cautioned.

'Yes, I truly want to know,' he assured her.

'Very well. Working girls, or those with a friend or relative who has a daughter who aspires to a different life, send them to me. Or sometimes I find them at the posting inns, where I try to intercept country girls who've come to town looking for work, before the bawds can spirit them away.'

Lady Vraux frowned. 'Isn't that dangerous? I imagine the bawds don't like being robbed of their pigeons!'

'I'm sure they don't,' Ellie agreed. 'When he learned what I intended, Lord Witlow insisted I have a burly man to accompany me. As it turns out, he engaged the bully boy at the house from which they obtained the girl meant to entrap Mr Tawny. It seems the man was sweet on her, and after Witlow helped her escape, was ready to trade his current employment for some honest work where he might be able to continue the acquaintance.'

'Well, it's commendable of you, my dear, setting up the school, but nobility does become rather dull. Surely you leave yourself some time for amusements—concerts, the theatre?'

Ellie smiled faintly, shaking her head. 'I don't go out much any more.'

'To avoid being pestered by gentlemen hoping to persuade you to let them take Summerville's place?' his mother guessed. 'Lovely as you are, I'm certain you've had offers! If you don't intend to open an establishment that will earn you a reliable income, you must find some other way to secure your future. Are you planning to take another protector?'

'No,' Ellie said flatly, the bleakness that swiftly crossed her face before she masked it suddenly recalling one of Christopher's earliest memories of her.

It must have been only a few weeks after they'd first met. Answering a summons by his mama to escort her home from a definitely disrespectable masquerade ball after her nominal escort had fallen into a drunken stupor, he'd encountered Ellie alone in one of the anterooms, weeping. Seeing him, she'd hastily wiped away the tears, insisted there was nothing wrong, and led him to his mother. Not knowing how to get her to confide in him, he'd let it go. But the devastation he'd read on her face then had struck him deeply—as did the glimpse of it he'd just seen.

No more certain now how to ask her about it, before he could speak, his mother continued, 'But how are you to live, if you do not allow another gentleman to provide for you? You have the house, and Summerville was certainly generous with gifts, but even if you sell some jewels, it won't cover your expenses for ever. Not with servants to pay, and candles, coal and all manner of victuals to be bought, to say nothing of clothing. To wrap your loveliness in outdated gowns would be a travesty!'

Ellie laughed. 'I think I can tolerate the indignity of wearing last year's fashions. Summerville *was* generous with his gifts, and thanks to your advice, I obtained that annuity and some other assets that will allow me to remain independent. I can maintain myself for a good long while before I have to worry about where my next meal is coming from.'

'Is it the notoriety of living outside wedlock that holds you back?' his mother persisted. 'I can't believe a lady as young and beautiful as you prefers to exist without...masculine attention.'

Again, Christopher caught a glimpse of distress before Ellie could submerge it. 'I've quite had my fill of "masculine attention" these last few years. Nor does the idea of additional notoriety bother me. I'm not naive enough to think I can erase the past; even were I to live the rest of my life as chastely as a nun, I will always be known as a kept woman.'

'We are all kept women, my dear,' his mother replied, a look of bitterness passing over her face. 'Some of us are trapped by wedding lines. You, at least, still have the power to choose your path. Don't discount that freedom.' Then, her face clearing, she said, 'But enough of this sober talk. Let me tell you something that is certain to amuse you. Christopher just announced he has taken it into his head to *marry*! Is that not the most ridiculous notion you've ever heard?'

'I'm so glad my intention to reform myself into a respectable gentleman inspires you to hilarity,' Christopher said wryly, as his mother went off into another peal of laughter.

'Come, you must dissuade him of the nonsensical idea, Ellie! You've encountered him in enough disreputable places and scandalous company to recognise he's not sober husband material. Christopher, remaining devoted to a single woman?' She shook her head. 'He ought to spare some earnest, virtuous virgin a lifetime of sorrow and abandon the notion forthwith.'

Although she didn't succumb to mirth like his mother, Ellie's lovely eyes were definitely dancing when she glanced at him. 'I must allow, Christopher, up to now, you've shown a preference for ladies more renowned for a…particular kind of skill than for their virtue, and an ever-changing parade of them at that.'

'Indeed!' his mother agreed. 'Remember that soprano from the Theatre Royal—was it a vase she threw at you, Christopher? You've still got the scar on your chin! And the time you stole Harrington's doxy out from under his nose, and he threatened to call you out! And then there was—'

'Please, must you list all my indiscretions?' Christopher protested, half-amused, half-embarrassed. 'I agree, I've not exactly been a…model of punctilious deportment, but a man can change. Can't he, Ellie?'

Instead of the witty riposte he expected, she stared at him—those magnificent violet eyes making his breath hitch, as they always did on the rare occasions when she gave him her full attention. 'I don't know, Christopher. I expect a *man* can reform, if he wants to badly enough.' A faint smile touched her lips. 'Unlike a female, even a truly notorious man can choose to turn respectable.'

Is that what caused the lingering sadness he saw in her eyes? Christopher wondered. She'd always seemed, and he's always treated her, as a lady, despite her position as Summerville's mistress. Had she once been respectable, and been robbed of that reputation by some cruel circumstance? He really must press his mother for more details about her background.

'You're young enough, you've plenty of time to change your mind,' his mother told her. 'When you meet a gentleman too charming to resist— or when you've run out of the ready.'

Setting down her teacup, Ellie made a face at her. 'I hope to avoid both outcomes. But now, I should be getting on. I must check on the school, then discharge some errands before Lady Lydlington meets me there tomorrow.'

'Giles's wife Maggie has taken an interest in your work?' Christopher asked, surprised.

'Yes. Though I've been giving Lord Witlow the credit, I'm fairly certain it was his daughter

Maggie who encouraged Witlow to provide protection for Mr Tawny's accuser, for me on my forays into the posting inns, and prompted him to sponsor the school. I doubt a man of Lord Witlow's position would have had any notion there might be a need for such things.'

Ellie shook her head, smiling. 'The first time Lady Lyndlington visited the school, I told her I couldn't believe her father would permit her to associate with me—or that her husband would, now that's she's in a delicate condition. She laughed, saying that since she'd married a radical, her papa already knew she wouldn't let a little thing like Society's disapproval stop her from helping a good cause. She found it fulfilling, she said, to assist to a better life girls who'd been born without the advantages she possesses. Her courage and graciousness remind me of you, Felicia. Though I don't mean to suggest *she* considers me a friend, of course,' Ellie added quickly.

'You did one of her husband's closest friends a great service. Why shouldn't she befriend you?' Christopher asked.

A slight flush coloured Ellie's lovely face. 'The daughter of an earl, the wife of a viscount and Member of Parliament, on intimate terms with… It's quite impossible, Christopher, and you know it,' she added, an unusual sharpness in her tone.

'Perhaps for Lady Maggie,' his mother inserted with a grin. 'She's far more respectable than I am!'

'Well I, for one, can only be glad you've chosen to be slightly scandalous!' Ellie said, leaning over to give Lady Vraux a hug. 'Now I must go.'

'Thank you again for the visit,' his mother said. 'Please, do come back soon! Even if it's only to ask for money to support your noble cause.'

Smiling, Ellie shook a finger at her. 'Be careful what you wish for. Next time, I might just come begging!' Turning towards him, she said, 'It was wonderful to see you, too, Christopher. Good luck getting your Reform Bill through the Lords this session. And with your other project. Despite your mama's objections, if you're set on reforming your rake's ways, I know you will make a success of it and choose a wife wisely.'

With a graceful curtsy to his bow, she walked out, Christopher unable to pry his gaze from her lovely form until she'd shut the door behind her.

He looked back to see his mama watching him, a speculative look on her face. He bent over the teapot and poured himself another cup to mask the heat he felt rising in his face at her scrutiny.

However, rather than teasing him about his obvious admiration for Ellie, when he looked back at her, she was frowning. 'I worry about her, Christopher,' she said unexpectedly. 'Despite what Ellie says, she can't have extracted enough jewels or blunt out of Summerville to support herself indefinitely. And despite my distaste for the married state, having a husband—even one conspicuous for his absence—does provide a woman with a layer of protection. The unscrupulous are less likely to try to take advantage if they know there is a man about who could hold them accountable for their behaviour. With Summerville gone, Ellie has no one. And she's far too lovely to be without a champion.'

As his mother perhaps intended, her words immediately called up Christopher's protective instincts. He didn't need his mother's warning to know there were many men who would feel a woman in Ellie's position was fair game. 'Is there someone in particular you suspect might be thinking of *taking advantage*?'

'She disappeared from the public eye immediately after Summerville's death, so I can't say for certain. But Viscount Mountgarcy and Sir Ralph Simonton have been sniffing around her for years, and they are both as dissipated as Summerville. As you well know, the two have vied over women and wagers since they left university. With their wealth and position, I can't see either of them believing they should take Ellie's refusal as a final answer.'

Christopher frowned. His mother was correct; neither would believe Summerville's former mistress would actually reject an offer from a man of their lineage and deep pockets. They'd likely interpret her refusal as a game, her way of bargaining between them to get better terms. 'I'll keep an eye out. Wouldn't want either of those dissolute characters laying a hand on her.'

His mother gave him another speculative look. 'Maybe you ought to do more than just "keep an eye out". She's not indifferent to you, Christopher—and you're certainly attracted to her. Even better, you *like* her. Were you to offer her *carte blanche*, I'm almost certain she would accept. It would be a far happier arrangement for you than marriage to some prune-faced virgin.'

He, Ellie's protector? He couldn't deny that the mere thought of possessing her sent a blaze of desire through him. In his many amorous liaisons, he'd never met another woman who touched him more deeply on a physical level. He was nearly certain they would make spectacular lovers. And as his mother said, they were already friends. He enjoyed her company, her good sense and intelligent observations, her calm demeanour that was often so in contrast to his emotional, volatile mother.

Protecting her from harm would be a privilege.

But taking a mistress wouldn't advance his career, nor help him fit in better with his married friends. Indeed, it would distance him further.

He really did need a wife to achieve both those aims. He resisted a sigh. No matter how tedious the idea of marriage sounded. He'd just have to talk himself into liking the idea better. Surely he could reshape his outlook, if he worked at it hard enough.

'I do admire Ellie—and I certainly find her desirable. But I also think it's time that I moved beyond temporary liaisons and made a permanent choice of companion.'

Could he take Ellie—and then walk away from her? If she were to become his mistress, and they later parted, how could he keep her as a friend?

Though his mother was correct about his tendency to move from one woman to the next, he couldn't imagine his life without the serene loveliness of Ellie in it.

'So you'll just leave Ellie to fend for herself?' his mother asked, jolting him from his thoughts.

'Because a woman who isn't chaste and dutiful deserves whatever she gets?' she added bitterly.

'No, of course not,' he flashed back, stung. 'How could you accuse me of thinking that? I've never treated any of the women with whom I've associated with less than courtesy and respect, and you know it! Just because I'm not prepared to make Ellie an offer doesn't mean I'm not concerned for her well-being. We're not as close as you and she have become, but I still consider her a friend! You may trust me to make sure she comes to no harm.'

'And just how do you mean to accomplish that, if she is not under your protection?'

'We're *friends*. I can stop by her school, and visit her at home.' He gave his mother a smile. 'It *is* possible for a man and a woman to be just friends, you know.'

She shrugged. 'Maybe if the man's a eunuch, or the woman a sour-faced virgin.' She heaved a sigh. 'But I shall stop, before you make me cross. Just promise to watch out for Ellie, and I won't tease you any further. Even though I think your desire to pursue *marriage* is a mistake.'

'That's easy enough to promise.' Setting aside his teacup, he rose. 'I must get along as well. But to demonstrate the sincerity of my pledge, I'll stop by Ellie's school this very afternoon. Check out her circumstances, make sure that bully boy is providing sufficient protection. I'll keep my eyes and ears open when I make the rounds of my clubs, too. If someone has disreputable intentions towards her, I'll put a stop to it.'

His mother opened her lips, then closed them. 'I'll not ask again how you think you can do that without staking a claim to the lady. Just know, I shall hold you responsible if anything untoward happens to her.'

'No more responsible than I'd hold myself,' he retorted. 'I watch out for my friends, Mama— even the ones who happen to be female.'

'See that you do. Now, go on with you. Some dreadfully dull committee meeting awaits, I'm sure.'

Chuckling, Christopher dropped a kiss on his mother's head and left her.

But despite his intent to focus on finding a wife, the enticing vision of Ellie in his arms was difficult to put out of mind.

Chapter Two

A short while after her visit with Lady Vraux, Ellie Parmenter stepped down from the hackney and approached the modest shop front she'd rented for her school on Dean Street. With space on the ground floor for classrooms, her office, and a storeroom, and bedchambers upstairs for the girls and the matron she'd engaged as chaperone and fellow teacher, it served excellently for its purpose.

'Afternoon, miss,' Jensen, her bully-boy protector-cum-butler, said as she entered. 'The post done arrived. I put it on your desk.'

'Thank you, Jensen. I'll see to it directly.' Nodding to the matron and calling a hello to the girls seated at tables, working on some stitchery, Ellie crossed the space towards the small room she used as an office. Laid out on the desk were several envelopes—that looked very much like bills.

She took a seat and opened them, confirming with a sigh that they were indeed invoices for coal, porridge, thread, and candles. Having gone from her mother's house to her protector's, she had little experience of the various and sundry expenses involved in running a household. She kept discovering, to her dismay, how many *more* of them there were than she'd anticipated.

Pushing away the unpleasant realisation of how quickly she was going through the sum Lord Witlow had invested in the school, she told herself they would manage somehow. After she finished with the bills and checked on the students, she would go out again and purchase some cloth. The two new girls she'd taken in yesterday, both children raised in brothels, needed more suitable clothing. She meant to use Witlow's funds as prudently as possible, and it would be cheaper to buy the material to make up the gowns.

Besides, Lucy had expressed an interest in learning the dressmaker's art. With time and training, she could perhaps be found a place with a modiste—especially if Lady Lyndlington gave her a recommendation.

All the wives of Christopher's closest friends, the Hellions, were uncommonly gracious. After she'd responded to his plea for help and located the girl involved in the plot to discredit Ben

Tawny, they'd insisted on having her dine with them so they might thank her personally.

She wouldn't have admitted it to Christopher, or even to his mother, but she would have been willing to do nearly anything *he* asked of her.

What an arresting figure he'd made today, the sunlight streaming through the gauze-curtained windows silhouetting his tall, muscled body, shimmering on his dark gold hair and highlighting the sparkle of those deep turquoise eyes!

She chuckled, remembering the quizzical twist of his lip as he protested his mama mocking his intention to marry, even as that aim sent a pang to her heart. His hold on her affections went far deeper than admiration for his handsome face and virile body, or the zing of attraction she felt whenever he came near. She would never forget, nor could she adequately repay him, for the unfailing kindness, sympathy and respect with which he always treated her, especially at the darkest moment of her life.

Just as well that he was set on wedding a proper young miss. Now that she was finally free of her obligation to Summerville, she didn't intend to become any man's mistress ever again. That firm resolve, however, might waver—if Christopher were the one offering her *carte blanche*.

Shaking her head at her foolishness, she told herself she mustn't even consider becoming more to Christopher Lattimar than a casual friend. It would be too great an irony if she agreed to a disreputable liaison with the one gentleman who'd always treated her like a lady, despite her position.

Besides, even if he should crook his finger and she were not strong enough to refuse him, such a relationship would only be temporary. How could she bear to have the warmth and courtesy he now showed her turn to polite disinterest, or worse yet, disdain, when he tired of her, as men always did of their mistresses?

Naturally, with him showing her kindness and respect at such a low point in her life, she'd fallen immediately into infatuation, seeing him as some sort of Knight in Shining Armour. But she was no longer an innocent eighteen-year-old, wrenched from home, family and all that was familiar and forced into a degrading role.

She smiled wryly. If Christopher could reform the rake, perhaps she could remake the romantic girl she'd been. Put those nostalgic fancies behind her and, now that her life was finally her own, turn herself into a sensible, mature woman. She had a few loyal friends like Felicia and important work in helping destitute young women build better lives to keep her occupied.

Having Christopher marry would end their friendship as effectively as if she were his cast-off mistress, she suddenly realised.

She was struggling to resist the wave of desolation that cruel thought produced when Jensen poked his head in the door. 'There's a man to see you, miss. Says he's from the landlord.'

'I suppose I shall have to receive him.' Gathering up the bills and thrusting them into the drawer, she said, 'Very well, show him in, Jensen.'

A few minutes later, a short, trim gentleman strolled in. After sketching a bow, he said, 'I'm Wilson, Miss Parmenter, agent for your landlord. Mr Anderson sent me to inform you that, the preliminary portion of your lease being up, as of your next payment, your rent will be going up five pounds a month.'

'Five pounds a month?' After rapidly figuring the percentage in her head, she exclaimed, 'That's a ridiculously high increase! Besides, the term of the lease was a year. He cannot raise the rent before the end of the term.'

Wilson shrugged. 'I wouldn't know about that, miss. I just knows he sent me to warn you that he expects the new amount to be paid when next it's due, lessen he take steps to get you evicted.'

Anger coloured her distress. 'I'm quite certain that your employer has no legal right to arbitrarily increase the rent.'

'I suppose you could talk to him, but dunno he'd change his mind. I know the bailiffs won't listen, if he sets them to throwing you out. Happen it be better if you just pay the increase, like he says.'

'*Happen* he is trying to coerce me into paying something I don't owe,' she snapped back angrily. The lease didn't allow for an interim increase—did it? Surely she would have noticed if the landlord were allowed to make such an adjustment.

'Wouldn't risk it, were it me, ma'am. Lettin' all them girls get put out into the street, with no place to go? Up to you, though.'

How could she determine for sure whether or not the threat was genuine? How could she keep the school going, if she had to pay so much higher a rent in addition to all the other bills?

Worry might be tightening her chest, but she didn't intend for this vile little man to glimpse her agitation. Schooling her face to calm, she rose in dismissal. 'Very well, you've delivered your message. You may tell your employer that

I have no intention of increasing my payment, and I very much resent his attempt to extort a higher sum from me. Good day, sir.'

A little smirk on his face, as if he knew she was bluffing, Wilson said, 'I'd think Mr Anderson's warning over careful. Hard life for them girls, out on the street.'

With that parting shot, he ambled out.

As if she didn't know just how hard such a life was, she thought, sinking back into her chair. Opening the bottom desk drawer, she rifled through until she found the copy of her lease.

Full of excitement at beginning the project so dear to her, she'd not paid much attention to the lengthy list of terms and conditions. She scanned it now, trying to make sense out of the stylised legal phrasing.

So absorbed was she in trying to decode the document, she only nodded distractedly when Jensen announced she had a visitor. Until a large masculine hand that did not belong to Jensen planted itself beside hers on the desk.

She looked up then, to see Christopher Lattimar smiling down at her. She sucked in a breath, surprise—and a heated awareness—making her nerves tingle.

'I might expect such rapt attention being given to a racy novel,' he said, 'but some dull legal document?' Then, as he gazed at her, the teasing smile faded. 'Something is troubling you, Ellie. What is it? And how can I help?'

There seemed little point in denying she was upset. 'Yes, I am…disturbed,' she admitted. 'But it's nothing that should concern you. How delightful to see you again! Will you take some tea? And what can I do for you?'

'I would love some tea,' he replied, taking the chair she indicated. 'And nothing in particular. Your enthusiasm when you described your school for Mama made me curious to see it, that's all. But I do wish you would tell me what's wrong. Something about that document, I'm guessing?'

As she walked past him to summon Jensen to fetch tea, she debated whether or not to reveal the situation. On the one hand, her problems had nothing to do with him. But on the other, he was a friend, and maybe could offer some advice. She could certainly use some!

'It's the lease on the school, Christopher,' she said as she resumed her seat. 'My landlord's agent just stopped by to inform me that my rent is being raised a very considerable degree.' Uncomfortably aware of the other bills tucked inside the desk, she continued, 'I don't *think* the lease allows it, but I must admit, I'm not sure.'

He took the document from her and scanned it, frowning. 'Although I work every day crafting legislation, my expertise doesn't extend to agreements about property,' he said, handing it back. 'I agree that the provision on changes doesn't seem to provide for an increase, but the wording is so vague, but I can't be sure, either. You ought to get a solicitor's opinion.'

'And how much would that cost? Probably more than the increase in rent, which is doubtless what the landlord is counting on!'

The maid of all work came in then, struggling under the weight of a heavy tea tray. Christopher rose and took it from her, setting it down on the desk. 'Allow me—'

'Sally,' she inserted bashfully.

'Sally. Wouldn't want such a pretty lady to hurt her back.'

'Oh, no, sir, I wouldn't never!' she breathed, standing motionless as she stared up, wide-eyed, into Christopher's handsome face.

'That will be all, Sally,' Ellie said drily, amused to observe Christopher's effect on the little maid. Not that she could blame the girl, she thought, suppressing a sigh. Gazing into those turquoise eyes had the same paralysing effect on her, which was why she generally avoided looking directly at him.

'Yes, miss,' the girl said, flushing. Dropping a curtsy, she hurried back out.

After several moments spent pouring tea and passing cups, he said, 'Now, where were we? Discussing a problem with the lease, I think.'

She grimaced. 'And the fact that, whether I pay the increase demanded or consult a solicitor, it's going to cost me a good deal of blunt I can ill afford. Or I can ignore it, hope my reading of the text is correct, and trust that Mr Anderson won't set the bailiffs to tossing my girls into the street.'

Christopher frowned. 'He threatened that? How…unhandsome of him!'

'Unhandsome indeed! But it might be a moot point. If I keep incurring so many unexpected expenses, I may be forced to close the school a-anyway,' she finished, her voice trembling as she confessed her deepest fear—for without the school, what purpose, what future was there for her?

'We can't let a shortage of funding affect your enterprise!' he said bracingly. 'Why don't you consult my solicitor? He's already on retainer. I'd be happy to escort you there.'

She hesitated, grateful, but unwilling to put herself under such an obligation. 'That's very generous. But I must warn you, I'm not sure when I'll be able to pay you back. Lord Witlow set up a generous endowment, which I find I'm having to spend much too quickly, and I hate to approach Lady Maggie, when she's already been so free with her time and support.'

'Don't worry over the repayment,' Christopher said, with a dismissive wave. 'Your backers believe in the school, and are committed to its success. They will invest whatever additional amounts are needed—and there's always my mother. As you may recall, she's waiting to be touched for a contribution.'

His words were heartening, but she wasn't sure she dared believe them. 'I wanted to do this myself, mostly from my own resources. I didn't want to become a charge on anyone else.'

'You're not a charge, and you don't have to do it alone.' Leaning closer, he put his hand over hers. 'You have *friends*, Ellie. It's their pleasure to help you—as it was yours, to help Ben Tawny.'

Her composure shaken by the threat to the school, worry over finances and a vague but deep-seated fear for her future, it took only that small gesture to immobilise her completely. She didn't seem able to move her hand from under the comforting clasp of his fingers. And as she gazed up at him, comfort turned to something more.

With her control so tattered, she was helpless

to resist the force of the attraction sweeping over her. Wonder about what it would feel like to have his lips on hers submerged every other thought. An urge seized her to claim just one kiss from this man she admired, a man who cared about her, a man she trusted. Because, for once in her life, *she* wanted that intimacy as much as his molten gaze told her Christopher did.

His gaze never leaving hers, he leaned closer. Her pulse accelerated like a horse spurred to a gallop, while heat from deep within spiralled outward in melting waves of sensation. A powerful urgency unlike anything she'd ever experienced coiled within, seeming to press her towards...*something*.

But as she sat motionless, chin raised, awaiting the contact of his mouth, he suddenly stopped. Dragging in a ragged breath, he moved away from her. She took a gulp of air herself, unaware until that moment that she'd been holding her breath.

'As I said, you have friends, Ellie,' he repeated, a slight tremor in his voice. 'I hope I may count myself among them. If it's convenient for you to visit the solicitor now, I would be pleased to escort you, so you might clear up the question about the lease without delay.'

Squelching an irrational disappointment at

being robbed of his touch, she told herself she should rather feel relief. Succumbing to that kiss would threaten the friendly camaraderie they'd always shared. It was disconcerting enough to discover just how powerful a physical hold he could exert when her guard was down. How urgently she'd wanted him to act upon the attraction between them.

And that wouldn't do at all. Having set his sights on finding a proper young maiden to marry, Christopher didn't need to be distracted by her. She mustn't tempt him—or herself—into a relationship that would be wrong for them both.

But oh, how delicious it could be, her senses argued.

Shutting her ears to that insidious voice, she focused on his offer. 'If you are certain I wouldn't be imposing, I could leave as soon as I give Mrs Sanders her instructions. I would prefer to discover at once whether or not I must pay the increased rent.'

'Then instruct away while I finish my tea.'

Chapter Three

Two hours later, Christopher assisted Ellie down the narrow stairs from Mr Worthington's office, trying not to notice the sizzle sparking from her fingers to his arm, despite the layers of gloves, shirt, and jacket.

He had to ignore it—ignore her allure in general. There was no way he could fulfil his pledge to his mother and keep watch over Ellie without spending time with her. Besides, he *enjoyed* spending time with her. He'd derived a good deal of satisfaction from having been able to help her today. Somehow, he was going to have to focus only on the warm camaraderie of their friendship—and avoid a repetition of what had almost happened in her office.

His visit to the school was the first time they'd been alone together since Summerville's death. Doubtless, knowing on some subconscious level that there was no longer any impediment to keep him from acting on his attraction, the desire to kiss her had overcome him before common sense could restrain it. At least he'd retained enough wits to draw back. Forewarned now, he'd be more careful in future.

Still, he was uncomfortably aware both of the strength of that desire and how quickly it had overwhelmed him—in spite of his resolve to focus on finding an innocent maid to marry. Persuading his intellect to follow that wise course was one thing. It appeared that retraining his automatic reactions would be a good deal harder.

He'd just have to manage it. Because if he could not keep himself from succumbing to temptation, he'd have to give Ellie up. And he had no desire to end their friendship until or unless he must.

As they reached the bottom of the stairs, he said, 'Do you feel better, having Worthington confirm that your lease doesn't permit raising the rent?'

'I do indeed! I also very much appreciate his offer to send my landlord a letter to that effect. Although, as he suggested, I think it likely Mr Anderson is well aware of the law, and simply thought he could frighten a lone, unprotected woman into paying an additional sum.'

'A letter from the solicitor will let him know you can't be victimised in such a manner. You're neither alone nor unprotected. I would be quite happy to call on Mr Anderson myself and reinforce that truth.'

'Hopefully that won't be necessary.'

'But you promise to let me know if the man, or his agent, give you any more trouble? Truly, it wouldn't be an imposition. Helping friends is a pleasure.'

As her gaze jerked up towards his, he regretted a choice of words that recalled that moment in her office, reminding them both how much more of a pleasure it had almost been. His body tightened and sweat broke out on his brow as attraction sizzled between them again.

Ellie pulled her gaze free first, shaking her head a little, as if to dispel the enchantment. After preceding him into the street, she waited until he'd reached the pavement beside her to say, 'I'll thank you once more, and send you on your way.'

'I can see you home,' he offered, not wanting to end his time in her company. Besides, he needed more practice if he was going to master the trick of ignoring the sensual pull between them.

'That's kind, but before going home, I need to purchase cloth to make gowns for some of the girls. With the Season soon to begin, the dressmakers and linen drapers are going to be mobbed with customers placing orders. I'd like to obtain what I need before they get too busy to bother with my modest requirements. I wouldn't want to bore you with such a mundane errand.'

'I wouldn't be bored. I've often advised ladies on clothing purchases.'

Your mother and sisters—or the women you've had in keeping? her enquiring look said.

'Mama says I have excellent taste,' he added loftily, and had the satisfaction of seeing her blush.

Looking tempted, as if she too were reluctant to end their interlude, she said, 'You're sure I wouldn't be imposing? I have to admit, it is more…agreeable to walk with an escort. Thereby eliminating most of the blatant looks and rude remarks I would otherwise receive.'

'I shall happily shield you from both. Although you must allow—and I protest in advance, this isn't gallantry, merely simple truth—when a lady as lovely as you are walks down the street, men *will* look at her. Having an escort just makes them think twice about approaching.'

'Then I thank you for guarding the approaches.'

Realising how perfect a conversational opening that gave him, he said, 'Are there any other approaches that need guarding? I don't mean to pry, but Mama is concerned about you, living alone now without protection. She worries that you may be…harassed by gentlemen who refuse to be dissuaded from pursuing you.' A fear he had to admit he shared.

Her delay in responding and the little frown that flitted across her forehead told him that concern was justified. His protective instincts fully roused, he said quickly, 'Who is it? Tell me, and I'll warn them away.'

She shook her head. 'I'm not really troubled by anyone. There have been…enquiries that I've turned away with the polite but firm response that I do not intend to accept any offer. Once they discover that I am not trying to pit one against the other in order to drive up the price, I expect they will desist. There are far too many lovely and willing women in London to persist in pursuing one who is not.'

Once a man set his sights on Ellie, he'd be tough to dissuade, Christopher thought. Trying to decide whether he should press harder, or respect her reticence to name names, he said, 'I hope that is another matter you would bring to my attention, should anyone begin to "trouble" you in truth.'

'That's kind of you, Christopher,' she said,

her eyes brightening before the glow faded and she sighed. 'But I really mustn't rely on you. I have no right to lay such claims, and as we both know, you need to turn your attentions in a different direction.'

Though that statement only echoed what he'd just been telling himself, he found himself driven to refute it. 'That may be true, but I have no intention of abandoning my friends. Besides, you'll be doing me a favour. Should someone try to harass you and I fail to prevent it, my mother would harass *me* for months.'

That earned him a chuckle, as he'd hoped. 'Very well, you may accompany me and apply your discerning taste to the choosing of material appropriate for the gowns of apprentice housemaids and seamstresses.'

Chuckling himself, he set off to procure them a hackney. During the transit to Burlington Arcade, he kept up a flow of light banter, pairing together such a ridiculous assortment of buttons with cloth and trimmings with fabrics that he kept Ellie laughing for the length of the transit— earning the satisfaction of seeing the worry fade from her face and the tension ease from her shoulders.

How it delighted him to see her looking more carefree!

A short time later, the hackney set them down and they proceeded past the beadle into the covered shopping street. An array of tempting shops awaited, from jewellers and hatters to dressmakers and dry goods' dealers. As Ellie had predicted, the walkway was thronged with fashionable ladies, some with wide-eyed maidens in tow, doubtless preparing themselves for the sartorial demands of the upcoming Season. Weaving in and out among them, Ellie proceeded to a linen draper's shop, Christopher following behind.

They were lucky enough to find one clerk free, though his enthusiasm muted when Ellie waved away the sumptuous fabrics he brought forward and stated her need for simple, unadorned material. After ushering them to the back of the shop, he left them alone to debate the merits of various plain cottons and woollens.

'I'm quite impressed,' she told him after she'd made her selection. 'Although I expected you might have some expertise about the expensive fabrics your mama—or your ladybirds—choose for gowns, I'm surprised you had useful advice about cloth appropriate for servants.'

'Mama prefers not to delegate the task of acquiring the female staff's annual allotment of cloth to the housekeeper. Believing it wise to acquaint a son who wouldn't inherit the wealth of the Vraux estate with the expenses involved in maintaining a household, she's been dragging me along on those expeditions since I was a boy. Although the sinecures I've obtained since joining Parliament give me greater financial security than she anticipated, I'm still grateful for that training.'

'I wish someone had done as much for me,' Ellie said ruefully. 'I'm continually surprised by a variety of expenses I hadn't anticipated.'

And why had no one ever trained her? he wondered. As Summerville's mistress, all bills for her household would have been sent to her protector. Was it because she was some peer's base-born daughter? Blood kin but not family, with no aristocratic mother to give her the instruction in household management she would have received had a conventional marriage been anticipated?

'Ask my mother. I'm sure she'd be happy to offer advice. Though, despite what Society may think, she's really a canny household manager.' *As she'd needed to be, with her husband uninterested in any household purchases beyond those for his art collections.*

After she'd paid for the material, he collected the paper-wrapped parcel and escorted her out. 'Back to Hans Place now, or have you other errands to run?'

'If you can endure one more shop, I need stiffening to line bonnets,' she said. 'The place across the way should have what is necessary. I promise to reward you with tea, or something stronger, when we finally reach Hans Place.'

The image of the reward he'd truly enjoy sprang to mind. Clearly, he thought with a sigh as he suppressed it, if he meant to court an innocent, he was going to have to work harder to divert the automatic direction of his thoughts. Or was it only because he was in the presence of a beautiful courtesan that he couldn't keep his mind from veering towards pleasure?

Former courtesan, he rebuked himself before replying, 'I'm amenable to one more stop, and a glass of brandy afterward would be quite welcome.'

'Thank you,' she said as she led him back into the throng crowding the Bazaar. Stopping before a shop that displayed an array of bonnets, she said, 'You may not realise this, but I wouldn't have been given such prompt or courteous treatment in that last shop, had you not accompanied me. Like most of the merchants hereabouts, he knew me as Summerville's mistress—and knows that since I'm no longer in keeping, I'm unlikely to provide him with such lucrative custom in future. But a man's wishes always command attention—even if it's just the purchase of a few yards of cotton.'

'Then you must include me on all your errands.'

She laughed. 'Fortunately for you, I'm too sensible to hold you to that offer!'

Though he had thrown out the remark to amuse her, he found it wasn't really such an exaggeration. With his Parliamentary duties now in a lull, he'd be quite happy to accompany Ellie, enjoying the simple pleasure of her loveliness... titillated by the simmer of desire being near her evoked.

It was certainly a more enjoyable way to spend his time than facing the daunting task of charming some Virtuous Virgin, a species about which he knew almost nothing.

They entered the bonnet shop, Ellie skirting around several clusters of patrons to reach the rack at the back that held hat-making supplies. Then, abruptly, she halted. Her breath escaping in a gasp, she stared towards the opposite corner of the shop, colour draining from her face.

Following the direction of her gaze, he took in a stylishly dressed matron who'd frozen in the process of tying the ribbons of a bonnet beneath the chin of a young lady who must be her daughter—and caught his breath as well.

Hell and damnation! The girl looked like *Ellie*—or a paler reflection of her. Younger, her hair lighter, her frame smaller, but with similar facial features and the same wonderful deep violet eyes. Before he could gather his rattled thoughts, Ellie brushed past him and almost ran out the door.

He rushed after her, having difficulty keeping her in sight as she darted around knots of shoppers and out of the Bazaar. He had to wait for a group of ladies to pass through the entrance before he was able to exit himself. After looking up and down the street outside, he caught a glimpse of Ellie headed west, towards Green Park, and set out in pursuit.

She didn't slow until she reached the outer reaches of the park where, finally free from the street traffic that had hampered him, Christopher caught up to her. Her face ashen, her eyes wide and startled, she looked back over her shoulder at him and stumbled.

He caught her and braced her against him as he led her to the nearest bench. 'What is it, Ellie? What frightened you so? *Breathe*, now!'

He sat her down and chafed her chilled hands, talking at her to make her focus her vacant gaze on him, all the questions churning in his head submerged as he worked to calm her.

Finally, she took a shuddering breath and attempted a smile. 'S-sorry,' she said, her voice unsteady. 'Running off like some mindless goose. You…saw the ladies I was looking at?'

'I did. But you needn't explain anything you don't want to.'

'The resemblance is so striking, I suppose much of the story must be evident to anyone with eyes. As I'm sure you already suspect, that…girl was my sister, and that lady, my mother.'

Though Christopher was surprised by the connection, he wasn't shocked. Given the strong resemblance between the two young women, he'd already figured Ellie must be the girl's half-sister. It was deplorable, but sadly not all that unusual, for a peer to sire a daughter on the wrong side of the blanket, farm her out somewhere to give her a genteel upbringing, but never acknowledge her. Which would explain both Ellie's ladylike qualities—and her ending up a viscount's mistress.

Until he realised the flaw in that explanation. Ellie had identified the girl as her sister—but the lady as her *mother*.

'You're not base-born?' he exclaimed before he could stop himself.

Infinite sadness in her face, she shook her head. 'You know me as "Miss Parmenter"—

my governess's name, by the way—but until ten years ago, I was Miss Wanstead of Wanstead Manor in Hampshire.'

Miss Wanstead of Wanstead Manor? So Ellie had been *legitimately* born a lady? Christopher thought, astounded. Then how under heaven had she ended up Summerville's mistress?

He looked down at her, her face expressionless as she stared into the distance.

Pain twisted in his chest. He'd long suspected Ellie was either illegitimate, or the offspring of a wealthy cit educated with the daughters of the Upper Ten Thousand at some elite academy. An innocent beauty who'd been beguiled by a seducer or compromised by a man who refused to marry her, stripping her of reputation and respectability.

But to be born a legitimate lady of quality and end up Summerville's mistress? What an enormous loss of position that had been! No wonder she had that aura of sadness wrapped about her like a cloak.

Though it was far from extraordinary for a family to disown a legitimate daughter who'd been ruined, he couldn't quell a rising anger at Ellie's father. No matter what she'd done, how could he have thrown her out to survive on her own, leaving her vulnerable to a man like Summerville?

She looked at him then. 'You've always been so kind to me, despite my...position.'

Simple kindness that had cost him nothing, given to a lady who should never have required it. 'I can't even imagine how—why—' he exploded, goaded into speech by anger and outrage. 'Sorry, you needn't explain,' he said, raising a hand in apology. 'It's not my right to question, and I don't want to pry.'

'You wonder how I came to be with Summerville,' she said quietly. 'I suppose no one else besides your mama has better right to an explanation. Since I might well not have survived the experience, but for you.'

He must have looked as puzzled as he felt, for before he could question that, she continued, 'You probably don't even remember the incident, but you...saved me once, from the depths of despair. At a masquerade ball, shortly after Summerville brought me to London.'

'But I do remember it!' he exclaimed. 'Mama had sent me a note, begging me to come and escort her home. While looking for her, I found you, distraught. But—I didn't *do* anything! I couldn't even take you away, much as I would have liked to, for Summerville spotted you while you were helping me locate Mama, and bore you off.'

With a look that said the younger man had better steer clear of the Viscount's woman. He'd often wondered what might have happened had he been older, and sure enough of himself to have taken up that challenge.

'On the contrary, you did something—*everything*—I needed,' Ellie was saying. 'Treated me like the lady I'd been born, reminding me of who I was, what I was. What I could in my own mind continue to be, despite my circumstances.'

'I always knew you were a lady. What...did happen to make Miss Wanstead of Wanstead Manor end up with Summerville?'

'Papa's debts. Not all incurred by him, to be fair; the estate was already heavily encumbered when he inherited. Apparently many in Society knew he was dished. Summerville visited Wanstead to talk to Papa about buying some land—and bought me instead.'

It took a moment for Christopher to comprehend that stark statement. 'You mean your father accepted money from Summerville in exchange for allowing him to take you as his *mistress*?' he said slowly, incredulous. 'That's...*criminal*! How could he?'

She shrugged. 'Papa summoned me to his study, told me he'd been offered one last chance to save the estate, provide my younger sister a dowry, and keep my mother from homelessness and penury. That it was my duty to the family to shoulder the bitter task of making all that happen. Then he left…and Summerville walked in.'

Christopher strangled a curse, curling his hands into fists to keep from reaching for her as her expressive face revealed the absolute bleakness of that moment.

'I didn't really understand, at first,' she said softly. 'I drifted through the early days of the arrangement in a fog of disbelief, certain I was trapped in a nightmare from which I must awaken. But that night at the masquerade, the first public event I attended as his mistress… the crude comments, the groping hands of his friends as they fondled and kissed me, Summerville looking on, laughing, finally broke through the cloud of abstraction with which I'd been protecting myself from the truth.'

She took a shuddering breath before continuing, 'I was a viscount's mistress. No longer a part of polite society, but a denizen of the demimonde. A harlot. The future I'd always envisaged irretrievably lost. Feeling I must crawl out of my skin in torment, I fled the pawing hands and suggestive comments and took refuge in that anteroom. Where you found me, and asked how you could help. Though there was nothing you

could do to put right the terrible wrong of my
world, you treated me with such courtesy and
gentleness! As if I were still the lady I'd been
b-born.' Her eyes sheened with tears, she continued softly, 'I truly didn't know what I might
have done that night, had you not given me just
enough hope that I would one day escape for me
to summon the courage to go on.'

As she told her story, tears had begun to drip
down her cheeks. Wiping them away, she sucked
in deep, uneven breaths, obviously battling to
regain her composure.

His heart aching for the youth and innocence
and position in life that had been stolen from her,
Christopher had to restrain himself from taking
her in his arms. If they hadn't been in a public
park, he would have.

Disordered thoughts and emotions tumbled
through his mind as he watched her struggle
for control. Fury at the man whose weakness
had forced his daughter into sacrificing herself for the family. Contempt for the unbending
rules of Society that punished a woman without
possibility of redemption for any lapse, whether
or not she was responsible for it. The anguish
of a man who'd dedicated his professional life
to righting wrongs and knew there was nothing
he could do to right this one. A sense of shame

that, had he not recently taken it into his head to marry, believing Ellie a courtesan who had *chosen* that profession, he too might have done her the insult of offering *carte blanche*.

'I'm sorry, I'm so sorry,' he murmured, as, with one last shuddering breath, she lifted her face to him.

Swiping away two final tears, she said, 'No, *I'm* sorry. I thought I was done long ago with weeping over what cannot be mended. I suppose this unexpected glimpse into a vanished past got past my guard.' She frowned. 'My time would be better spent figuring out about what I mean to do about that glimpse.'

'Do about it?' he echoed. 'Why need you do anything?'

'There could only be one reason for my sister to be in London. She must be—eighteen now! I should have foreseen that, at some point, she might be given a Season. Only recall how strong an impression was made on you, seeing me and my sister in close proximity. Should anyone else see us and note the resemblance, it could ruin Sophie's debut before it even begins. I shall have to avoid the fashionable shopping areas until the Season is over.'

'You mean to avoid buying essentials until the family that abandoned you departs from the metropolis?' he asked, furious on her behalf that she would be so concerned for the welfare of relations who had treated her with callous neglect. 'Why should you further deprive yourself for their benefit?'

'None of what happened was Sophie's fault. Indeed, she was devoted to me.' Her gaze lost its focus, as if she were looking back through the years. 'What an enchanting child she was! And what a strikingly attractive young woman she's grown to be. I'd rather starve than do something that would ruin her chances to make a respectable marriage.'

Before he could remonstrate, she waved a hand. 'But there's no need to turn this into a melodrama. Though I should avoid areas where the *ton* shops, most of my purchases nowadays involve coal or candles or victuals. A young lady embarked on her first Season is hardly likely to frequent establishments that sell those. And if for some reason I should need a new gown or bonnet, I'm sure your mother would be happy to find one for me.'

'Mama never needs much excuse to look for gowns and bonnets,' Christopher agreed.

'Very well, Sophie is in London, but I should be able to stay out of her path.' She gave her head a little nod, as if finished coming to terms with the shocking development. 'I think I'm ready to proceed back to Hans Place.'

But as she tried to rise, she swayed, then sank back on to the bench. 'I seem unaccountably dizzy. Perhaps I should rest a bit longer.'

'Little wonder, after such a shock! The Gloucester Coffee House is just down the street. With all the coach traffic coming and going, they always have freshly made victuals. Why don't I get us a flagon of wine and a meat pasty? Some sustenance will revive you.'

She looked up at him gratefully. 'Thank you. That sounds very appealing.'

'Very good. You rest here; I'll be back in a trice.'

With that, after another concerned glance at Ellie, Christopher strode off in the direction of the Gloucester.

Chapter Four

Hҽis mind still on Ellie and her shocking revelations, his hands full with a flagon of wine and the meat pasty, Christopher had just exited the Gloucester when some sixth sense alerted him. Stopping abruptly, he turned to see a ragged urchin attempting to slip one thin hand into his jacket pocket, where the change from his purchases jingled.

The urchin pulled his hand free and scuttled backward. Before he could take to his heels, a furious Christopher jammed the pasty into the hand with the flagon and grabbed his arm.

The child struggled, trying to pull away from him. 'Didn't mean you no harm, guvn'r! I was jest moseying by. You leave go of me now, woncha?'

'I'll be leaving you with the nearest magistrate!' he snapped back. But the arm twisting in his grasp was so thin, the huge eyes looking up at him under a worn cap so frightened and desperate, Christopher realised there was no way he could turn this child in—to be jailed, transported or hanged.

They were already attracting the notice of passers-by, several patrons of the Gloucester emerging to gawk.

'Aye, take 'em to the magistrate straight away!' one cried.

'Too many thieving scum like him about, preying on their betters,' said another.

'You hang on to 'em. We'll get the landlord to send his boy for the magistrate,' said a third.

He'd better make away with the child before someone did just that. 'Thank you, good friends, but I'd rather handle this myself,' Christopher told them as, tightening his grip on the lad, he dragged him off towards Green Park.

'Wh-what you meanin' to do with me?' the child cried, still twisting to break free.

'Not call the magistrate—yet. But someone else may, if you don't stop yelling and fighting me.'

Apparently realising the truth of that, the boy ceased his struggling and began matching his shorter stride to Christopher's longer one. Perhaps, Christopher thought, he recognised they were headed to the park and figured he'd have a better chance of getting away once they reached it.

He held his tongue, too, remaining silent as Christopher led him towards the bench where Ellie rested. She spotted them as he turned into the park, and watched with puzzled curiosity as he approached with the child in tow.

'That's quite a meat pasty you've brought me,' she said as they halted before her.

'Yes, seems they are serving up a new variety in the vicinity of the Gloucester.'

As he spoke, the child suddenly yanked at his arm and twisted. Had Christopher not been expecting another attempt at escape, the lad might have broken free.

'Lemme go!' he shrieked, the pitch of his voice going ever higher as he struggled against Christopher's hold. 'You're thinkin' to murder me and leave me corpse in them bushes! I didn't do ye no harm!'

'Hush, now, nobody's going to be murdered. Although I might have to go back on that promise if you don't stop your caterwauling,' Christopher retorted. As the boy continued yanking away, the much-jostled meat pasty mashed against the wine flagon finally broke apart, one piece falling to the ground. 'Now you've ruined the lady's meat pie,' he added in exasperation.

'So's you *will* be turnin' me in?' the lad said in a quieter voice. Two tears tracked down his cheeks, leaving light trails through the grime. 'Kin I have that bit on the ground afore you does?'

Christopher had scarcely begun to nod before the child fell to his knees and grabbed the scrap, stuffing it into his mouth without even attempting to brush off the dirt. While he and Ellie looked on, aghast, he rubbed a grimy thumb carefully over the grass, popping out a few more crumbs he plucked up carefully and devoured.

Ellie's troubled gaze met his over the child's head, and he knew he wouldn't be turning the starving lad over to the law. But what *was* he to do with him?

Feed him, first. 'Here, have the rest,' he said gruffly, easing his grip on the remaining piece of pasty so the boy could pry it free. After a frozen moment, as if not sure he'd heard Christopher correctly, he tore the meat pie from Christopher's fist and stuffed it whole into his mouth.

'Thankee, sir, that be right kind,' the child said when he'd swallowed the last morsel. 'Guess I'm ready for you to take me in. Might be safer in Newgate, at that.'

A long lock of hair fell from under the lad's battered hat as he straightened. Christopher glanced over at Ellie, who was studying the child intently, her gaze examining him from hat to tattered shirt, patched jacket and shabby, too-large trousers, to the thin legs and bare feet.

She leaned forward, grasped the child under his arms, and lifted him on to the bench beside her. 'Heavens, you scarcely weigh anything at all! Why don't we start with you telling us your name, Miss…?'

Panic flitting across her face before she turned it into a look of bravado, the child wrapped her arms around her chest in a telling gesture. 'Don't know whatcha mean, ma'am. It's Joe. Joe's me name.'

'Short for Josephine, perhaps?'

'A girl? Are you sure?' Christopher murmured to Ellie.

'I suspected when I saw the hair. But I knew for certain when I lifted her, and felt those. Look closer.'

Doing as instructed, Christopher discovered what Ellie had spotted—the slight swell of budding breasts beneath the shirt as it rose and fell at the child's rapid, frightened breaths, along with hands and legs too slender and shapely to be a boy's. 'By Heaven, I believe you're right!'

'Are you wearing boy's clothing for protection?' Ellie asked her. 'And how did you come to be in this part of the city—alone? It's well-known the beadles at the Pantheon Bazaar don't allow beggars to linger—and establishments like the Pulteney and the Gloucester keep a sharp watch out for pickpockets. Besides which, pickpockets generally operate in groups.'

When the girl remained stubbornly silent, Ellie gave Christopher a rueful look. 'It appears I may have found another candidate for my school.'

To their surprise, at that pronouncement, the girl leapt up and would have raced off, had Christopher not collared her again. 'Lemme go!' she shrieked. 'I ain't going to no school like that. I'd die first! Was it Gentleman Bob what sent you to the Gloucester?' she cried, looking accusingly at Christopher. 'And I thought you was a nob!'

'Hush, now,' Ellie soothed. 'He *is* a nob, and he has no connection with Gentleman Bob. Nor is the school I run anything like the Schools of Venus operated by Sister Mary or Mrs Pritchard.'

Finding herself unable to break free, the child subsided with a whimper. 'Please, ma'am, lemme go!' she pleaded, looking up at Ellie. 'Me mum'd turn over in her grave if I was to become such.'

Seeing what must be a look of incomprehension on Christopher's face, Ellie turned to him. 'Gentleman Bob is the underworld boss who runs the gangs of pickpockets that infest the West End. He also sponsors some of the bawdy houses that specialise in very young girls.' Disgust coloured her voice. 'Establishments sometimes known as "Schools of Venus".'

Turning back to the girl, she said, 'Did you belong to one of Gentleman Bob's gangs? And struck out on your own when you got old enough that he thought you'd be more profitable to him in one of the "schools"?'

The girl stood silently for a moment. Finally, brushing the lock of hair from her face again, she said, 'Me and me brother Joe worked with one of his thieving gangs. Until Joe died last month, and the Gentleman started looking at me funny. Then one day, he run his hands over me chest and…and started rubbing me, there.' She gestured towards her small breasts. 'His eyes started glowing, like, while he done it, and he said it were time for me to go to Sister Mary's. That night, I changed into me brother's clothes and run off. I came here 'cause, like you say, he keeps his teams away from the fancy hotels and shops hereabouts, on account of the watchers, so I thought I'd be safer. But it's harder to thieve, too, and the pot boys at the Gloucester kept running me off.' She heaved a deep sigh. 'If you ain't from the Gentleman, fixing to snatch me back, what are you going to do with me?'

Ellie held out her hand, and after some hesitation, the girl gave her hers. 'My name is Ellie Parmenter,' she said, shaking it. 'Pleased to make your acquaintance, miss...?'

'Artis. Artis Gorden. After me da' went away—he were in the army in India—me mum took in washing, mostly for the theatre folks around Covent Garden. She took my name from one of them theatre signs. Joe was seven and I was six when she died, and we joined up with the Gentleman. Been there ever since.'

'Pleased to meet you, Artis. And this is Mr Lattimar, a good friend, who is also a Member of Parliament.'

'Cor!' the girl breathed. 'And I tried to pinch your coppers! You coulda had me transported!'

'As if I would do that to a starving child,' Christopher murmured, moved with both compassion and outrage for a plight that was all too heartbreakingly common.

Ellie smiled reassuringly at the girl. 'I used to be in keeping to Lord Summerville—who occasionally joined friends with a taste for that sort of thing on a visit to Sister Mary's school,' she explained. 'During my time with him, I met a lot of girls in the trade. I left the business after Summerville's death last autumn and started a school for other girls like you, who didn't want to be pulled into the life. I teach them to read and write and train them for respectable positions as shop girls, seamstresses and housemaids. Would you like to accompany me there? I can offer you a good meal, a bath, and some clean clothes. I promise, no one will harm you and you may leave again straight away if you wish. Though I do hope you will stay.'

Artis stared at Ellie incredulously, as if she didn't trust what she'd just heard. 'You'd…take me in? Feed me, learn me my letters, and how to be somethin' 'sides a pickpocket?'

'If that's what you want.'

The girl's eyes glowed in her thin face. 'Mum taught me to write my name, and do some sums, but…to *read*? Do you have books at your school, ma'am, like the ones in the shop windows? With the pretty leather covers and lettering all in gold, looking like treasures waitin' for someone to open?'

'Yes, I have books. Primers, for teaching you to read, and leather-bound treasures, too.'

The glow faded a bit as the girl looked down and inspected herself, then looked back up at

Ellie, hope and despair warring on her face. 'Are you sure you want *me*, ma'am?'

The simple words hit Christopher like a punch to the chest, knocking free a series of devastating images. Escaping his nurse and tracking down his regal father, holding out a treasured rock to the man he'd been told collected treasures, only to have Lord Vraux brush past him without a glance, as if he didn't exist...being accorded a slight, cold nod on the few occasions the governess was instructed to bring the children down for his inspection...receiving not a single word of farewell from Vraux when he was sent off to Eton.

Do you want me? Could the language contain a more poignant phrase for a love-starved child?

He looked from the girl to see on Ellie's face the same desolation those words had caused him, and was struck again by her pain.

He, at least, had always known a mother's love. She had been completely abandoned by all her nearest relations. Cast into a world where 'do you want me?' had taken on a wholly different, degrading meaning.

He wished he could wrap his arms around her and hold her until his warmth burned away all memory of that cold-blooded betrayal.

'Yes, I'm sure I want you,' Ellie told Artis,

gently wiping a tear from the girl's grimy cheek. 'I want you very much.'

'Then…then I'd love to go with you, ma'am! Lemme carry your parcel.' Looking down at it with an expert eye, Artis said, 'Cloth from Merriman & Company, in the Bazaar? Bet I could find you some jest as good and heaps cheaper in Petticoat Lane! 'Tis where all the dressmakers round Bond Street get the materials what they sell at ten times the price to the grand Society ladies.'

'Do you know where to get other household provisions?' Ellie asked. 'Coal, candles, soap, needles, thread, flour, tea, salt?'

'Oh, yes, ma'am. And should you need somethin' lifted, I could do that, too.' The girl looked over at Christopher. 'If'n I hadn't been so tired and weak today, I'da had them coins from your pocket, and you never the wiser.'

Ellie exchanged a wry look with Christopher before saying, 'Thank you, Artis, but we would have you display your gratitude in more, um, legitimate ways in future.'

As sympathetic as he was to the girl's plight, at that reminder of her origins, Christopher caught Ellie's eye to mouth silently, *Are you sure*?

At her emphatic shake of the head, he shook his. 'Very well, then. Dean Street it is.'

* * *

To his amusement, during the transit back to Ellie's school, Artis kept up a steady chatter, asking Ellie what sorts of supplies she might need in future, and naming off a list of establishments at which she could procure the goods at a bargain price. She was still proclaiming her gratitude after their arrival, as Ellie introduced her to Jensen and had Mrs Sanders bear her off with the promise of a meal, a good wash and clean garments.

Leading Christopher into her office, Ellie said, 'I'm afraid I have only wine, rather than the stronger spirits I promised. But my thanks for your help today is no less sincere.'

Accepting a glass, Christopher said, 'You're very welcome for the assistance with the landlord. I'm not so sure I want to take credit for the urchin. I have a terrible suspicion you may one day find she's stolen you blind and run off.'

Ellie shook her head. 'I doubt that. She's been a thief for certain. But many of us, given a chance to escape doing what enabled us to survive, prefer to take a different path. I think she will, too.'

Christopher shook his head dubiously. 'I hope you're right. But after so many years thieving, I suspect she knows as much about conducting herself as a law-abiding citizen as I do about properly courting a Virtuous Virgin.'

'After spending all your formative years among ladies of the demi-monde?' she replied tartly. 'A gentleman's behaviour towards innocent maids must certainly be quite diff—' She went silent, her hand with the wine glass halting halfway to her lips. 'You truly don't know what to say or how to act around innocent maids?'

'The only females of that description I've ever spent time with are my sisters. Since our conversations generally involve them plaguing me until I feel like giving them a slap, I doubt that experience will prove very useful.'

'Definitely not,' she agreed with a chuckle. 'You must know how grateful I am for your many kindnesses over the years. Artis's desire to repay my help inspires me to want to repay yours as well. You may find the offer ludicrous, coming from me, which I would totally understand, but... But as you've learned today, I used to be just the sort of innocent maid you need to court. If you think it would be helpful, I could school you in what to say, how to behave, the kinds of compliments you can pay and gifts you can offer. Warn you against the sort of remarks and behaviours that must come naturally after your long experience among the demi-monde, but which would be disastrous if directed towards a respectable female.'

Before he could think how to respond, she rushed on, 'You possess a well-earned reputation as a rake. Having neither a title nor great wealth to offset that drawback puts you at a disadvantage in the search for a suitable bride. The most well-bred and accomplished of the available maids will be pursued by a crowd of admirers, most of them with unsullied reputations. To win the superior lady you desire, your speech and behaviour must convince not just the maidens, but also their sceptical mamas, that you have truly reformed your rake's ways. I could help you do that.'

'School me into becoming the sort of gentleman who could win the hand of a Virtuous Virgin?' he asked, torn between amusement and interest.

'Exactly,' she replied. 'It's only a matter of altering behaviour and language —as I well know, you already possess a sterling character, else you'd not have treated me with such compassion and kindness all these years. I'd be honoured to repay that debt by helping you find a wife worthy of one of Parliament's rising leaders.'

As useful as that service might prove, he felt a deep, gut-level resistance. But that was foolish. If he truly meant to follow up on the notion of taking a wife, he needed to master the intricate rules of acceptable behaviour with unmarried ladies. Besides, his friends had all found respectable ladies as lovely and fascinating as the women of the demi-monde he'd admired, women to whom they believed they could remain devoted for a lifetime. Why should he not, too?

Ellie was correct; he had little doubt that his 'well-earned' reputation would precede him. He would need help to overcome his rake's ways and be seen as a serious suitor, capable of devotion and fidelity.

Was he capable of becoming such a man? He had to admit he shared his mama's doubts about his ability to limit himself to only one woman— a dull, virtuous one at that! But while he struggled to resolve that problem, it only made sense to acquire the tools that would convince Society his rake's days were behind him.

Besides, accepting would allow him to see Ellie frequently, giving him more time to figure out how to ignore his automatic responses to an alluring woman. He'd also be able to delay courting actual Virtuous Virgins until a time when, with Ellie's help, he was better equipped to confront that foreign species.

'It is an outrageous idea,' he said, setting down his wineglass.

'But…' she prompted.

'But it's ingenious, too. And I can't deny I have need of such lessons.'

'So we've a bargain, then?'

'We have a bargain, Miss Wanstead of Wanstead Manor. I am grateful for your offer and will do my best to learn well.'

'Excellent!' she said, looking delighted. 'I must remain here and help Artis settle in. Why don't we begin your lessons at my house in Hans Place tomorrow afternoon, if you are free then?'

'I am. I shall be delighted to call upon you tomorrow afternoon, Miss Wanstead.'

'I shall be delighted to have you call, Mr Lattimar.'

She held out her hand. As he shook it, sensation zinged from her fingers to his, automatically tightening his grip. Gritting his teeth, he loosened it.

Trying to purge *this* from his mind was going to be difficult. But somehow, he could manage it—and keep Ellie as a friend.

Ignoring the little voice that whispered *friend* might not be enough, he bid her goodbye and walked out of the office.

Lessons in wooing a virtuous wife—given

by a former courtesan, he thought as he strolled towards the hackney stand. His mother would appreciate the irony, even if she'd disapprove of its object.

Though he was glad to have left Ellie in a more cheerful frame of mind, Christopher wasn't so sure he wouldn't come to regret the bargain he'd just made.

Chapter Five

The next afternoon, Ellie gave the parlour one last inspection, noting with approval that the maids had dusted every surface, straightened all the furniture, and set the fire burning properly. Smoothing her dress with trembling fingers, she tried to suppress her excitement and trepidation.

It was just Christopher coming by, she scolded, trying to still the flutters in her stomach. They'd talked together on a variety of subjects times out of mind over the last ten years.

But never alone, with you in your own home, free from your bondage to Summerville, the little voice whispered back. *Never with him in the guise of suitor, and you the woman he is wooing.*

Except she was not an innocent maid, and he wouldn't be wooing *her*, no matter how well she played the part. She suppressed a wave of sadness. She'd long ago accepted that a respectable marriage was no longer possible for her. But she could equip Christopher to make one for himself—and that would be a worthy accomplishment. As his friend, of course she wanted what was best for him.

Seeing him often would be helpful for her, too. She still needed to master that lingering schoolgirl infatuation with her 'Knight in Shining Armour.' Meeting him day to day, surely she would discover he was just a man like any other. With noble traits, to be sure, but also with the inevitable flaws that would tarnish that knight's armour for good and set her free from his spell.

She should keep a list of the faults she discovered, to remind herself when she was tempted to turn dreamy-eyed. Then, having put him in proper perspective, she could regard him only as a valued friend.

She sighed. Except for that unexpected, unwanted sensual pull between them.

Much as she knew about sexual congress, she knew almost nothing about how to deal with desire. Being compelled to give herself to Summerville so young had ruined the experience of passion for her. She'd often silently marvelled when other courtesans frankly discussed their lovers, some boasting of the pleasure given them by younger swains, some lamenting the lack of technique or consideration among the older protectors.

Summerville had certainly been a member of the old school. She'd often suspected of outright invention the women who rhapsodised over the heights of fulfilment to which some man had taken them. For herself, after having been punished on several occasions for resisting Summerville's instructions, she'd tried to mentally remove herself as much as possible from what she was doing and what was being done to her as she followed his directions.

In any event, he'd been thirty years her senior, his ageing body not a subject to inspire lust.

Christopher Lattimar was a man in the prime of health, strength and virility.

Just recalling his handsome face, the strong arms that had held her, evoked that distinctive ripple of what she now recognised as desire. Recalling their almost-kiss, she felt a stirring of the *yearning* that had consumed her then.

That must be what those satisfied women had been talking about. That intensity of feeling, as if her nerves were on fire, all her senses striving towards some pinnacle of pleasure. With Christopher, she'd wanted more and more of it, and been awed—and disturbed—by the strength of her disappointment when it was denied her.

Soon she'd be spending more time alone with Christopher. She knew he desired *her*. With privacy, and opportunity, she could probably break through the barriers of his control, sweep him into kissing her, touching her, and fully experience what he'd made her crave.

Except, she'd promised herself she'd never again be any man's convenient—and that was all she could ever be for him. She had also offered to give him, not a tryst with a not-so-reformed courtesan, but lessons from a once-virtuous maiden.

It would be a betrayal of their friendship to promise that, and then attempt to seduce him.

It would be a betrayal of her character to seduce him, and become again what she'd only just escaped.

Even if it meant she would most likely be turning her back for good on discovering all that pleasure meant.

No wonder her stomach was tied in knots!

But if she meant to salvage her dignity and self-esteem, she must master her craving for him as she mastered her infatuation. Submerge all feeling but the pure affection of a concerned friend, and offer him only what he *really* needed from her—not temporary pleasure, but the skills to win the wife who would stand by and support him for the rest of his life.

Thus resolved, she chose a book from the stack of suitable volumes she'd assembled for his lesson and set to reading.

She'd gone over the same paragraph six times when the front doorbell sounded. Quelling the nerves that skittered in her belly, she made herself look at the book again while she waited for Tarleton to escort Christopher in.

But the words of greeting dried on her lips when she glanced up and saw, not her good friend's smiling face—but her mother's grim one.

'Lady Wanstead,' Tarleton announced, giving her a curious glance—no doubt as astonished as Ellie to be called upon by this obviously respectable matron.

Ellie closed her lips before she could blurt out 'Mother'. 'Tarleton, would you bring us tea, please?' she said instead. Giving her unexpected visitor a stiff curtsy, she said, 'Won't you have a seat, my—my lady?'

After Tarleton closed the door, her mother said, 'Miss Parmenter, I believe you're calling yourself?'

Years of anguish rushed back, and she struggled to control a sudden surge of anger. 'It would have been a bit impolitic to call myself "Miss Wanstead", don't you agree, *Mama*?'

'Your father knew we could count on your discretion,' Lady Wanstead replied, a surprisingly bitter edge to her tone.

Determined to extract as much information that might prove useful in protecting her sister as she could from what would surely be a short interview, Ellie said, 'You're here for Sophie's comeout, aren't you? Who will be sponsoring her?'

'Your Great-Aunt Marion. She has…looked after us since your father died.'

Surprise and a twist of conflicting emotions—anger, disgust, a wisp of sadness mingled with a child's anguish over a parent's inexplicable betrayal—held Ellie momentarily silent. 'He's dead?' she said at last, unable to make herself say 'Papa'.

'Yes, five years ago now. He was never the same after we…lost you. Officially, he died after taking a fall from his horse—but he was castaway at the time. He was always in his cups, sometimes locking himself in his study for days at a time. Ravaged by grief, probably, over what became of you.'

'Or guilt?' Ellie suggested, still working to master that anger. 'Did you go to live with Aunt Marion then? As I recall, Wanstead Hall was in ruinous condition. Enfield Place would have been more comfortable.'

'Soon after. Despite your father's…condition, the estate actually prospered those first years after you—left. New hangings and furnishings for all the rooms, smoking chimneys repaired, the tenant farms put in better order.'

'I'm ecstatic that sacrificing me meant you could dine without the smell of smoke,' she spat out.

Ignoring that gibe, her mother continued, 'Wanstead's cousin Reginald, who inherited, would have allowed us to stay in the Dower House, but I preferred to accept Aunt Marion's offer. After what had happened, I never wanted to see Wanstead again.'

'I am moved by your pain,' Ellie said.

'What exactly do you think I could have done to prevent it?' her mother snapped back. 'My dowry was long spent. I had no resources of my own. I didn't even know what Wanstead intended until after Summerville had taken you away! By then, it was too late. Even if I'd had the means to follow, you would have already been ruined.'

Hearing her mother's words changed what she'd believed all these years. She'd thought her mother an equal partner in the outrage committed against her.

Staring at the woman who'd fallen silent, her face averted, Ellie hesitated, unsure what to say, how to feel. 'If…if you didn't approve his actions, why didn't you try to find me after his death?'

Her mother shrugged. 'What would have been the point of that? The moment you arrived in London with Summerville, you were lost to polite Society. Dead to me. There was nothing I could do for you, and I had your sister to protect.'

Dead to her. True as the words were, they should not have hurt so much. But despite what her logical mind argued, her heart recoiled in anguish at this second rejection. A reviving fury burned it away. 'Then why bother to come now?'

'After I recognised you at the bonnet shop, I hurried Sophie out, hoping the proprietor hadn't got a good glimpse of the two of you together. But at several of the other establishments we visited, the shopkeepers kept staring at her, or remarked how familiar she looked. I told Aunt Marion about the encounter as soon as we returned home. She immediately consulted a good friend from her own debut Season, Lady Sayleford, whom she says practically runs society.'

'Lady Maggie's great-aunt,' Ellie murmured.

'What?'

'It doesn't matter.'

'In any event, Lady Sayleford advised that since the resemblance is so strong someone might eventually make the connection, and since you are no longer a…a kept woman, it would be better for us to quietly recognise you. Not, of course, take you with us into Society, or do anything that might call attention to the bond. Lady Sayleford instructed Aunt Marion to bring you to call, so that if one of Sophie's suitors should learn about you, the Dowager Countess could assure the young man she was aware of the relationship and approved of Sophie, despite her… unfortunate sister.'

Her unfortunate sister. Battered by another wave of hurt and loss, she struggled to recapture the fury. *Why should you put yourself out for the family that disowned you?* Christopher had said. Taking strength from his angry words, she rallied her bruised spirit.

Had her mother been asking for herself, she would have refused. But this was for Sophie. What good would it have been to sacrifice her own future, if she refused to protect her little sister's now?

'Very well,' she replied, still struggling to suppress the pain.

'That's settled, then.' Her mother rose. 'You needn't see me out.' As she walked towards the door, Ellie watching with an aching heart, all the old wounds torn back open, her mother hesitated. Turned back towards her. 'You look...well, Tess. Still so beautiful. If only you had been less beautiful.'

Ellie swallowed the tears that threatened. 'If I had been less beautiful, Sophie wouldn't have a chance at a future either.'

At that moment, a knock sounded at the parlour door, followed by the entrance of Tarleton. 'Sorry, ma'am, but you've another visitor. Mr Lattimar.'

With the shock of her mother's unexpected call, she'd completely forgotten she'd been expecting Christopher for his first lesson. He followed Tarleton in, then stopped short, his smile fading as he recognised Lady Wanstead.

Meanwhile, her mother was looking him up and down with blatant suspicion. Turning back to Ellie, she said, 'I was told that after your... association with Summerville ended, you'd not formed any further...arrangements. Was I misinformed?'

Hanging on to her temper, Ellie disdained to answer. 'Mother,' she said coolly, 'let me present Christopher Lattimar, Member of Parliament for Wiltshire and son of Lord and Lady Vraux. Mr Lattimar, my mother, Lady Wanstead.'

Christopher made a curt bow. 'As you may be aware, Lady Wanstead, Miss Parmenter runs a school for disadvantaged girls, for which my mother is one of the sponsors. Along with the Earl of Witlow and his daughter, Viscountess Lyndlington. Excuse me for intruding upon your meeting with your mother, Miss Parmenter. I came about the donation for your school that my mother promised.'

'I will not hinder your business,' her mother replied, looking relieved. 'You will receive an invitation to call on Lady Sayleford,' she said, turning to Ellie. 'I trust you will make yourself available.'

'For Sophie's sake,' Ellie said evenly.

'Naturally. Miss—Parmenter, Mr Lattimar.' According them a brief curtsy, Ellie's mother turned and, ramrod straight, walked out.

She wasn't aware she was trembling until Christopher stepped over to seize her arm. 'You're shaking like a thistle in a windstorm. Are you all right? Let me help you to a seat.'

She did feel unsteady—not surprising, after her mother's revelations and demands had stirred up ten years' worth of anguish, anger, grief and resentment. 'Thank you,' she said after he'd helped her to a chair. 'Tarleton was supposed to have brought tea. I can't imagine where that got to.'

'Let me ring.'

Before he could reach the bell pull, Tarleton poked his head in the door. 'Are you all right, miss? Sorry about the tea, but that woman looked so fearsome, I was afraid to go off and leave you alone with her, so I loitered in the hall.'

Touched by his solicitude, Ellie said, 'Thank you for your concern. But as you can see, I'm in good hands now. And I would like that tea.'

'At once, miss.' With a nod, the butler bowed himself out.

'What was that visit about—if you don't mind my asking?' Christopher said, careful, she noted, to take the chair adjacent, rather than a spot on the sofa beside her.

Ellie gave a mirthless laugh. 'It seems the black sheep is to be brought back into the fold—though the "fold" will remain well outside the drawing room! I must have made more of an impression on various modistes of the *ton* than I thought, for apparently several, upon seeing my sister, were struck by the impression they'd seen her before, and said as much to my mother.'

'I'd bet they knew exactly who the girl reminded them of,' Christopher said. 'The question is, what will they do about it?'

'Gossip, eventually. I suspect my mother also fears they know, or will soon figure it out. Wanting to head off an "unfortunate revelation" down the line that might scare off Sophie's suitors, she consulted my great-aunt who, apparently, is a bosom friend of Lady Maggie's Great-Aunt Lilly. The upshot is, the "Grande Dames" recommended that the family quietly recognise me.' She laughed again. 'I'm to make myself available to accompany Aunt Marion to meet Lady Sayleford.'

Christopher frowned. 'Curious that Maggie's aunt didn't inform her you are already acquainted. Although Maggie does say her aunt likes to *know* more than she *reveals*, especially to people outside the family. Did you tell your mother?'

'No. At least I'll have the satisfaction of watching her surprise when Lady Sayleford acknowledges we've already met.'

'Not just met, but dined together.'

'Only because Lady Maggie included her when she and the other Hellion ladies invited me in thanks for my assistance to Ben Tawny. It's not as though I dine with her frequently!'

'You might,' Christopher pointed out. 'She often attends Lord Witlow's political "discussion evenings", which include a great range of personalities from all walks of life. You know Maggie has urged you to attend, and I'd be happy to escort you.'

Ignoring that—for she'd known even before their almost-kiss that it would not be prudent to become too used to Christopher's company—she said, 'Mean-spirited though it may be, I might not have told her even if I'd had the opportunity. Were it not for the harm it could do Sophie, I might refuse to co-operate at all. She doesn't *really* want to recognise me as her daughter, merely head off any potential problems my existence might cause.' She ought to leave it at that, but with the hurt of it still making her heart bleed, she couldn't keep herself from adding, 'She said as far as she is concerned, I am still d-dead to her.'

'She *said* that? Wretched woman!' With a muttered curse, Christopher reached over and seized her hand, compassion—and understanding—in his gaze.

For once, she welcomed the zing of connection that flowed from his hand to hers, that little shock enough to check the tears stinging her eyes. 'She vowed she had no idea my father intended to turn me over to Summerville until after I was gone. Though it is also true, as she claimed, there wasn't much she could have done to stop him, even had she known.' She sighed, trying to knit her ravelled emotions back together. 'At least I won't have to brace myself to encounter my father. He died five years ago.'

'Good. That saves me the trouble of shooting him. Murder committed by a Member of Parliament is severely frowned upon, you know.'

Knowing he was trying to cheer her, and grateful to him for trying, she managed a smile.

Tarleton came in then with the tea tray, and Christopher sat back, releasing her hand. Wistful at the loss of his touch, Ellie couldn't help feeling regret that she would never have the right to command it.

That right would belong to his wife. She should pull herself together, put behind her the ugly past stirred up by her mother, and get on with his lesson.

And at the same time, remind herself he was not here to court her, but to let her equip him to court someone else. At which time, he would transfer his heart, his compassion and his support to his new wife.

Before that happened, she needed to pry him out her heart, mind and senses.

Chapter Six

While Ellie performed the ritual of pouring tea, Christopher tried to submerge his fury and think of something to ease her distress. Which was difficult when what he'd really like to do was find her mother and strangle her for her thoughtless cruelty.

'Shall we begin your lesson?' Ellie asked as she handed him his cup. 'Should you be invited to take tea at a young lady's home—a signal honour, especially early in your acquaintance—the procedure will be much the same as taking it with your mother. The lady of the house, or the young lady upon whom you are calling, will pour. Take a chair opposite—never presume to sit right beside her. As for proper topics of conversation—'

'Before we get started,' he interrupted, 'let me say something.' Driven to try to ease the pain she'd submerged beneath a brittle smile, he continued, 'The subject is doubtless too personal for a social tea, but I hope it won't make matters worse.'

Looking puzzled, Ellie set down her cup. 'Go on.'

'You are a lovely, gracious, compassionate woman, a lady to your toes, as your friends and everyone who comes into contact with you knows. That your mother refuses to recognise that is her loss, not yours.'

She blinked rapidly against the sheen of tears glazing her eyes. 'You're being kind, as always.'

'Not kindness, just simple truth.' The smile he attempted became more of a grimace as he continued, 'Despite those fine words, I know from my own experience with Vraux the power some individuals have to hurt us, even when we tell ourselves they shouldn't.'

'Lord Vraux...never warmed to you?'

He hadn't intended the conversation to veer towards his experiences, but if describing the anguish of his fatherless boyhood distracted her from the sorrow her mother had caused, he'd force himself to relate what he normally avoided remembering.

'No,' he said shortly. 'Vraux never had any interest in being my father. Though to be fair, he showed little enough interest in Gregory, his heir, even though he acknowledges him as legitimate offspring. Unlike me and my sisters.'

'Do you know Sir Julian Cantrell well?' Ellie asked curiously.

Another exploding cannonball of an enquiry he normally sidestepped. But as she'd listened, the tenseness of her body had relaxed, the frown on her forehead less pronounced. Since this conversational diversion seemed to be working, he made himself continue, 'I've met him several times. Mama…never talks of him. Once, when I was especially angry with Vraux, I pressed Aunt Gussie to tell me about him. She said he was the only man my mother had truly loved. Single at the time of their affair, Sir Julian went on to marry and sire a family. Daughters only, though—which is probably why he was willing to grant Mama's request and sponsor me for Parliament.'

'I always thought there was a great deal of sadness below your mama's veneer of flirtatious charm. Vraux…never objected to all the attention paid his wife by other men?'

'Apparently not, according to Aunt Gussie. Once Mama had provided him with a son and heir, Vraux was happy to busy himself curating his inanimate treasures, leaving her to amuse herself as she chose. Lonely, and despairing of ever attaining her husband's interest, she looked for affection in a series of lovers, and in her children. Even when Mama flouted her lovers, Aunt Gussie said, she got no reaction from him. I've tried to ignore Vraux as he ignores all of us, and build my life around Mother and my friends.'

'You are right; we shouldn't hold on to pain we didn't earn or deserve, but shrug it off and move forward. For my part…wounding as Mama's words were, I *do* inhabit a different world, and now always will. In a very real sense, I *am* dead to her. Were she to become more involved in my life, she would put Sophie's future in jeopardy. Better to concentrate on making sure her remaining daughter gets respectably settled, and avoid the heartache of being torn between two irreconcilable worlds.'

'By demanding you agree to a limited recognition, she's asking *you* to do that,' he pointed out, his anger over that fact reviving.

She sighed. 'Once I accepted that my abrupt departure from life as I'd always known it was permanent and irreversible, I worked hard to block out the past and resist the temptation to discover what was happening to those I'd left behind. I didn't want to hate them—not even my father. Just not…think of them any more. Seeing Mama shattered that barrier of separation. I may be inviting more heartache, but I...I truly wish to see Sophie. Even on a "limited" basis.'

Christopher recalled his glimpse of the girl who resembled Ellie so closely. 'She was devoted to you, you said.'

Tears glimmering on her lashes again, Ellie nodded. 'She used to follow me about like a chick after its mother hen, chattering all the way. Seek me out in the library and tease me to put down my book and tell her a story. I helped her sew her first sampler and comforted her when storms woke her in the night.' She sighed again. 'But it's been ten years, and I mustn't expect she'll be as interested in seeing me as I am in seeing her. In fact, she may well be appalled that she's expected to acknowledge her relationship to a harlot.'

'Don't!' Christopher said sharply. When she jumped, her eyes widening at the harshness of his tone, he couldn't restrain himself any more. Moving to sit beside her on the sofa, he took her by the shoulder and tipped her chin up. 'Don't ever describe yourself in such terms! What Summerville did to you is not your fault. You still possess all the purity, the integrity, the loveliness you had the day your father sacrificed you on the altar of your family's advancement.'

Swallowing hard, she nodded. 'Thank you for that.'

He'd meant to release her immediately, but as he stared down into those mesmerising violet eyes, he couldn't move away. Desire and tenderness swelled in his chest. 'You are the essence of loveliness, inside and out.'

'Dear Christopher,' she whispered, reaching up to touch his cheek. A touch that sizzled and burned against his skin. And then, as he watched her, unable to breathe, she tilted his chin down, angled her face up, and kissed him.

It was just a simple brush of her closed mouth against his, so sweet, so innocent, one might think her a maid like her sister rather than a practised courtesan.

All the same, that touch fired his simmering desire into white heat. He had to exercise every bit of self-control to keep his arms at his sides and resist the urge to bind her against his chest and ravage those plum-sweet lips.

He was trembling and breathless from the effort when she leaned away.

'Oh, dear,' she whispered. 'Pray forgive me. I really hadn't intended… But…you cannot imagine how much your good opinion means to me.'

He rose and took an agitated turn about the room, trying to get a grip on rampaging senses that screamed at him to return and kiss her again. 'My fault as much as yours,' he said shortly. 'I should know better than to touch you. Too much temptation.'

'And that is my fault! I vowed to help you reform and move towards the future you must embrace. Not tempt you to backslide into old habits.' She gave a strained laugh. 'Kissing a female after she pours you tea may do for a courtesan, but it's definitely not permissible behaviour with an innocent young maiden.'

That maiden could never be as irresistible as you. His senses still urged him to lead her up to her bedchamber, let him demonstrate just how much he cherished her loveliness.

But upstairs was where her protector had led her. Lamb to the slaughter, trapping her in a life she'd never wanted. If and when he ever made love to her, it wouldn't be in the bed where Summerville had taken her in lust.

He blew out a frustrated sigh. 'No kissing of tea-pouring maidens. Right.' *And no touching of maidens who make you crazy with wanting*. 'I'd have to apologise to that innocent maid for taking such liberties. Though I am not sorry. I've wanted to kiss you for years. Still, since I'm *trying* to reform my behaviour, please accept my apology for overstepping the bounds.'

plored his face, travelled up and down his body, before returning to his lips. After a time-suspended minute, she gave her head a little shake and looked away, a blush colouring her cheeks as she stood up.

'It goes without saying that such a remark—any remark that touches on a lady's garments, other than a general compliment on her loveliness—is strictly forbidden—especially given the reputation you are trying to overcome! Say something like that, and your young lady's mama will have you shown the door before you can finish the sentence.'

He nodded. 'Understood. Forgive me again. To the other dictates, I shall add "Edit speech before uttering".'

She gave him a sympathetic look. 'Few of us can control our thoughts. But all of us must learn to manage how, when and whether to express them. Let me fetch my pelisse and I'll rejoin you in a minute.'

Were her 'uncontrolled thoughts' producing the same visions his were? The image of that candlelit chamber recurred as she walked from the room. If so, heaven help them both.

Maybe taking lessons from a courtesan was not such good idea.

Quickly he backed away from that conclusion.

Being with her was the best way to learn to control his behaviour—if not his thoughts. Because proximity to a beautiful, desirable woman called up all the comments and instinctive reactions he needed to retrain. Just this short time today had demonstrated how much he had to learn.

Besides, he knew he couldn't make himself give up the last encounters he'd have with her before he must move on to court that Virtuous Virgin. There would be no cancelling of lessons unless *she* requested it.

A short time later, Christopher helped Ellie alight from a hackney in the Covent Garden market. 'Although the area is known for its theatres,' Ellie explained, 'it also houses some of the best flower shops.' Leading him to one off the main square, the area before it filled with containers of colourful blooms, she continued, 'Let's say you danced with an intriguing young lady at a ball last night. What flowers would you send her the next day?'

Christopher inspected the varieties available—jonquils, tulips, various shades of heather, violets, bluebells, delicate crocuses, sweet pinks, wood irises, lilies of the valley, and sweet peas, with bins of ivy, fern, holly a green foil to their brighter hues. 'I *would* choose roses, but they don't appear to be in season yet. Maybe some jonquils,' he said, pulling out a stem. 'With bluebells for contrast?' he said, choosing that, 'and a bit of fern or ivy?'

She nodded. 'Fern would be good, for that signals you are fascinated by the lady, and daffodils also signal your regard. Bluebells indicate humility, which is always a courteous way to present yourself, but best avoid ivy when you're just getting to know the girl, for it signifies wedded love—a sign you may not be ready to give on such slim acquaintance!'

Christopher hastily returned the sprig to its bin as a salesgirl, who'd been busy with another customer, hurried over to greet them. 'Can I fix you a bouquet, sir?' she asked.

'Yes. Several stems of each of these, please, wrapped up in blue ribbon.'

The shop girl had finished the bouquet, and Christopher presented it to Ellie. 'Payment for my first lesson. To complete your instruction, though, is there anything else here—besides ivy—I'd need to avoid?'

'Crocus indicates "cheerfulness", which might tell the lady you're not really interested, merely being polite. Pinks in general are good, signalling fascination, but avoid the striped—those say "no, I'm not interested". Sweet peas can indicate gratitude—but also "thank you and goodbye".'

'So, if I want to tell the lady the dance was pleasant, but nothing more? Would I send crocus, striped pinks and sweet peas?'

'If you're not interested, better not to call or send flowers at all,' Ellie said.

'But isn't it considered impolite to dance with the girl, and then not call on her?' Christopher asked, trying to pull up some long-ago instructions from Aunt Gussie.

'Better for the lady to think you rude than raise hopes you don't expect to fulfil. Paying attention to a lady will lead to expectations that you have serious intentions. If you do not, and later stop seeing her and pursue another, it would damage her chances of obtaining a respectable offer.'

Christopher frowned. 'In what way?'

'Society—and other prospective suitors—will wonder why, after getting to know her better, you broke off your pursuit. Unfairly or not, they will conclude you felt there was something lacking in the lady.'

'A girl's prospects could be blighted on so flimsy a ground?' Christopher exclaimed.

'I'm afraid so. Which is why you must carefully select which ladies you call on, dance with, or take in to supper at balls. Society is always watching, and the amount of attention accorded a girl by her escorts closely scrutinised.'

'I never realised courtship was so filled with hazards,' Christopher said. 'Ruin a girl just because you stop paying her attention? Be thought ready to ask for her hand because you dance too often, or send a bouquet full of ivy? Makes me glad I've avoided it all these years. Giving presents to experienced matrons requires much less discrimination.'

'Sadly true. Carriages, jewels, gowns—anything is permissible. Although more taxing on the purse.'

'Ah, but the reward is immediate.' Instantly, his thoughts flew back to her kiss—and how much he'd like to sample more of her.

Irritated that he'd just lapsed again, he once again stifled the desire that seemed to escape restraint at every opportunity. 'So I must add to the list "call after dancing only if I want to continue the acquaintance" and "send the proper sort of flowers". What other presents are permissible, and when would I send them?'

'None, immediately. Remember, your calls upon the young lady will be brief, and you will never, ever be left alone with her, so it will take longer than with…other sorts of ladies…to become well enough acquainted to decide if you wish to pursue her. Although, as with any female, there will be clues in her behaviour to help you make that choice. Women of the demimonde can display their interest quite blatantly, but even an innocent maid will give you signs—subtle, but observable, if you're paying attention.'

Christopher raised his eyebrows sceptically. 'What "subtle" reactions must I watch for?'

'Notice whether or not the lady looks directly at you. If she does look, observe *how* she looks at you. A very shy girl probably won't look at you at all, and will defer to her chaperone. Which might be a sign she's not the right wife for you. A gentleman involved in politics needs a hostess with the intelligence and self-assurance to draw out her guests, ensure a good flow of conversation, and deftly deflect or defuse any budding disagreements. It's quite an art.'

'I suppose it is. Maggie does it so well, one doesn't notice how expertly she manages her guests. It would be advantageous to acquire a wife with such skill, so I don't have to impose on Maggie whenever I need to gather a discussion group for dinner. So, observe the lady during my call, and eliminate the shy and retiring.'

'Of course, if a shy girl touches your sensibilities, I'd not rule her out simply because she might not make a perfect political wife. A lady who wins your heart would be the best choice of all. As much as possible, personal preference should be given full weight.'

If only he could choose by personal preference alone. Unfortunately, Society had rigid requirements for a woman to be considered suitable to become the wife of a baron's son and Member of Parliament.

'If the lady does take part in the conversation,' Ellie had continued, 'notice whether her comments add something of interest or value. Since she will be on her best behaviour, hoping to attract a suitor, having her prattle on about matters of no consequence would indicate she possesses a shallow mind. No matter how beautiful she might be, at some point your dinner guests will tire of having to show a polite interest in trivialities. That would be a worse failing in a hostess than shyness! Having previously been associated with only the cleverest of demi-mondaines, I doubt you have encountered either shy or garrulous ladies, so be on your guard.'

Christopher shook his head. 'I can only imagine what Ben would do, were he seated next to a female who spent the entire meal talking about the trimming of her bonnet.'

Ellie nodded. 'Exactly. You also want a lady

with enough self-confidence to meet your eye or even flirt a little, while avoiding any who are *too* flirtatious. A good political hostess needs to feel comfortable in mostly masculine company. But a lady who seems intent on attaching every gentleman around her, as if she must always be the focus of attention and conversation, would make a taxing wife. You don't want to spend your dinners frowning away every gentleman she attempts to beguile.'

Christopher recoiled. 'How would I conduct any business, if I had to waste all my time keeping tabs on my wife?'

'Exactly.'

'So, during the short duration of a call, I need to carefully observe the female's behaviour so as to rule out any who are too shy, too shallow, or too flirtatious.' He shook his head with a groan. 'The task grows more daunting with every new instruction. Indeed, I feel the need for some restorative. There's a tavern at the next corner—can I offer you a glass of ale?'

'You can certainly invite me to have a glass—but you could never invite an innocent maid into a tavern.'

Christopher sighed in exasperation. 'So if we are strolling, and it is warm, we must expire of thirst?'

Ellie laughed. 'You could leave the lady in the care of her maid or footman and fetch refreshments, as you did for me in Green Park. But the only public place at which an unmarried lady might take refreshments *with* you would be Gunter's. Even there, you likely order tea, cake or ices for the waiter to bring to you in the square, rather than going into the shop.'

'Remain out in the open, to demonstrate no improprieties are occurring.'

'Precisely.'

'Then let's go there now. It's too chilly for ices, but you can show me the proper place to bring a lady for tea and cake.'

Ellie grinned at him. 'I thought you needed ale.'

'When the lesson is over, I'll escort you back to Hans Place and you may offer me a brandy.' *Where remembering I'm in Summerville's house will keep me from wanting more.*

Chapter Seven

Another hackney ride brought them to Berkeley Square, where Christopher gave their order to a waiter and escorted Ellie to a bench. As Ellie had predicted, there were a number of carriages under the plane trees in the Square, their occupants sipping tea and nibbling cakes.

Christopher scanned the vehicles, noting several contained turbaned matrons seated beside young ladies in pastel-coloured pelisses, the gentlemen—some of whom he recognised—on the backward-facing seat, conversing with them.

Some appeared to be *very* young ladies. Alarm spiking through him, he murmured, 'Heaven forfend! Some of those chits look scarcely old enough to be out of the nursery. How could I woo one of them? It's almost as bad as visiting one of those "schools" Artis feared.'

'Some are quite young,' Ellie admitted. 'But

generally they have some say in who they marry, and at the end of it they will be respectably settled.'

Her expression clouded, and Christopher knew she must be thinking of her own circumstances—being very young, having no choice, and ending up ruined. Before he could say anything, her brow smoothed and she said, 'Besides, not every unmarried lady will be straight from the schoolroom. Families of higher rank or those who can provide large dowries don't feel compelled to marry off their daughters in their first Season. An older girl with several years' polish would probably appeal more to you.'

'Or an experienced, but respectable widow?' he suggested, recalling his talk with his mother.

'There's not so many of those, but there would be fewer restrictions on how and when you could meet with her. Though, of course, most of the rules of proper behaviour would still apply.'

His instinctive distaste for the whole business suddenly welling up, Christopher made a face. 'Maybe I'll skip courtship altogether and elope with her.'

Ellie laughed at his disgruntlement. 'You'd ruin even the widow's reputation if you did that!'

After a halt in the conversation when the waiter brought their tea and cakes, Ellie continued, 'There's no need for anything so drastic. Once you learn the proper techniques, you'll find that getting to know a respectable lady is no more daunting than becoming acquainted with… more accessible females. And I'd not have you set your mind against someone just because she's young. A self-confident, well-educated, intelligent girl with far-reaching interests and a lively curiosity might well capture your heart with her freshness and purity, as you capture hers. It's what I most wish for you,' she added quietly, tenderness in those magnificent violet eyes as she gazed at him.

A girl like she had been, ten years ago? How he wished he might have known her then, when she'd been pure and innocent and eager, poised for a bright future. Before a father's weakness and an aristocrat's lust had ruined her dreams, leaving her available now only for the one thing he must not have. 'What I wish is altogether different,' he murmured.

She didn't pretend to misunderstand. 'It's foolish to wish for what can never be,' she replied, the warmth in her eyes turning to sadness.

He gritted his teeth against the urge to take her hand in comfort. Before he could commit that mistake, a sardonic voice said, 'What's this? A tête-à-tête under the trees?'

Christopher looked up to see Lord Mountgarcy on horseback at the edge of the square. His mild irritation increased to full-blown annoyance as he recalled his mother mentioning the Viscount as one of the men who might be pursuing Ellie. 'Mountgarcy,' he acknowledged the man with a nod. 'Returning from your night's revels?'

'Merely a refreshing morning ride before beginning again,' the older man replied as he swung down from the saddle. Handing the bridle to the urchin who came running, he strolled over.

Christopher raised his eyebrows. 'A bit late for a "morning" ride, I should think. The afternoon's nearly gone.'

His smug expression broadening to a smile at Christopher's hostile tone, the older man halted beside them, his gaze roaming from Christopher to Ellie—who ignored him. 'Didn't know you were entering the lists in the competition for the lovely Ellie. Wouldn't have thought you had enough blunt.'

'There are no "lists" to enter, my lord,' Ellie said, according the Viscount a cool nod. 'I thought I'd already made that very clear.'

'So you *said*,' Mountgarcy replied, subjecting her to a full and insolent appraisal that had Christopher itching to jump up and punch him.

'How often a lady says one thing, while her behaviour demonstrates just the opposite! As one might assume from your appearance here in the company of Mr Lattimer, who is famed for his associations with only the loveliest of demi-mondaines. If you *are* beginning your search for a new protector, surely you won't forget the many inducements I can offer.'

'Miss Parmenter,' Christopher said, emphasising the formality, 'is a close friend of my mother, who is one of the sponsors of the school for indigent girls she now occupies herself running.'

Mountgarcy raised his eyebrows. 'A "school" for girls? That's something that could interest me, though I generally prefer my pigeons a bit older. You do have two sisters, don't you, Lattimar? Given your mother's reputation, I'm not surprised they are thinking of joining Ellie's sisterhood. If they are as pretty is she is, they should be quite successful.'

Rage at the double insult—to Ellie, to his family—so blinded Christopher that he barely restrained himself from punching the Viscount on the spot. Only the fact that the older man was obviously trying to goad him allowed him to keep the fury under control. 'I find those remarks so insulting,' he replied, managing an even tone, 'that I should be pleased to invite you to a round of fisticuffs at Gentleman Jackson's. Unless you care to apologise?'

Doubtless realising Christopher could pummel him into a pulp, disquiet flashed in the Viscount's eyes. 'No need for violence,' he replied in a genial tone. 'Forgive me if I gave offence.'

Christopher was about to call him on that blatant falsehood, but a glance at Ellie's strained face had the sharp remark dying on his lips. As much as he'd been angered, how much more humiliating had it been for her to be described as the matron of a brothel—with several carriages close by, their occupants easily able to overhear?

'Mr Lattimar, I believe I am ready to leave,' she said, only a trembling lip betraying her agitation. 'There's a bad odour here.'

'Of course, Miss Parmenter.' Rising, he offered Ellie his arm.

'But you've not finished your refreshment,' Mountgarcy said, gesturing to the half-empty cups

Turning to stare the Viscount straight in the eye, Christopher said, 'I think we *are* finished here. All of us.'

Mountgarcy waved off that warning with a chuckle. After a significant glance at the bouquet Ellie had set on the bench beside her, he said,

'So it's to be all sweetness and innocence, is it, Ell—*Miss Parmenter*? Very well, I can play that game too—when the outcome also promises to be so…sweet.'

He gave them a nod neither acknowledged as Christopher led Ellie from the square towards the nearby hackney stand. 'Insufferable man!' she exploded once they were seated in a carriage. 'I wish *I* could meet him at Gentleman Jackson's! The only good thing about being ruined is not having to be polite to an ass like the Viscount.'

'I'm sorry you were subjected to that. It probably was a mistake for me to insist on taking tea in the open. Mountgarcy was correct in pointing out that being seen with me does not strengthen your claim of having no interest in finding a new protector,' Christopher said, regretting for perhaps the first time his well-earned reputation as a rake.

'Nor does being seen in public with *me* give the impression you are ready to abandon your rake's ways. No young lady would willingly enter a union with a gentleman she suspects is still involved with a courtesan.' She sighed deeply. 'Perhaps it would be better after all—'

Before she could finish the sentence, Christopher interrupted to protest. 'But I'll never be successful at pursuing a respectable miss if you don't finish my training! We'll be more careful about where we appear in future—to avoid encounters with men of Mountgarcy's ilk.' Besides, he needed to continue seeing her to make sure the Viscount refrained from creating any further unpleasantness.

Looking relieved, as if she were happy he'd found an excuse not to end their association, she nodded. 'Many men with a well-established rogue's reputation have been able to convince Society they've truly reformed. Once you are fully equipped to begin your quest, we shall end our public association in enough time for such a transformation to be believable.'

Putting out of mind the unpleasant notion of ending their time together, he concentrated on the part he preferred to hear. 'Then we shall continue the lessons?'

She nodded. 'Yes, we will continue them. But...would you mind terribly if I reneged on that offer of brandy? This afternoon has been rather taxing. Would you simply escort me home, and meet me again another day?'

It might be wise to avoid the temptation of being alone at her home with her—temptation that would take some resisting, despite Summerville's malevolent spectral presence. 'Of course.

You are doing *me* the favour, after all. I'll see you safely home, and wait for you to let me know the place and time for my next lesson.'

A short time later, the hackney halted before her town house in Hans Place. After handing her down, Christopher walked her up the steps. 'I am very grateful, you know. When I finally launch off into the world of Virtuous Virgins, I'm much more confident of having success.'

'You'd have found your feet eventually, without lessons,' Ellie replied. 'However, having some knowledge of what to expect and how to respond will help you achieve your goal of bewitching a suitable bride more quickly.'

His goal. Yes, he needed to keep reminding himself that what he really wanted was to find the ideal wife. He just needed to keep repeating that until inclination believed what reason kept telling it.

Tarleton opened the door for her. Christopher was about to reluctantly bid her goodbye when the butler leaned forward, holding out a note. 'A footman brought this urgent message for you, miss. He's waiting in the hall for a reply.'

Christopher halted on the steps. 'Something... alarming, Tarleton?'

'I don't know, sir. The lad just said "urgent",

and that his mistress had commanded him not to return without an answer.'

Frowning, Ellie motioned him into the house as she took the note from Tarleton, quickly scanned it, then looked up at Christopher with a grimace. 'It's from Aunt Marion, informing me the call on Lady Sayleford is set for tomorrow afternoon. I'm to present myself at my aunt's town house at three.' She took a deep breath. 'Into the lion's den. I only hope I emerge with a whole skin.'

She looked so troubled and apprehensive, the words slipped out before he knew what he meant to say. 'Would you like me be present at Lady Sayleford's? So you won't have to beard the lions alone.'

She paused, looking uncertain. 'I should refuse. My moth—Lady Wanstead already insinuated she thought I'd taken you as my new protector.'

'But we both know I'm not. I'll ask Maggie to come, too—as your sponsor at the school, and an added buttress to respectability. With your permission, I'll acquaint her beforehand with the facts of your background, so she understands the purpose of your call on Lady Sayleford. I know she'll be as shocked and outraged as I was, and eager to assist in whatever way she can.'

'You may certainly inform her of my background, if you think she would be interested. I hate to bother her, but...it would be helpful to have a few friendly faces on hand when I arrive with Aunt Marion. But wouldn't Lady Sayleford be annoyed at having extra guests arrive uninvited?'

Christopher shrugged. 'It's an afternoon call, not a dinner at which the numbers need to be even. Being her niece, Maggie is always welcome. And Lady Sayleford likes me. She's always had a soft spot for a rogue, Maggie says.'

As he'd hoped, Ellie chuckled at that, looking relieved and more confident. 'Very well, I gratefully accept reinforcements, and will see you there.' Her eyes brightened and she laughed. 'We shall turn it into a lesson! My mother is already suspicious of you. With your reputation to overcome, you're bound to encounter other matrons, zealously protecting their innocent darlings, who will be equally suspicious. Meeting her and Aunt Marion will be good experience in figuring out how to disarm dubious chaperones.'

Christopher grimaced. 'I shall gird myself for the challenge. And be even more grateful to have Maggie at my side. So, assuming she's free, I'll collect Maggie tomorrow and see you at Lady Sayleford's, about half-three?'

Ellie nodded. 'Lady Sayleford's at half-three. And thank you, Christopher. I did enjoy our outing today—except for that last part. And I do think I managed to impart some useful information.'

'Now I just need to memorise it,' he replied, nodding a farewell. *And suck every morsel of delight from being with you before I have to implement it*, he thought as he walked out.

After Christopher's departure, Ellie dismissed Tarleton and wandered into her sitting room. Feeling in need of reinforcement, she poured herself some wine before moving on to the sofa.

She glanced again at the terse missive from her aunt. Grateful as she was for Christopher's promise of reinforcement, she couldn't forestall a wave of apprehension at the mere thought of meeting her mother, Aunt Marion and perhaps Sophie at Lady Sayleford's.

It was quite possible those Society leaders would subject her to a quick session of stilted introductions, then order her to make herself scarce. There was a good chance Sophie would not even be present.

In which case, the shorter the meeting, the better. Being around her mother raked up the distressing mix of fear, shame, pain, hurt, abandonment, sorrow, anguish and fury she'd spent a decade burying. Complicating that turmoil was a tiny niggle of compassion that said she ought to forgive her mother. And she wasn't sure she could.

As for Aunt Marion—she had no idea what the woman thought of her now.

As a child, she'd loved going to Enfield Place. With her widowed great-aunt's own children already grown by the time Ellie and Sophie had come to visit, Aunt Marion had welcomed them with hugs and treats, laughing when Mama chided them for coming in after roaming the grounds with leaves in their hair and grass stains on their gowns. She'd ordered Cook to make their favourite treats, read them stories, and allowed them to peer down from the gallery at the adults dining in their finery.

Would she be greeted with a kiss for the child she'd been? Or a brief, cold nod for the disgrace she'd become?

Somehow, it hurt more to envisage her aunt's coldness than it did to recall her mother's. She was suddenly, overwhelmingly glad that Christopher and Lady Maggie would be present at Lady Sayleford's to support her through whatever would come.

She counted too much on Christopher's support, though, she thought with a sigh—which was exactly what she needed to *stop* doing. Fortunately, his next lesson would be conducted in the stifling company of Aunt Marion, her mother and Lady Sayleford—a mix of personalities would surely churn up enough tumult to distract her from his presence.

Or would it? She was always so acutely conscious of him. The way he moved, his expressions, the whole...aura that he radiated, drew her attention and drew *her*, the proverbial moth to the flame. As if some invisible force tethered her to him whenever he appeared, like iron fragments pulled to a magnet.

Was it wise to continue his lessons and subject herself to the temptation of being near him? Much as she tried to convince herself she'd been satisfied by that one kiss, in truth, it had only made her hunger for more.

Kissing him had been...wonderful. The subtle friction of his mouth against hers, skittering flames of sensation to every extremity of her body. But even more, how wonderful to kiss him and know with absolute certainty that he would press his caresses only as far as *she* wanted them to go.

After being pawed by lechers and possessed by a man whose only concern was satisfying his own needs, such assurance was heady. With

Christopher, she just *knew* intimacy would be entirely different. She had this growing yearning to taste more, confident she could experience pleasure at her own pace, stop whenever *she* willed.

But she mustn't. She hadn't offered this arrangement so she might discover what other courtesans sighed over. She must provide Christopher only the lessons she had promised, immerse herself in the work of her school, and watch him march off into the future for which he was destined—with someone else.

Since that was both necessary and inevitable, she should dedicate more time to eradicating her romantic imaginings about him.

Carrying her wine glass to the secretary, she trimmed a pen and took out a sheet of paper. *Christopher's Deficiencies*, she wrote at the top, and under it, a number one.

She took another sip and stared at the blank page. Surely he'd done something today to disturb or annoy her. When, after a few minutes, nothing came to mind, she wrote, *He tempts me.*

She let herself envisage him—his handsome face, that tawny-wheat hair she itched to run her fingers through, his tall, solid body, and the warmth and strength and tangy spicy scent that enveloped her when he held her. Desire spiralled

within, fierce and strong. Yes, he tempted her—
an undesirable trait in a man for a woman who
intended to leave the courtesan's life behind her
for good.

What else?

Adding a number two, she wrote, *He makes
me long for things I cannot have.*

She wasn't an innocent girl any longer, despite
how she'd felt while play-acting with him today.
There would be no respectable marriage for her,
at least not to a man from the class into which
she'd been born, and for his career to prosper, he
absolutely must have a bride who was his social
equal. Allowing herself to dream about anything
else was just as great a hazard to her well-being
as desiring him.

Maybe it was the wine, but she didn't seem
able to come up with any other faults. By the
time she'd finished the glass, feeling rather desperate, she scrawled, *He uses women for pleasure.*

Although it wasn't really fair to accuse him
of that. All men 'used' women for pleasure. The
telling point was who, and how. Lovingly embracing a wife, or a female who'd freely, eagerly,
invited the intimacy, was completely different
from taking a woman—or a wife—without her
permission or any regard for her needs. Worst of

all was a man like Summerville, who considered any woman he wanted 'available'. Whose conscience hadn't even been pricked by the knowledge that he was ruining her.

In contrast, despite meeting her as Summerville's mistress, Christopher had unfailingly treated her like a lady. She didn't know any of the Society matrons with whom he'd been involved, but he had a reputation among the demi-mondaine for being a kind, generous, and appreciative lover. There was always a competition among them to win his favour.

Frowning, she struck out the sentence and thrust the list back into a drawer.

After tomorrow's interaction, she surely would discover more faults to add to her list—and make better progress at rooting out of her heart the pesky weed of her infatuation with Christopher Lattimar.

Chapter Eight

At three the next afternoon, Ellie arrived at the home of the Dowager Countess of Enfield, and was shown into a small anteroom where she found her mother and her aunt awaiting her.

Though she looked frailer, and her hair had turned entirely grey, Aunt Marion still had the commanding figure and vital presence Ellie remembered. Nervously, she made her curtsy.

'Miss Parmenter, I believe you're calling yourself?' the Countess said.

Trying not to be disappointed by her aunt's chilly tone, Ellie chose the most formal reply. 'Yes, Countess.'

Her aunt looked over at her mother. 'She's presentable enough, thankfully.'

Apparently, she wasn't even to be addressed directly. From out of the hurt stabbing her heart, a defiant burst of anger emerged. 'You expected me to appear in feathers and a bodice cut down to the nipples, like a proper courtesan? So sorry to disappoint.'

Her mother gasped and the Countess's eyes widened in surprise. 'Still sharp-witted, I see,' she said.

'With only myself to rely on, I had to be, didn't I?' she shot back, the anger still smouldering.

To her surprise, her aunt laughed. 'I suppose you did. Well, let's not pull caps, shall we? Whoever is at fault for what become of you—and there is a good deal of blame to go around—we can't change that now. We can, however, ensure that the misfortunes of the past do not continue into the future to ruin Sophie's chances. I presume you agree?'

'If I did not, I wouldn't have come.'

At a nod from her aunt, both ladies rose. 'I'm pleased you were prompt. The carriage awaits.'

Once they were seated and on their way, Ellie said, 'May I ask what you wish to accomplish by calling on Lady Sayleford, Countess?'

'I expect those vulgar shopkeepers in Burlington Arcade are already sniggering behind their sleeves at discovering Miss Wanstead is the sister of Summerville's former mistress. Ordinarily, my support would be all that was necessary to see Sophie well launched. But given the…unique circumstances, we shall need reinforcement at the highest level. No one in Society wields more power than the Dowager Countess of Sayleford. If *she* approves your sister, in the full knowledge of her…unfortunate connection, the rest of Society will do so as well. To bc sure, there's no longer any possibility of her making a grand match, but—'

'And that is my fault?' Ellie burst out.

'As I said, fault can be apportioned in several places.' Her aunt gave her an appraising look. 'The girl I remember would never have interrupted me to defend herself. You've grown quite forthright, my dear. And, yes, I suppose you had to, so you needn't remind me.'

Ellie's anger subsided, leaving her feeling drained and empty. 'What *do* you want me to do for Sophie?'

'That will be up to Lady Sayleford. I imagine she means to inspect you, and determine the best way forward. She might recommend that you leave London until the Season is over. Would you be prepared to do that?'

'I hardly see how that would assist matters,' Ellie argued. 'The shopkeeper has already seen us, and will either gossip about it, or not. I'm perfectly prepared to avoid shopping in the fashionable areas for the duration, but I'm not prepared to leave town. Others here depend on me.'

'That wretched school,' her mother muttered.

'Yes, the school,' Ellie said evenly. 'A place designed to give girls without other resources basic skills and training—so they won't end up as I did.'

'I hope you will not show yourself so defiant to Lady Sayleford!' her mother cried.

The outburst offered her a chance to inform the ladies that Lady Sayleford was already acquainted with her—and her school. She wasn't sure why the Dowager Countess had not told her aunt about their prior acquaintance, but since she had not, Ellie didn't intend to, either. She'd wait and see how the situation developed.

She took a deep breath, the knots in her stomach loosening. Aunt Marion had treated her coldly at first, but was thawing a bit. And once they reached Lady Sayleford's, she'd have Maggie and Christopher's support to ease things further.

A few minutes later, the carriage arrived in Grosvenor Square and they were shown into an elegant blue salon. Though her mother and aunt halted on the threshold in surprise, not expecting other callers to be present, Ellie was delighted to see Christopher standing beside the sofa on which Lady Maggie sat with her aunt.

He gave her an encouraging smile as she entered, the glint in his eyes turning sardonic as Lady Wanstead recognised him and recoiled. Ellie, however, felt her spirits lift. Just knowing he was present calmed her. And ridiculous as the notion was, she couldn't shake this gut-level conviction that with him near, no injury could befall her.

Her aunt, however, paid no attention to the other occupants, coming straight to the Dowager Countess and leading the ladies in a curtsy. 'Lady Sayleford, thank you for finding time in your busy schedule to see us on such short notice. But we don't want to intrude. We can wait until your other visitors leave.'

'No intrusion at all, Lady Enfield,' Maggie's aunt said. 'Since the matter at hand is deciding how best to present Miss Wanstead, I asked them to come.'

Looking puzzled, Ellie's aunt opened her lips as if to question Lady Sayleford, then closed them. 'Very well, I bow to your expertise. May I present my niece, Lady Wanstead, and my great-niece, Miss... Parmenter.'

Lady Sayleford and Maggie both rose, returning the curtsies. 'Lady Wanstead,' the Countess said, nodding. 'Miss Parmenter. And may I present my great-niece, Lady Lyndlington, and her husband's good friend and fellow Parliamentarian, Mr Lattimar.'

After another set of bows and curtsies, Lady Sayleford turned to Ellie. 'How are you, my dear? Things are going well at the school, I trust?'

'They are, Countess. We have several students now, and a programme of instruction in place. Lady Lyndlington and her father have both made substantial contributions towards its support, for which I cannot thank them enough.'

'Excellent! As I told you when we dined, I find it both brave and highly commendable of you to take on running such an enterprise. Shall we be seated? Harris,' she said, turning to the butler, 'would you bring tea, please.'

Ellie couldn't help feeling a bitter gratification at the shocked expressions on the faces of her mother and aunt. *So the fallen woman knows some respectable people.*

As soon as the butler had withdrawn, Aunt Marion said, her tone not entirely masking her irritation, 'Why did you not tell me you were already acquainted with my great-niece, Lilliana?'

'You never asked,' Lady Sayleford said. 'Only told me of a *problem* you would need my assistance to circumvent, so that the after-effects wouldn't ruin the prospects of an innocent girl. An aim of which I approve, which is why I asked you to call. Shall we proceed?'

'Of course,' Aunt Marion said faintly. 'What do you recommend?'

'As you can see, Miss Parmenter is already supported in her current endeavour by several well-regarded members of Society. Naturally, she can't accompany you to Society events, but it's not as if she'd been a dancer on the stage. When word of the relationship gets out—and sooner or later, it's bound to—simply acknowledge it. You may add that I am aware of the circumstances and have given Miss Wanstead my full approval. Send the curious to me, should they have further questions.'

'Thank you, Lilliana. That is most gracious.'

Lady Sayleford shrugged. 'If you wish to receive Miss Parmenter at your home privately, I envisage no difficulties. Though I doubt you will avail yourself of that opportunity. After ten years, you must hardly know each other. If I've been correctly informed, there has been no communication with her whatsoever in all that time.' The Countess looked over at Lady Wanstead. 'Not even from her mother.'

'Th-that's true,' Lady Wanstead stuttered in alarm, 'But I hardly see how—'

'You were in a difficult position, Lady Wanstead,' the Dowager agreed. 'In the country, without any means, with another daughter to protect. But really, Marion,' she said, turning her reproving gaze on Lady Enfield, 'how could you have let the silence extend so long? And don't try to tell me you had no idea what was going on. Sayleford was still alive when it happened, and rumours of Wanstead's difficulties and what he'd done to recover from them permeated the clubs like a foul odour.'

'Of course I knew!' Aunt Marion cried. 'But what could I have done? She was already *ruined* by the time I heard of it!'

'Send her a note to see if she was well? Or if you feared having a written connection to her, place a maid in the household to watch over her, so you would know if she were in need. Something. *Anything* other than turn an innocent over to Summerville and cut her off from everything and everyone she'd ever known. Merciful Heavens, Marion, she was your flesh and blood!'

Continuing in a quieter tone, Lady Sayleford said, 'Were it not to protect her innocent sister, I might refuse my assistance. I do intend to lend my support to Miss Parmenter. In fact, my dear, I should like to become a contributor to your school. Helping girls without any resources to preserve their virtue and honesty is a worthy goal.'

Before Ellie could respond, Lady Sayleford turned towards the door. 'Ah, here's Harris with our refreshments,' she said in a pleasant tone, as if she hadn't just reduced Ellie's mother and great-aunt to shocked, red-faced silence. 'Since we're agreed on the way forward, let's have our tea. Maggie, will you pour?'

Her heart pounding, almost as shaken as her relations at the Dowager's fierce attack and unexpected sympathy, Ellie looked at Lady Sayleford, surprise, gratitude, and a turmoil of other emotions holding her speechless. The Dowager gave her a wink and a quick, conspiratorial nod.

Then Ellie looked at Christopher—and found him trying hard to suppress a grin. 'Bravo, Aunt Lilly,' he murmured under cover of Maggie handing him his cup.

'You have a new girl at the school, Mr Lattimar was telling me,' Maggie said as she gave Ellie hers. 'Quite a character, it seems.'

'Having your pocket picked by a scamp wearing boy's clothing is not generally the introduction you want to a girl you invite to join your students,' Christopher said.

'To be fair, she didn't actually pick your pocket,' Ellie protested.

'Only because, as she put it, she was "too tired and weak".'

'A thief, Miss Parmenter?' Lady Sayleford said. 'Are you sure she can be made into an honest citizen?'

'What else was she to do after she lost her family, Countess? I suspect most of us would choose thievery, if the alternative were starvation. But she's very much interested in books and learning, so I think she can be saved. I intend to at least try.'

Before the Dowager could reply, the sound of raised voices by the door distracted them, followed by the entrance of Harris. 'Excuse me, my lady, but there's a Miss Wanstead here, demanding admittance. I told her you were busy, but...'

Before he could finish, a young female edged around him and darted into the room. 'Sophie!' Ellie's mama gasped. 'What are you doing here?'

'I knew I should have suspected something when you positively shoved me out to go shopping. But when I returned to have Basker tell me you'd gone on an important call with Aunt Marion, I—'

As the girl's gaze left her mother's face to scan the room, she broke off abruptly. 'Tess!' she cried. 'It *was* you in that shop! Mama tried to persuade me otherwise—but oh, I *knew* it!'

Without realising she was doing so, Ellie set down her cup and rose to her feet, her gaze drinking in every detail of her little sister's face and form. 'How lovely you've grown, Sophie.'

And then the girl ran to her, flinging her arms about Ellie in a ferocious hug before pushing back to gaze up once again into Ellie's face, tears in her eyes. 'They told me you were *dead*, Tess. That you'd sickened with a putrid fever, and they sent you away to protect the rest of us. Oh, I've missed you so much!'

'I've missed you, too,' Ellie whispered, hugging her tight again.

'Sophie, you shouldn't have come,' Aunt Marion scolded. 'If your presence were required, we would have brought you. Apologise to Lady Sayleford for bursting in uninvited, and leave us at once.' She turned an angry gaze on Ellie's mother. 'We'll deal with the matter of your talkative maid later.'

'I'm very sorry to have intruded, Lady Sayleford,' Sophie said, dropping a curtsy deep enough to grace a royal drawing room. 'Although I am not at all sorry to have discovered my sister. Where have you been all these years, Tess?'

'That's quite enough, Sophie,' Aunt Marion said. 'This matter will be better discussed at home.'

'But if you are discussing my future, why should I not be present? And I want to know what happened to Tess. And why you lied to me!'

'You don't seem to have much control over your other great-niece either, Marion,' Lady Sayleford observed. 'From what I've just seen, if you're thinking of pawning her off with some facile explanation for Miss Parmenter's disappearance, I doubt it will work. I recommend you tell her the truth—finally.'

Sophie sank into another curtsy. 'Thank you, Lady Sayleford. But if my sister is here, you must know the truth, too. Can you not just tell me straight away? When I thought she was dead, I was heartbroken. I'm not a child any more. I think I deserve to know what happened.' She paused for breath and a quick frown. 'And why did you call her "Miss Parmenter"? That was our governess's name!'

A smile tugged at Ellie's lips as she watched her sister use all the persuasive charm that had usually induced Ellie to grant Sophie whatever she was pleading for. From the amused expression on her face, it appeared the Dowager was not proof against it, either.

'Why don't we let Miss Parmenter explain,' Lady Sayleford said, gesturing to Ellie.

Tell her—and forfeit her loyalty and admi-

ration? Like all girls of her class, Sophie would have been brought up to look upon courtesans with disapproval and disdain. Ellie wasn't sure which would be worse: having someone else relate what had become of her, or confessing that shame herself.

Would Sophie's joy at finding her turn to revulsion when she learned what Ellie had become? If so, how could she bear it? How could she bear *Christopher* seeing it?

For a moment, she considered asking to delay, as Aunt Marion had advised. But she knew what it was to live with half-truths and evasions. The little girl who had adored and mourned her *did* deserve the truth. And better it come from her.

'I'm afraid it's rather shocking.'

And so, Ellie gave a short account of Summerville's visit, his disreputable offer, and her father's acceptance of it, concluding with the fact that she'd lived in London as the Viscount's mistress until his death the previous autumn.

Though her sister's face paled, she kept her gaze focused on Ellie throughout the brief narrative. After sitting silently for several moments after Ellie finished, she turned to her mother.

'How could Papa have done something so… *monstrous*? How could all of you just…let her go?' Wheeling to Ellie, she cried, 'I would never have abandoned you! I won't abandon you now! Having found each other, can we not be sisters again, openly?'

'You have no idea what it would cost to acknowledge her,' Aunt Marion flashed back angrily. 'We're trying to *preserve* a future for you! Not have it destroyed before the Season has barely begun!'

'I appreciate your loyalty, darling Sophie, but Aunt Marion is right,' Ellie said. 'One ruination was enough; let us not have this reunion lead to another. My disgrace provided the funds to restore the estate and fund a dowry to see you respectably married. Don't let my lost reputation be for nothing.'

'If the truth about you ruins my chances with *ton* suitors, so be it! I wouldn't want to marry a man so concerned about Society's approval that he expected me to deny my own sister.'

'Commendable words, my dear, but you must also be realistic,' Lady Sayleford interposed. 'I see no reason you should not meet your sister in private, but an open and public association would, I'm afraid, mar your reputation irretrievably.'

Sophie turned a pleading gaze on Lady Sayleford. 'My aunt says you are the most influential lady in all the *ton*. Surely you see how unfair it is for Tess to suffer because of what our father did to her! Could you not right this wrong, and get her reinstated into Society?'

The Dowager sighed. 'I only wish I *could* right it. But though I wield enough authority in Society to ensure that you will be able to make a respectable match, even I cannot persuade others to change their inflexible standards. No matter how unjust the situation may be, there truly isn't any way to restore your sister to her rightful place.'

Sophie's chin quivered, but she nodded. 'If *you* cannot do it, then I expect it cannot be done. But you said I would be able to see Tess?'

'If you meet her privately at the home of a respectable member of Society, I don't see why not.'

'An excellent idea, Aunt Lilly!' Maggie said. 'You may call on me, Miss Wanstead. Miss Parmenter will often be present, consulting with me about the school.'

'But, Maggie dear, you're not always up to receiving visitors.' Lady Sayleford smiled at Sophie. 'My niece is expecting, and is often unwell. You must call on *me*, Miss Wanstead and Miss Parmenter. I also expect you to keep me abreast of developments at your school. I don't suppose Society would object to your niece calling here, do you, Marion?' she asked, turning to Ellie's aunt.

Lady Enfield forced a smile. 'No, Lilliana, no one in Society could object to my niece visiting you.'

'Either of them,' Lady Sayleford said drily, before turning her gaze to Ellie and Sophie, seated side by side. 'What a charming picture the two of you make. Perhaps I shall commission a portrait.'

Ellie's mama gasped, Christopher almost choked on his tea—and a laughing Sophie clapped her hands. 'Please, do so, Lady Sayleford!'

'Vraux will want to buy it, to add to his treasures,' Christopher said.

'You should come entertain them while it's being painted,' Lady Sayleford told Christopher. 'Sitting for a portrait is so tedious.'

'Lady Sayleford!' Ellie's mother cried. As the Dowager raised her eyebrows, Lady Wanstead rushed on, 'I suppose it's acceptable for a married lady to associate with her husband's friends, or a…woman like Tess to be escorted by him, but to allow an innocent maiden to associate with *him*? Surely you're aware of his reputation!'

Before an indignant Maggie could fly to Christopher's defence, Lady Sayleford put a hand on her arm. 'Mr Lattimar has earned himself quite a naughty reputation,' the Dowager replied. 'But having recently decided to marry, he is in the process of reforming his behaviour. Your daughter stands in no danger from associating with him. In *my home*,' she added mildly enough, but with a look that said she didn't appreciate having her judgement questioned, especially by a woman who'd deserted her elder daughter.

'You've decided to marry?' Maggie asked a clearly startled Christopher. 'Giles will be so pleased!'

'With Mr Lattimar's well-known charm, good looks, pedigree and important connections,' Lady Sayleford continued, 'I expect he will be quite sought after. There's nothing quite so attractive to the ladies as a reformed rogue. *If he's truly reformed*,' she added *sotto voce*, raising a warning eyebrow at Christopher.

'To think, you were planning something this important, and Giles didn't know—but Aunt Lilly did,' Maggie said with a laughing glance at Christopher. 'I swear, Aunt, you must have spies in every household in London!'

Lady Sayleford lifted an imperious eyebrow. 'One must stay informed. But now I've finished my tea, and it's time to rest. Marion, you can be assured that your little "problem" is solved. Girls, I do look forward to seeing you again soon. You come, too, Maggie, if you're feeling up to it. And you, Mr Lattimar. The best of luck with your courtships.'

With that, she rose, and perforce the other guests did as well. After bows and curtsies, the Countess made a grand exit, her callers trailing in her wake.

Ellie followed her friends out. 'That went off better than I could have dared hope,' she said, catching up to them. 'Thank you both so much for being here to support me.'

'With as forceful a champion as Aunt Lilly turned out to be, our support wasn't necessary,' Maggie said. 'But we were pleased to offer it.'

'Did you know the Dowager was going to… champion me?'

'With that blistering indictment of your mother and aunt? No,' Maggie said. 'But I'm not surprised. She's ferociously devoted to family.'

'How did she find out I'd decided to start looking for a wife?' Christopher asked.

'You know she didn't hear it from me,' Ellie said with a rueful glance.

Maggie laughed and shook her head. 'Aunt Lilly knows everything! She really must have a spy in every household in London.'

'Can we see you home?' Christopher asked Ellie. 'As splendid as it must have been to see your relations so thoroughly routed, dredging up those memories cannot have been pleasant. Besides, with your mother and aunt having just experienced a thorough dressing down, you might rather not share a carriage with them.'

'Goodness, no!' Maggie said. 'Ellie, you must make your excuses and come with us.'

Ellie shuddered. 'Truly, I wouldn't mind missing that carriage ride! Give me a moment to talk with Sophie, and I'll gladly accept your offer.' Especially since she'd have the heady delight of Christopher's proximity, with Maggie's presence to check the temptation to do something about it.

She dearly wanted another kiss, she thought as walked back up the steps to consult her sister. And had been arguing with herself since last night, as she tossed and turned, trying to capture an elusive sleep, about whether she should or shouldn't indulge in one before their lessons ended.

After all, this would almost certainly be her last opportunity to experience intimacy with a man she admired and desired.

Chapter Nine

After she'd obtained a promise from Sophie to send her a note so they might arrange a time to meet, Ellie bid goodbye to her glowering aunt and walked back out. The footmen Christopher dispatched had already obtained a hackney, and handed her in to join her companions.

'So, Christopher, when did you decide to pursue wedded bliss?' Maggie said as soon as the vehicle set off.

Christopher groaned. 'I suspected you would tax me about it. Go ahead, make merry at my expense. My mother has already mocked my intentions, giving her opinion that I'm not suited to matrimony.'

'You're as well suited as Ben,' Maggie said. 'He was just as much enamoured of the demimonde until he met Alyssa. It's the right lady who makes the difference.'

'So I've told him,' Ellie said, suppressing the silly longing that she might be such a lady. 'I've observed quite a few womanisers, and you don't fit the mould, Christopher. You aren't like the men who view women as tools for their pleasure, to be charmed until they agree to yield their bodies, nothing more. You've always displayed too much genuine concern for a woman's well-being to fall into that category.'

'Well said, Ellie,' Maggie agreed. 'You "like the ladies", truly *like* them. Once you meet the female who inspires you to *love* her, I have no doubt you'll give her the respect and devotion necessary to make your marriage a success.' With a sidelong glance, she added, 'As long as you've chosen this course because it's what you truly want—not just because you're the lone bachelor left among your friends. In any event, Giles and I—all the Hellions—stand ready to assist, however we can.'

'Don't bring on the parade of eligibles yet,' Christopher said with a laugh. 'Lady Sayleford praised my "charm", but I've spent my adult life charming women around whom a man can conduct himself rather freely. I need to learn how to behave properly around vir—respectable young ladies. Fortunately, Ellie has volunteered to school me.'

'Ellie is giving you courtship lessons?' Maggie asked, her eyes widening.

'You may think that highly inappropriate, given my...recent occupation,' Ellie said hastily, hoping Maggie wouldn't think her presumptuous.

To her surprise, Maggie reached over to take her hand, tears glittering on her lashes. 'I think you are wise and kind, and incredibly brave and resilient to have survived what you did. To have been turned over to Summerville at sixteen... I can't imagine.'

Ellie blinked back the tears that stung her own eyes. 'Thank you. It's been a long time since I was an innocent maid, but with my family's finances at such a stand that I didn't have much more to offer than beauty and breeding, my mother felt it imperative that my behaviour be the absolute model of a virtuous, pretty-behaved maiden. You can imagine with what intensity all the lessons of proper conduct were drummed into my head!'

'Then you know far more about it than I do,' Maggie said. 'I grew up a hoyden, trailing after my brother and Robbie, our closest neighbour. Since I was barely in my teens when he and I decided we would marry, I didn't see any need to learn to behave like a "proper young lady", despite my mother's scolding.'

Sadness briefly crossed her face before she laughed. 'My papa would say I never did learn, even after I lost Robbie and came to live in London. Acting as hostess for his political dinners, meeting mostly his associates in Parliament, I spent very little time among Society ladies. So what have you been learning, Christopher?'

'I know which flowers to send to the maiden I've danced with at a ball, and which to avoid,' he replied. 'I'm starting on—'

The carriage hit a rut, throwing them back into their seats. Maggie immediately leaned forward, her face paling as she put a hand to her mouth. 'I'm afraid I'm suddenly feeling very unwell,' she whispered.

Christopher leaned out the window and called up to the driver, 'Slow them to a walk, if you please.' Looking back to Maggie, he said, 'Better?'

Though she gave him a quick nod, she kept the hand to her lips. Frowning as he inspected Maggie's white face, Christopher said, 'Why don't we go directly to Upper Brook Street? It's only a few streets more. While you get settled more comfortably, I'll see Ellie home, then come back to consult Giles.'

'I would appreciate that,' Maggie said.

'There's no need,' Ellie said. 'I can make my way home from Lady Maggie's.'

'Certainly not,' Christopher said. 'When a gentleman invites a lady for a drive, he always sees her safely home. That's the rule, isn't it?'

'Well—yes,' Ellie admitted.

'End of discussion.' Leaning out again, he gave the jarvey the address.

Soon after, they arrived at Lyndlington's house. 'I'll turn Maggie over to her maid and be back in a moment,' Christopher said.

'Is there anything I can do?' Ellie asked.

Maggie shook her head. 'I'll feel better after I lie down. Or not.' She sighed. 'Quite annoying at times, this business of making heirs. Come see me again soon.' After pressing Ellie's hand, she let Christopher help her down.

In her concern for Maggie, it didn't occur to Ellie until after the pair walked away that she would now be alone with Christopher for the rest of the transit to Hans Place.

A different kind of agitation began to swirl in her belly, and the opposing voices that had been nattering at her last night resumed their argument. By the time Christopher returned, she was so nervous she jumped when he took the seat beside her.

Trying to distract herself from the urge to sidle closer, replacing the warmth emanating from him with the feel of his thigh, arm and shoulder against hers, she stuttered, 'D-did you get Lady Maggie settled?'

Christopher chuckled. 'Her maid came running, took one look at her face, and whisked her away, talking of weak tea and stale biscuits. The last I heard was Maggie grumbling that she didn't want to be wrapped in cotton wool.'

A bleak image struck Ellie, the memory of a time she'd been ill while Summerville's mistress. Learning she was indisposed, her protector took himself off to find other amusement. After asking if she required anything, the maid he'd engaged to serve her swiftly withdrew. Aching and feverish, Ellie wrapped herself in a shawl and dragged a chair near the fire, her only companion the tick of the mantel clock.

How many years had it been since anyone had cosseted *her*, sick or well?

'It's good to have friends and family to watch over you,' Christopher said quietly, seeming with uncanny understanding to sense the source of her sadness. 'You have friends like that now, Ellie. If you are ever ill or troubled or in need, you must call on them.'

She nodded, her throat too tight for speech. And when Christopher took her hand, she couldn't resist any longer. As if she belonged there, she lay her head against his shoulder.

Lacing his fingers with hers, he wrapped his other arm around her to pat her shoulder while she forced away the grim memories. 'Thank you,' she murmured a few minutes later, as he moved his arm away.

She ought to let go his fingers, but the aching tenderness of being comforted was so sweet, so rare, she couldn't quite manage it. She looked up at his face, trying to summon words to express how much his compassion meant.

Within an instant, gratitude turned to yearning. With everything in her, she wanted to pull his head down and recapture the lips she had briefly touched before, that simple caress setting her afire with need and urgency. She shoved her hand beneath her skirts before she did just that.

As if equally unable to look away, his turquoise eyes studied her. With a little thrill, she recognised when concern deepened to desire. Breath hitching in her throat, she angled her head up, unwilling this time to make the first move, desperately hoping he would.

Instead, he drew away. She stifled a sound of bitter disappointment. Then, he turned back and cupped her chin in his hand. 'Bloody hell,' he muttered, and kissed her.

A shock of sensation rocketed through her as, with long, slow strokes, he tasted her, licking and nibbling at her lips. He didn't probe at them, demanding entry, but after a moment of feeling the exquisite hot wet plush of his tongue against her mouth, she just had to learn the feel of it inside. With a whimper, she opened her mouth to him.

Once again, he didn't rush, but entered gently, tentatively, not moving to explore until she brought her tongue to meet his. Ah, then, wrapping his arms around her and pulling her closer, he explored her with relentless precision, the lazy scouring of his tongue over her teeth, her tongue setting off a series of little explosions, like a string of fireworks.

Her heartbeat stampeded as her body seemed to heat and melt under his touch. The throbbing intensity at her centre built and built, until she was pressing against him, desperate for more.

The carriage hit another rut, jolting them apart. Steadying her back on the seat with trembling fingers, Christopher held her at arm's length, his eyes closed as he steadied his breathing.

Only as the carriage slowed, signalling they were near their destination, did her brain finally emerge from the miasma of sensation that had swamped it. Remorse as intense as her disappointment over the interruption overwhelmed her, cooling the heat of passion.

'Sorry,' she whispered. 'I didn't mean to tempt you again.'

He deposited a kiss on her hand before releasing it. 'It appears neither of us is very good at resisting temptation. But we'll have to do better. Just the few things I've learned so far have made me realise how much I need more lessons.'

Ellie wasn't sure she could do better. Seat her beside him in a covered carriage, away from watching eyes, and she knew she'd be driven to beg for more of his marvellous kisses.

Fortunately, before good sense could browbeat desire into doing the prudent thing and ending the lessons straight away, the vehicle halted at Hans Place. Perhaps as eager as she was to avoid thinking about the implications of what had just happened, Christopher jumped out, then held out a hand to help her down.

'You needn't walk me in.'

'A gentleman always walks a lady in.'

She hesitated a moment, not sure she wanted to confront the issue. 'Even when she hasn't acted like a lady?'

'Maybe not like an innocent maid,' he allowed. 'But very much like a beautiful, courageous, desirable lady. You'll be occupied, meeting your sister tomorrow?' he asked, skirting away from the dangerous topic.

'I'm not sure yet. I need to spend time at the school. With my family coming to town, and the...lessons, I've been neglecting it.'

He nodded. 'Send me a note when you're ready to resume. Now that the Reform Bill has passed the Commons, the focus has shifted to the debate in the Lords. I'm consulting with Giles and the other Hellions today, to see what we can do to persuade some of the members.'

'Vital work, to be sure. Lessons can wait.'

He hesitated, as if to say something more, and she had an instant's terror that he'd reached the same conclusion she was resisting, and would tell her they should discontinue the lessons entirely.

Instead, to her guilty relief, he smiled. 'Lessons are important, too. You'll send me a note, then?'

She nodded. 'Yes. And thank you again for your support today. I... I can't truly express how much it meant.' *How much you mean.*

'And you can't begin to know how much a pleasure it was.' With that, he tipped his hat and motioned her towards the door Tarleton held open for her. 'Goodbye, Ellie.'

After bidding him farewell, Ellie walked up to her sitting room. Christopher's final statement must refer, at least in part, to the kiss they'd just shared. Had it been as difficult to resist for him as it had been for her?

Should she heed prudence, and call off the lessons? That single first kiss hadn't been enough to satisfy her, and the second, even more marvellous one, just whetted her appetite to explore further.

Tasting pleasure with him would allow her to blot out the bitter years of forced intimacy, replacing them with images of passion as something shared, tender and desirable. But could she taste a bit more, and a bit more, and a bit more, without both of them abandoning the vows they'd made to move on to a new life?

As she fell ever further under his sensual spell, the barriers she'd erected to refuse another offer of *carte blanche* were beginning to crumble. If she gave in to temptation, took him for her lover, what would be left for her when, inevitably, they parted?

Emptiness, sorrow, and the bitter knowledge that'd she'd betrayed her own better self. Quite likely, the disdain of ladies she'd begun to look on as friends and the loss of their support for her school. Realities that would be far more difficult to live with than the ugly memories of her bondage to Summerville.

For without the school, what future would she have?

She'd be reduced to living on the few resources she'd eked out of the arrangement with
Summerville. The call at Lady Sayleford's had
made quite clear that, save for Sophie, none of
her family had any interest in her welfare. She
would be really and truly alone.

And Sophie! Resuming her life as a courtesan would ruin Sophie's chances, too. She would
rather starve in the streets than have Sophie discover what it felt like to be treated as unworthy
of a mother's love, an aunt's respect, or Society's
approval.

By no means the least consideration, by tempting Christopher back to a life he'd vowed to leave
behind, she'd be betraying the man dearest to
her.

There must be a better way. She need only
apply herself to devising a method of instructing
him that eliminated any opportunities for dalli-
ance. No carriage rides alone, no meetings in a
private chamber with just the two of them present. She could meet him only in public places,
like their stroll through the market and tea at
Gunter's.

With others around them, she could even take
his arm and savour the energising warmth he radiated, without danger of desire getting out of
hand. She'd be able to claim his escort a while

longer, build a mental keepsake of joyful interludes to remember and relish after he went on
to his new life, and she threw herself fully into
hers, teaching her girls.

She could do it, and she must. The losses she
would sustain otherwise were—unthinkable.

Feeling better about the future, she moved to
her secretary to write the note to Sophie. Opening the drawer to find a card, she saw the list
she'd begun of Christopher's faults. Sighing, she
drew it out.

Had she discovered anything she could add?
He'd been attentive and courteous today, acting
in every way as she'd described him to Maggie,
a man who truly liked women, not a womaniser.
He'd not arrogantly monopolised the conversation, or attempted to flirt with her lovely sister.

He'd even been courteous towards her mother,
who'd insulted him.

It would be hard going over rough ground to
overcome her infatuation, if she couldn't do better than this at discovering some faults.

She looked over to the bouquet he'd bought
her, its vase holding pride of place on the side
table. Though he'd teasingly treated her as his
Virtuous Virgin during their lesson, she had no
illusions that he would ever offer her more than
the chance to become his mistress.

Picking up her pen, she wrote at number four, *He doesn't think I'm good enough—to be a wife.*

Not that she held that against him. *I'm really not good enough—now. But I'm still too good to become anyone's mistress—even yours.*

She stared at the line for a long time, feeling something wither inside as she faced that stark reality.

Could there be any more convincing argument for expunging him from her heart and mind?

Chapter Ten

A disgruntled Christopher hopped back in the hackney after instructing the jarvey to return to Upper Brook Street. Just when he thought he was doing better at resisting Ellie, something happened to deflect him. This time, it had been her obvious sorrow over the contrast between the loving care Maggie received and the cold, friendless existence she'd suffered. Touched on the raw, angered anew at those who had failed her, he'd been overcome by the need to comfort her.

But all it took was a touch, no matter how innocently begun, and the beguiling being that was Ellie wove itself into his senses, disengaging thought and intellect, and letting the driving imperative of passion take over. Only a man made of iron, with ice for blood, could have resisted when she offered him her lips!

As numerous years of riotous living had proved, he was not such a man. Would he be able to quell his sensual nature enough to pursue a wife?

But he knew his friends enjoyed lusty love lives with their wives. It wasn't so much that he needed to curb the sensual—though that was certainly necessary to avoid offending an innocent maid while he was courting her. It was curbing his desire for *Ellie* that he needed to master.

Before he knew who she was and where she came from, he might have invited her to become his mistress, but he couldn't possibly insult her with such an offer now. Still, unfair as it was, she was no longer a suitable wife for a man in his position. Somehow, he needed to drum the fact that he couldn't have Ellie into his brain with enough force that it convinced his senses.

Somewhat to his surprise, he realised that, except for Ellie, he now felt little desire to pursue another woman from the demi-monde. On some deep level, he wanted to experience the joy and companionship and comfort that came from living with a woman who delighted one, body, mind and soul—a lady he could trust to be his companion and helpmate for life.

He could become a man worthy of such a lady...couldn't he?

He hadn't needed to hear Lady Wanstead's dubious opinion of his character to realise that, saddled with his rake's reputation, his behaviour would be scrutinised more closely than other men's. Any breach of protocol would prove to watchful mamas that he hadn't and never would reform. As Ellie had already warned him, being seen as a potential danger to a maiden's virtue would limit his access to some of the most eligible single ladies—one of whom might be the ideal wife he needed.

He didn't want to reduce his choices only to those so desperate to marry that they were prepared to take any risk to snag a husband.

To avoid making costly mistakes in courtship, he truly needed Ellie's lessons. But how to learn from her, without putting them both at risk of succumbing to the temptation neither of them seemed able to resist?

Perhaps he should take Lady Saylebrook up on her invitation and meet Ellie at the Dowager's. No sane man could consider committing improprieties under the very nose of the Dowager Countess.

By the time he reached that conclusion, the hackney was halting once again at Upper Brook Street. Paying off the driver, he loped up the front stairs, and was shown into the study where

Maggie's husband and the other two Hellions had already gathered.

After greetings all round and glasses of port distributed, the friends settled by the fire. 'So, Giles, what did you hear from Winterbury about the session in the Lords today?' David Tanner Smith asked.

Giles made a face. 'A number of tedious amendments are being suggested to hold up passage of the bill. The most harmful seeks to cancel or delay the stripping of votes from the rotten boroughs and their redistribution to the new industrial districts.'

'Can't Grey come up with a device to counter that?' Ben Tawny enquired.

'I've heard a rumour that he may urge the King to appoint new peers to the Lords—diluting it with enough supporters to ensure the bill's approval. Heaven knows, if they don't pass it, there will be devil to pay in the countryside! The riots and burnings when the second bill failed last autumn should be fair enough warning of that.'

'Only rumours?' Davie said. 'You should spend more time at White's, where the power brokers gather. You, too, Ben, now that Alyssa's father had you voted in. Find out all you can, so we can arm ourselves with better arguments to convince the Lords.'

'I know, I've been remiss in attending,' Giles admitted. 'With Maggie feeling so unwell, I've been spending more evenings at home.'

'I'll stop by every day, at least until the bill gets approved,' Ben offered. 'Alyssa is off on another sketching expedition anyway.'

'Thank you, Ben, that will be most helpful,' Giles said. 'Why don't we delay determining which points we want to bring up at Lord Witlow's dinner next week until you've done some more sleuthing? Which means we can turn instead to the personal—and find out why Christopher has been holding out on us about making the most momentous decision of his life.'

Christopher felt his face redden as three sets of eyes focused on him.

'You're giving up wine?' Davie asked with a grin.

'No, if it's truly momentous, he must be forswearing women,' Ben said.

'Actually, you're not far off,' Giles said. 'I had it from Maggie today that Christopher has decided to reform his wandering ways and find a wife.'

There was a moment of shocked silence, followed by Ben's hearty laughter. 'Shame on you, Christopher, teasing a lady in Maggie's delicate condition!'

'No, he's serious,' Giles insisted. 'They had quite a chat about it while he escorted her home from a call at Lady Sayleford's.'

'You truly mean to look for a wife?' Davie asked.

Blowing out a breath, Christopher braced himself for the harassment bound to ensue and said, 'It would benefit my career to be...settled. I'd like to have a hostess of my own to be able to entertain colleagues. And, after observing the three of you, I've concluded that matrimony might not be the...tedious affair I'd always thought it.'

'Providing you choose the right lady,' Giles said.

'And providing you truly want to take this step,' Ben added.

'If so, we can only wish you the best of luck,' Davie said.

'What, Ben, nothing more from you?' Christopher asked. 'I expected to be ribbed unmercifully.'

Ben shook his head. 'Not by me, my friend. Marrying Alyssa was the wisest thing I've ever done. No one more devout than a converted sinner.'

'You'll have to start attending Society functions—something you've always avoided,' Giles said. 'I'm sure Maggie would be happy to introduce you around—when she feels up to it. Even better, she could ask her Aunt Lilly to intervene on your behalf. No one wields more influence among the *ton* than Lady Sayleford.'

'Or knows more about everyone in London,' Christopher said wryly. 'I plan to enlist the help of my Aunt Gussie, too. She doesn't possess quite the clout of Lady Sayleford, but she is well connected. I'll talk to them both—when I'm ready.'

'Ready?' Ben said, raising his eyebrows. 'Birth, good looks, position. What else do you need?'

'A better sense of how to conduct myself around unmarried ladies of quality,' Christopher said wryly. 'As you well know, there are few behavioural restrictions when consorting with ladies of light virtue—the only kind of female, saving your lovely wives, of which I have any experience.'

'Fortunately, I never had to brave that gauntlet,' Giles said. 'Davie and I both married widows, and Ben's Alssya is unique unto herself. Maybe you should get advice from your Aunt Gussie before you begin.'

'Actually, I'm already getting some help. Ellie Parmenter is tutoring me on the correct way to court an innocent maid. But wait—'

He held up hand to restrain any comments. 'We've not met for a fortnight, so you won't have heard. I recently discovered that Ellie isn't at all what she appears.'

'I know she is a gracious lady who went out of her way to save my career,' Ben said.

'There's more—a lot more.' Christopher went on to explain what he'd discovered about Ellie's background, her true identity, and the call he and Maggie had made to support her at Lady Sayleford's.

'Hell and the devil!' Giles cried when he'd finished. 'Lord Wanstead's behaviour was *criminal*! I always knew our zeal to limit the power of the aristocracy was well founded. If only it could extend into the social realm! Summerville should have been prosecuted for what was virtually kidnapping and rape.'

Davie shook his head. 'Venality isn't limited to the aristocracy. There is evil—and nobility— at every social level.'

'Damn, the idea that she's barred from resuming her rightful place in Society for ever is hard to swallow,' Ben said. 'We may be able to change the course of government, but it's the matrons of the *ton* who make the rules excluding her.'

Christopher nodded, bedevilled by the same

frustration. 'Lady Sayleford admitted to her sister that even she couldn't manage it.'

'Still, we should do all we can to support her,' Davie said. 'She's begun a school to train indigent girls for respectable positions, something Faith told me she'd mentioned at their dinner last autumn. Why don't we encourage all our wives to support it?'

'Bring her to Lord Witlow's discussion evenings, too,' Davie suggested. 'Even a commoner like me is admitted, so I know he'd have no objection to Ellie.'

'Yes, do that,' Giles said. 'With Maggie overseeing the conversation, she's sure to be accepted.'

'I will,' Christopher said, energised by his friends' support of Ellie—and the idea of her joining their camaraderie during one of the free-ranging discussions that were the hallmarks of the Earl's discussion gatherings.

'Excellent,' Giles said. 'Davie, there was a point of law I wanted to ask you about, something that might offer us a bargaining position with the more moderate Lords. Take a look at Blackstone's with me, won't you, and see if you agree?'

'Of course,' Davie said. 'Discovering an ancient law of the aristocracy that we could use to bludgeon them into submission would be most satisfying.'

While Giles bore their friend off, Ben turned a penetrating gaze on Christopher. 'You're sure you truly want to marry?'

Christopher shrugged. 'I admit, when I first considered the idea, it was more about putting the dissipations of youth behind me and setting myself up to best advance my career. But as I've thought more about it—and seen the joy the three of you seem to have found in marriages—I've grown more enthusiastic about the idea.'

He hesitated, wondering if he should confess the whole. But who better to ask about his doubts than the friend who'd recently been in his same position? 'I do worry I may miss having my freedom, and possibly resent being tied down to just one woman,' he admitted. 'You ended up wedding Alyssa before you'd even contemplated getting married. How did you know you'd be able to make a success of it?'

'True, I was more or less coerced by duty into offering for her. Nor did I fall in love with her immediately, though she did intrigue—and drive me crazy with need—from the minute we met. Though, given the way she'd been treated by her family, I felt a fierce desire to protect her, at first. I, too, worried about whether I'd be able to remain faithful to just one lady for the rest of my life. But as we spent more time together, she just so fascinated and enthralled me that, before I realised it, she'd come to fill every corner of my heart and mind. So much so that I found I truly had no desire to pursue other women.'

Ben shook his head wonderingly. 'Mere words can't describe the sense of peace and belonging and...*rightness* I feel, being with her. When I compare the shallow pleasure of my carousing days to what I have now—well, I'd never go back. I can only echo what the others have said. Find the right lady, and your doubts will disappear.'

Unfortunately, the lady who intrigued, attracted, and called up *his* fierce protective instincts was out of the running. Pushing past his annoyance over that fact, Christopher said, 'Thank you for giving me an honest answer, rather than the ribbing I half-expected.'

'I hope you know I'd never harass you about a matter this important. However...' Ben hesitated. 'Are you sure a virginal innocent will be right for you? We spent our salad days around sophisticated, knowledgeable, sensual, females. As Giles pointed out, he and Davie married widows, and Alyssa, though virginal, was hardly an innocent. I don't know that the sort of sheltered, inexperienced maid to be found on the Marriage Mart would suit you.'

'But marrying an innocent girl of good birth will ensure my own children never have to endure having their schoolmates whisper about their mother, or come to blows with bullies who question her virtue. Not that I don't love and respect Mama,' he added. 'She weathered the unfortunate circumstances of her own marriage as best she could. But I would spare my children some of the harassment I suffered growing up.'

'I know it was hard on you. I suppose you won't know if an inexperienced virgin will suit until you test the waters. And for the sake of your career, you would do better to marry a girl with a sterling reputation. The damage I had to repair back in my district after that brush with scandal, even when I could prove I was blameless, isn't something I'd wish to repeat. I can recommend without reservation marriage to a woman who inspires you to passion, devotion, and contentment.'

At that moment, Giles and Davie returned, the volume of Blackstone's in Davie's hand. 'We need your opinions,' Giles said. 'Our philosopher here agrees with me that the law in question might be useful, but proposes twisting it in a very different way than I envisaged. Look it over and tell us what you think.'

Christopher accepted the book Davie held out, the matter of marriage superseded by the political discussion that had brought them together. Reassured by Ben's avowal that, with the right lady, he could enter wedlock with every expectation of finding marriage enjoyable and fulfilling, he was happy to put aside that nagging concern.

And push away the fact that, when he thought of discovering an intelligent, passionate lady of wide-ranging interests who would intrigue him, it was still Ellie's image that came to mind.

Chapter Eleven

In the late morning two days later, Ellie sat in the front room at the school with her pupils, having just concluded a lesson in arithmetic. 'You may put up your slates, girls, and retrieve your sewing from Mrs Sanders. We'll continue with reading tomorrow.'

'Will you tell us a story later, miss?' one of the girls asked.

'If I have time when I return from the marketing,' Ellie replied, giving the girl an affectionate pat.

Whenever she was in danger of feeling sorry for herself, Ellie knew she need only remember how much she had in comparison to these girls. A home and family growing up, an education, and after some hard times, a house, an income, and the means to assist others.

Having come from so little, her students were

appreciative of so many small things she took for granted—being read a story, or knowing how to total the sum of two stacks of pennies without having to count each one, or how to stitch a straight stem and do embroidery. It humbled her and gave her a sense of satisfaction to be able to help these eager girls acquire simple skills, a satisfaction that, thanks to the kindness of her benefactors, would continue to give her life purpose for the rest of her days.

Her lonely days, after Christopher went on to *his* new life.

Sighing, she stifled that thought as Artis came over to her. 'You be going to do the marketing, miss? Happen I can help you.'

Ellie smiled at the girl. Never had she been more glad of having established the school than after finding Artis. With the grime washed off and dressed in suitable clothing, the girl had turned out to be surprisingly pretty. Though still alarmingly thin, her hollow cheeks had begun to fill out, and with her pointed chin, sparkling grey eyes and mass of curly light brown hair, she had a piquant charm.

She was also a bundle of energy and curiosity, Mrs Sanders had reported, interrogating all the girls about their backgrounds, teasing Jensen to tell them about his days as a 'flash man' at the brothel, and inspecting every inch of the school.

'Would you like to come along and help carry the baskets? Jensen would appreciate having an assistant.'

'I could. But mostly, I thought to show you places to shop. I'm powerful grateful for all you done, takin' me in like you did, givin' me the finest clothes I ever had, and learnin' me my letters so's soon I'll be able to read all for meself! I been looking at all the provisions and asking Mrs Sanders and Jensen where you got what, and I know I can help you do better.'

'Indeed?' Ellie said, both amused and interested. 'In what way?'

'Mrs Sanders says you gets your wine from Berry's in St. James's, your tea from Twinings in the Strand, and cheese from a fancy shop on Jermyn Street. Well, I ain't never been to none of them fine places, but when she told me what was paid for beer and cheese, I was prodigious amazed! Since I scarpered up to Piccadilly, I been going to the market up on Tottenham Court Road, hardly a hop and a skip from here! Lots of costermongers there, who buy direct from the farmers and fishermen, so everything from fish to meat be blood-fresh! Kin I take you there and show you? I know I kin save you enough blunt to pay for my keep, so's you'll not be sorry you took me in.'

Touched that the girl was so eager to prove her worth, and suspecting she would hurt Artis's feelings if she brushed aside her offer, Ellie replied, 'Yes, I'd very much like to see the bargains you can find.'

Until recently, Ellie had never shopped for domestic items, and knew very little about the markets beyond the expensive couturières and bonnet-makers of Bond Street and St. James's. It would be interesting to explore a new part of the city, with this knowing child as her guide.

'Fetch your shawl, and I'll get my bonnet and pelisse.'

The girl bounded out of the room, but before Ellie could gather her outer garments, a knock came at the front door. Jensen being occupied in the kitchen, one of the girls ran over to open it. Her mild curiosity over who might be calling was superseded by distaste as the elegant figure of Lord Mountgarcy entered.

With his habitual mocking smile, he inspected the room. 'Good day, *Miss Parmenter*,' he said, emphasising the formal greeting. 'So, this is your little project. I have to admit, I'm quite impressed.'

All Ellie could think about was getting his polluting presence away from her innocent girls.

Waving out of the room the two remaining ones, who were gazing curiously at the visitor, she replied, 'I suppose I should say "thank you"? Although I must add that I cannot appreciate a visit here by a man of your…proclivities. I'm afraid I must ask you to leave. Immediately.'

'Now, now, Ellie,' he protested, holding up his palms in a placating gesture. 'I may be a man about town, but as I assured you earlier, I've no interest in the infancy. My tastes run to mature fruit, not budding blossoms.' He ran his eyes over her figure, and she had to resist the urge to slap him. 'Ripe, fully developed, and like fine wine, aged enough to have developed complexity and staying power.'

'Then I suggest you head off to a wine merchant. There is no such fruit available here, at any price.'

'If I must, but first, allow me to apologise for my rather boorish behaviour at Gunter's the other day. The wine fumes from the night before had not fully cleared from my brain, alas, and I made some rather…unfortunate remarks.'

'I would rather describe them as "unforgivable".'

He shook his head. 'I had spent the night in riotous company, and my tongue hadn't reverted to conversing with more…genteel persons. As

I see you are striving hard to become. I asked around, and it appears this school is not only legitimate, you've obtained the backing of some quite prominent Society figures. I must say, learning about this side of you makes you even more intriguing, my dear.'

'I am not your "dear", nor will you develop an acquaintance with any side of me. Can I make it plainer than that?'

There was another knock at the door, and ready to welcome any interruption that would speed Mountgarcy's departure, Ellie walked over and yanked it open. And then stopped, sucking in a breath, to find it was Christopher who had come visiting.

For a moment, she simply stood there, her avid gaze taking in his handsome face, the beautiful turquoise eyes gazing at her with warmth and concern—while awareness flashed through her, setting her senses humming in response to his nearness.

'Mr Lattimar!' she said, finding her voice at last. 'Please, come in. Lord Mountgarcy was just leaving.'

Christopher's smile evaporated as he jerked his gaze from her face to where the Viscount stood, watching them. 'Mountgarcy,' he said coldly, giving the older man a nod.

'Lattimar,' the Viscount replied. 'Still maintaining your interest in the…school, I see. Another discussion on behalf of your mother, who, I understand, is in fact a benefactor of Miss Parmenter's enterprise?' Looking back to Ellie, he said, 'Perhaps I would receive a warmer reception, were I also to become a supporter. I'm no stranger to philanthropic causes. I have a deep purse, a wide reach, and might be able to do you a great deal of good. Which could be…enjoyable. For both of us.'

'If you truly are interested in joining this philanthropic cause, you should apply to Lady Sayleford. She's to be the head of the governing board,' Ellie replied.

Mountgarcy laughed. 'Ah, you trump carnal interest by playing the card of the most eminently respectable Society matron of them all! Well done. The game grows more interesting by the day.'

Ellie nearly ground her teeth in frustration. 'How can I convince you there is no game?'

'You'll never do that, my dear,' he said, and strolled towards the door. As he passed her, he suddenly ran a finger under her chin. 'Like silk,' he murmured. 'Good day, Miss Parmenter.'

Furious that he'd managed to touch her, Ellie slammed the door behind him, rubbing at the spot on her chin. 'Detestable man! He claimed he came to apologise, but I think he only wanted to see how the ground lay, that he might scheme ways to bring me to capitulate.'

Christopher frowned. 'You're not alone and friendless any more, Ellie. There is no possibility of him manoeuvring you into a position where you would have to "capitulate".'

Shutting out of mind the one way Christopher could with absolutely certainty prevent that, she said, 'I know. I have my school, and enough supporters to ensure its future. It would take a catastrophe indeed to make me desperate enough to resort to sheltering with the likes of *him*.'

'I intend to make sure you never suffer a catastrophe that serious!' Christopher declared.

'Enough about that unpleasant subject. What brings you to the school today?'

'I called at Hans Place, but Tarleton said you were here. I hadn't heard anything yet about when we might have our next lesson. No rush about it—I won't be engaged on the political front until after the dinner at Lord Witlow's next week. I… I just wanted to make sure you hadn't changed your mind about teaching me.'

So he'd been worried she might listen to the voice of prudence, and pull back? She ought to have enough sense to do just that, she thought, half-resigned, half-regretful. So far, spending time with him had turned up little reason to think less of him, beyond the indisputable fact of the unsuitability of their being together—a fact she'd already known, but still seemed to have trouble facing. She felt a futile satisfaction that he was apparently as drawn to continue spending time with her as she was to him.

'No, I haven't changed my mind—even though it would be more sensible. But I mean to honour my pledge to help you. I only just heard from Lady Sayleford that it would be convenient for her to lend me the Blue Salon tomorrow afternoon at three to meet Sophie, and received Sophie's confirmation she could be there. I was about to write and request that, if your schedule will permit, we meet at two. Lady Sayleford has a fine pianoforte. Since your young ladies will surely perform at musicales and after dinners to display their skills, you will need to know what is required of gentlemen as such gatherings.'

'Yes, I can be at Lady Sayleford's tomorrow. An eminently safe venue.'

She looked up to meet his rueful gaze. 'Exactly,' she said drily, trying to submerge her regret that they must be safe.

'I'd much prefer for us to be foolish,' he said softly, echoing the words of her heart, and giving her a look that so mirrored her yearning it resonated deep within her.

It took her a moment to fight free of it. 'All the more reason to be wise,' she replied resolutely.

'Regrettably true. In any event, I will look forward to hearing you play.' He paused, as if uncertain whether or not to continue. 'Did you enjoy music growing up?' he asked finally.

She had a sudden vision of the old music room at Wanstead Manor, the couch covers worn and the window hangings faded, but the pianoforte kept in perfect tune. 'I adored it. The last governess we had, before Mama had to let her go, was quite proficient, and taught me all she knew. There was no coal for the hearth, and we dared burn only one candle, but oh, how many evenings after dinner we'd bundle up in our shawls and retire there, me with mittens on, playing from memory for Mama and Sophie! Thank you,' she said softly. 'For so long, I've blocked out all thought of Wanstead. But despite our poverty, most of my growing up there was happy. I'm glad to recover one such memory.'

'I'm glad to make you glad,' he said with a smile, reaching out to clasp her hand.

Awareness jolted through her anew, stimulating nerves from the tip of her head to her toes. She should drop his fingers, step away, but the contact was so delicious, both arousing and comforting, that she couldn't help indulging herself for a few brief moments.

Soon enough, he'll be gone, and all I will have is this memory.

Artis came bounding into the room, stopping short at the sight of them, and giving Ellie the resolve to pull away.

'Be you ready to go, miss? And is the nob going to escort us, too?'

'Good afternoon, Miss Artis,' Christopher said. 'I trust you are getting along well here?'

'Oh, yes, your Honour! 'Twas me lucky day when I tried to get me fives a-going into your pocket!'

'And you've proved to your satisfaction that you're in no danger here?'

Flushing, the girl looked at Ellie. 'Right sorry I am, miss, to have thought you an abbess and this place a School of Venus! I can't thank Miss Parmenter enough, sir! All the rum prog I can eat, and jest look at me!' The girl twirled, laughing with irrepressible delight. 'Dressed up fine as fivepence! And being taught me sums and letters. Don't imagine heaven be any nicer.'

Christopher shared an amused glance with Ellie. 'Glad to hear you say so. Now, where is it I'm supposed to be escorting you?'

'Artis is going to show me a market area where I can buy provisions at a bargain. Jensen will accompany us, so you needn't waste your time on such a commonplace mission.'

'On the contrary! As I told you, my mother insisted I learn about the products needed to run a household and where to obtain them. I'm as keen to guard my pennies as any thrifty housewife. Which market are we exploring?'

The clock ticking in her head warned that all too soon, she would finish his lessons, leaving her no further excuse to seek his company. With him professing his eagerness to go with them, Ellie couldn't quite force herself to turn him down.

'The markets up Tottenham Court Road,' Artis answered him. 'Just wait till you see the bargains there! Better than Cheapside!'

'Late morning as it is, we should depart at once, then, before all the prime offerings are gone. No need for Jensen; I can carry the baskets.' Giving Ellie a wink, with a sweeping motion, he herded Artis to the door.

Chapter Twelve

A short time later, their hackney set them down where the stalls of the street market began. *If his cronies at the gaming houses with deep play and light ladies could see him now*, Christopher thought with a grin. Bear-leading an urchin and a reformed courtesan to purchase brooms, scouring powder and cabbages.

But if it meant spending time with Ellie, he'd look at tooth powder and coal scuttles.

They had not gone more than a few steps when the competing voices of the merchants and salesmen crying their wares and the hustle-bustle of a diversity of people engaged his interest on their own behalf. 'What an assembly!' he called to Ellie over the hubbub, both of them pacing to keep Artis in sight as she darted in and out around pedestrians, stalls, wheelbarrows and donkey carts.

'Fascinating!' Ellie said, her eyes alight with curiosity. 'I would never have expected such a vast array of goods at a street market.'

Seeming to have a destination in mind, Artis led them past stalls hung with tin saucepans, displays of glassware shiny as mirrors that caught and reflected the bright sunlight, bins of china and pottery in different hues. They tiptoed along the kerb to avoid tripping over a line of second-hand shoes, while an assortment of shirts, trousers, and vests pinned to a cord flapped in the breeze at them.

Artis finally stopped before a baker's stand in one of the busiest sections. 'Best bread and buns you ever tasted,' she announced.

'Right you are, young miss,' the baker called back. 'How many loaves can I get you, my lady? And maybe an extra bun for you, miss, for crying my wares for me?'

'Six loaves, please,' Ellie said, retrieving her purse.

Artis reached out for the roll. 'Thankee, sir. Didn't used to treat me so nice when I hung about, hoping to filch a bun while yer back was turned.'

The baker leaned closer to peer at her. 'Why, you be that starving scamp of a boy I had to keep chasing off!' he said in amazement.

'Aye. Don't do no filching now, but ye should be thankful I did afore, else I wouldn't have known to bring you this lady here. Mind now, don't you be charging her more than tuppence a loaf—I heard ye calling it out often enough.'

'It's a right fine lass ye make,' the baker said as he parcelled up the loaves and handed them to Artis, who tucked them into her basket.

'Thankee. I'm a student at her school now, and she's got seven mouths to feed every day. Be worth yer while to send a boy there every morning.'

'I expect so, if you'd like an order every morning, ma'am?'

'For tuppence a loaf I would,' Ellie replied.

After giving the baker the address on Dean Street, Artis led them off, happily munching her roll. And eating it daintily, Christopher noticed—a far cry from the starving urchin who'd torn into the damaged meat pasty like a wild dog that day in Green Park. What a service Ellie was providing, in truth!

'Thank you, Artis,' Ellie was telling her. 'The loaves are excellent, and it's half what I usually spend for bread.'

Artis nodded. 'Told you so. There's more coming.'

She continued to lead them from stall to stall,

costermonger to costermonger, obviously having closely observed all the sellers in the bustling market and picked out her favourites. Ellie chose oranges from one wheelbarrow, butter and eggs from the back of a donkey cart, green and purple cabbages from a stall, turnips and onions from braided display. By the time they'd wound their way through the busiest section, their baskets were brimming with the addition of nuts, apples, cheese and a fine yellow haddock for the girls' dinner.

'Thank you, Artis,' Ellie said after she'd tucked the last bit into their full baskets. 'We've enough provisions for today, staples to last the week, and a promise from several vendors to come by Dean Street. All for significantly less than I have been paying.'

Artis nodded, her cheeks glowing at the praise. 'Like I promised, miss. Nothing fancy here, just good honest grub at a fair price.'

The food stalls had given way to a lane offering household items, a coal shed side by side with a stall selling boot-blacking, another with combs, brushes and shaving gear. Beyond that stood an old wooden stall displaying used books.

'Be ye needing any of these, miss?' Artis asked. 'I used to stand here and just look at them, all them pretty-coloured covers with the letters stamped out in gold. How I wished I could read one! Now, thanks to you, soon I will.'

Christopher ran a quick eye over the selections on display. Old sermons, hymnbooks, some novels, and a copy of *One Thousand and One Nights*. Plucking out that volume, he said, 'If you like tall tales, you'll like this one, Artis.'

The girl took it from his hand, the look on her face reverent as she carefully turned the pages. 'That be wonderful, sir. Mebbe some day I'll own a real book.'

Before she could put it back, Christopher produced a coin and flipped it to the bookseller. 'You own one now. In thanks, for helping Miss Parmenter save so much blunt.'

The girl's eyes widened. 'Truly, sir? I kin *keep* it?'

Christopher smiled as her obvious delight. 'Truly. It's a gift. And mind, I shall want to hear a dramatic reading of the story of Scheherazade, once you've mastered your letters.'

Artis looked at Christopher with awe. 'Never had nobody give me nothin' afore. I'll treat it tender as a newborn babe, sir. And thankee!'

After stroking the leather binding, Artis opened the book, rapt as she slowly flipped through the pages. Watching her, Christopher was moved—and humbled.

'We have so much, and count it so little,' he said to Ellie beside him, her gaze also on Artis.

'So I was thinking this morning. And realise even more, walking through this market. Such a variety of common folk, all busy about the tasks that keep this great metropolis running,' she said, gesturing towards the throng hurrying by. 'The costermongers with their wares, of course, but all who buy from them, too—boot makers and bakers and butchers, blacksmiths and mechanics and sweepers, maids and cooks and footmen, coachmen and ostlers and keepers of public houses. People *you* serve, and want to give a fairer voice in determining their government. What noble work you perform!'

Her praise warmed, but also surprised him, that she recognised and appreciated his goal. What a dedicated reformer *she* would make! 'You're right, I would like every able-bodied man to have a vote—and women, too, eventually. But no cause for adulation yet. We're far from achieving that. The Lords are kicking up a fuss about fairly apportioning even the votes that now exist.'

'It's a beginning. Those in power would never have initiated change, had you and your fellow reformers not dragged them down that path. What immense satisfaction that must give you!'

'It does. Much like, I imagine, rescuing girls like Artis gives you.'

Gesturing to the girl, still raptly regarding her book, Ellie said, 'You've certainly made a friend for life there. It was so kind of you to give her—' she broke off, her eyes widening and her lips curving into a smile '—a book! We shall squeeze a lesson out of this shopping expedition after all.'

'Training me how to carry a market basket for a young lady?' he teased.

'As if you'd bring a gently born young maiden into this mob!' she replied with a laugh. 'I'm in earnest! As we already discussed, you cannot give a lady jewels or any sort of apparel, but books are quite permissible.'

'Improving sermons, guide books to London, biographies of the kings and queens of England?' he suggested.

'Yes. No fiction, of course. Also, gifts of oranges, like those,' she said, gesturing down the street towards one stall, 'or such fine apples and pears as those,' she continued, pointing out another, 'or a basket of nuts would also be welcomed by the household.'

They'd been following Artis, who strolled along with most of her attention focused on her book. As they reached a crossroads, she looked up to get her bearings—and stiffened, an expression of alarm on her face.

'What is it, Artis?' Ellie asked.

'N-nothing, miss,' Artis said. 'Need you anything else? P'haps we oughta get back.'

Exchanging a puzzled glance with Christopher, Ellie said, 'Very well. We have all we need today.'

Nodding, Artis set off again at a brisk pace, leading them this time down a side lane away from the main road of the market. Not until they were several streets along, after peering behind them, did she slow her pace. 'There's a good tea shop here, if you want a spot of refreshment.'

Refraining from asking why, after hurrying them along, she was now inclined to linger, Christopher said, 'What say you, Ellie? Would you ladies care for some tea?'

'Have you tasted the tea here, Artis?' Ellie asked.

The girl nodded. 'Once, when I lifted…um… found a handful of coppers. Warm and sweet and wonderful it was, miss!'

'Then let this be my treat,' Christopher said, stepping into the shop to procure a cup for each lady. 'Not Gunter's, but permissible?' he asked as he handed Ellie hers.

'Permissible—' she smiled '—since you'd

never bring your young lady down this narrow back lane either.'

'What a dull life she must lead, that poor, pretty-behaved young maid.'

'Restricted, certainly. But with books, music, rides, walks, agreeable companionship, worthwhile work to do, and knowing nothing of the wider world she's missing, such a girl could be content. There are…benefits to remaining innocent.'

'Definite benefits to not being suddenly cast out of a sheltered existence into an indifferent world you've been given no training or preparation to survive,' he agreed with some heat. *As she had been.*

Tea finished, they picked up their baskets and resumed walking out of the maze of market streets, Artis clutching her book possessively. But as they were passing a stall displaying shirts, shifts and chemises, the girl halted, pointing to an elegant, beribboned corset.

'What kind of skirt goes with that, miss? Cor, but that's the prettiest thing I ever did see!'

'It's a corset, Artis. Worn over the chemise, but beneath the gown,' Ellie explained, sure Artis had never seen such lace- and ribbon-trimmed undergarments.

'You wears it *under* the gown?' Artis asked. 'All them pretty ribbons and flowers don't even show? What a bleedin' waste of lace and thread!' Shaking her head, Artis picked up the pace again.

'I know, I mustn't envisage you wearing it,' Christopher murmured to Ellie—although that was exactly where his nimble mind had leapt as soon as he saw the garment. Unable to resist the temptation to tease, he added, 'Or picture removing it.'

To his delight, that naughty comment earned him a blush. 'I hardly need mention that's not a remark you could make to your innocent maid. Indeed, if you should accompany her while she is shopping for gowns at a boutique that happens also to sell undergarments, you will pretend not to notice.'

'Another rule,' he said with an exaggerated sigh. 'No noticing of beribboned corsets—or envisaging the lady in or out of them.'

'Wretch! I imagine you have more experience getting a lady *out* than getting one *in*,' she returned tartly.

'Not as much as you might suspect. Most of my *chère amies* had already removed such impediments to passion before I arrived. Although it can be a delicious game, taking one's time to slowly remove each garment.' Grinning at having pushed her so far, before Ellie could reprove him again, he held up a hand. 'I know, enough! Artis may not be a marriageable miss, but she is little more than a child.'

'I'm more worried about sparing *my* blushes,' Ellie retorted. 'Artis might not recognise the purpose behind a decorated corset, but raised where she was, I doubt she has much ignorance left about anything else to do with the process.'

'She knew enough that she never wanted to end up in one of Gentleman Bob's schools,' he said grimly. 'After so many years thieving, though, do you really think she'll stop?'

Ellie inclined her head to where Artis trotted in front of them, using a sort of sixth sense to navigate while keeping most of her attention on her precious book. 'She has something she loves more now.'

Could he find something he'd love more?

Would that person be enough to make up for losing Ellie's companionship?

The thought of that potential loss burned like a hand placed too close to a blazing hearth. His mind recoiling from the prospect, as they reached the main area at Tottenham Court Road, he said, 'I'll fetch us a hackney. I know now it's not far to Dean Street, but these baskets are heavy.'

He wouldn't think any further about the fact

that marriage would inevitably mean the end of their interludes together.

Over this last week, he'd grown accustomed to seeing her almost daily. Just the prospect of losing the warmth and brightness she brought to his life made the world seem a little colder and darker.

After engaging a jarvey, he brought the vehicle to where the ladies waited, helped them in and loaded the baskets.

'Thank you again, Artis,' Ellie said to the girl as the vehicle set off. 'I shall certainly know where to look the next time I'm in need of any sort of item.'

'I enjoyed exploring it with you,' Christopher said. 'But I'd not recommend that you return there alone.'

Ellie nodded. 'I'll make sure to take Jensen, or Tarleton if I'm buying supplies for the house— if,' she added with a smile, 'you're not available and in need of another lesson.'

'Call upon me any time,' he replied. *As often as possible—before it no longer* is *possible.*

All too soon, the hackney pulled up in Dean Street and Christopher reversed the process of unloading. Telling the driver to wait, he walked the ladies in, Ellie calling for Jensen to help Artis carry the baskets down to the kitchen. The girl showered Christopher with another round of effusive thanks before running off, doubtless eager to show off her treasure.

'So, I'll see you tomorrow at Lady Sayleford's?' Ellie said.

'Tomorrow, at Lady Sayleford's,' he confirmed.

'Thank you again for accompanying us. I can't remember when I've enjoyed shopping more.'

'Good company makes any task lighter. Well… I'd better get along. I promised Giles I'd look over some papers with him.'

'Give my best to Lord and Lady Lyndlington, then.'

'I'll do that.' *Hell and damnation, just leave*, he told himself, fighting the desire to find another excuse to linger. 'Until tomorrow.'

Another precious day to look forward to—and extract every morsel of pleasure from while this temporary association lasted.

Chapter Thirteen

The following afternoon at two, Christopher presented himself at Lady Sayleford's home in Grosvenor Square. Although in the past, he and Ben usually excused themselves to seek more carnal delights when Maggie played for the company after a dinner gathering, he did enjoy music. He remembered listening with rapt enjoyment as a child, as his mother played.

He was also curious what type of music Ellie preferred. What had she played from memory for her sister in the frigid near-darkness at Wanstead Hall? The mathematically intricate arrangements of Mozart? Folk tunes and romantic ballads of star-crossed lovers? The grandiose, structured precision of Handel? Or the difficult, passionate interludes of Beethoven?

She was in turn all those things—logical, romantic, precise, and ah, yes, passionate. A passion that her forced introduction to intimacy had stymied. But if she were able to explore her inclinations, at her pace, as *she* wished? Everything about the intense connection between them promised she possessed hidden depths of desire, just waiting to be unleashed.

How he wished he could be the man to loosen those fetters!

'Lady Sayleford is resting, and regrettably will not be able to join you,' the butler informed him as he ushered Christopher in. 'But Miss Parmenter has already arrived, and is waiting for you in the Blue Salon.'

Christopher followed him up the stairs, until he halted before one of the doors. 'You needn't announce me,' he said before the man could knock.

'Very good, sir,' the butler said, and bowed himself away.

Christopher entered the room noiselessly— succeeding, as he'd hoped, in catching a glimpse of Ellie before she was aware of his presence. He halted, indulging in the rare opportunity of openly staring at her loveliness.

She was seated at the pianoforte, facing away from him. As she scanned the music on the stand before her, occasionally she turned her head, offering him a glimpse of her profile. She wore a plain gown—her gowns were always plain, he realised—but then, she had no need of elaborate trimmings to enhance her beauty. Not when the sheen of the gown did such a good job, echoing the sparkle in her eyes, and the sweep of the bodice from her shoulders to her waist emphasised its smallness so cleverly. He could span it with two hands, he thought, the idea jolting his pulse and making his mouth dry.

She was running her fingers experimentally along the keyboard, as if appreciating their feel and texture. He could imagine running his own fingers over the porcelain beauty of her skin. Hunger gnawed at him, sparking the urge to walk over and kiss the curve of her neck bared when she inclined her head towards the keyboard.

He stopped himself before he could act on the impulse. Damn and blast, he didn't seem to be doing a bit better at restraining his thoughts, if not his actions.

Lose control of those here, and he wouldn't need to worry about a repetition—an outraged Lady Sayleford would ban him from the house. He recalled her sharp, *sotto voce* reminder that rakes were attractive only if they had truly reformed.

As he was resolving to do better, Ellie must have sensed his presence, for she turned on the bench. 'Christopher!' she said, giving him the lovely smile that never failed to lift his heart. 'I didn't hear you come in.'

'I hoped to hear you play a bit before you were aware of me,' he said, admitting only part of what he'd been doing.

'So I wouldn't be nervous? As well I should be, having not practised in so long.'

'Why haven't you?' he asked, curious. 'I know...an instrument would have been provided, had you requested it,' he continued, avoiding the name—as he increasingly wanted to avoid recalling that she'd ever been bound to another man.

'It would have been,' she replied, apparently no more eager than he to mention particulars. 'But music, and performing on the pianoforte, belonged to another life. Silly, I suppose, but I thought it would be easier to survive the new one if I kept the two entirely separate. Fortunately, musical performances weren't a part of my new duties,' she added drily.

'If you played by heart at Wanstead, I wager you'll still recall the notes,' he said, wanting to pull her thoughts away from what they would both rather forget.

'I may recall the music, but after a decade without practice, don't expect me to perform it well! Before I make the attempt, how often have you attended a musical evening among the *ton*?'

'Never. Mama played occasionally when we were children, and Maggie sometimes plays for us after one of her father's political dinners. But that's the extent of it.'

'For a musical evening designed to display the talents of young ladies, there will probably be some refreshment and conversation before the performances begin.'

'Polite conversation on appropriate topics?'

She nodded. 'You might begin by complimenting the hostess on the excellence of her refreshments, the decoration of her home, or her appearance—nothing too extravagant, lest you be thought insincere. You may ask the young ladies about sites of interest they have visited in London, or the types of music they prefer.'

Christopher walked over to join her at the instrument, and bowed. 'Miss Parmenter, how lovely to see you again. What a charming gown! How have you been enjoying London? I understand the markets are without compare.'

Her lips quirking in amusement, Ellie said, 'I'm so pleased you could attend, Mr Lattimar. Yes, I've discovered some quite unusual markets of late. Though it is partly the excellent company that made the visit so delightful.'

'Excellent company always enhances an adventure.'

'Have you any requests, Mr Lattimar? Lady Sayleford has a good selection of music. Although I cannot promise to be able to play all of it.'

'I'm sure whatever you choose will be delightful.'

'You may live to regret that invitation,' she murmured, injecting a note of truth into their patterned exchange as she pulled several sheets from the stack she'd assembled. 'Would you be so kind as to turn the pages for me, Mr Lattimar? This piece was a particular favourite of my sister's.'

'I would be honoured.' Moving into position beside her, Christopher looked down to discover she had chosen a Beethoven piano concerto.

'Being in practice, your young lady would begin immediately, but I have need of a warm-up first. You will indulge me through a few scales?'

'Of course.'

She took a deep breath, as if beginning an arduous endeavour, he thought with a smile. But the pianoforte had such a lovely sound, and her rapt attention as she began slowly, then gradually increased the speed and difficulty of the exercises, had him listening in appreciation even before she began the work itself.

Which was marvellous. What a shame she had not played in so long, for even with a few missed notes and misplayed keys, her performance was mesmerising. The music itself in its sonorous complexity was engaging enough, but her rendition of it, by turns passionate, explosive and tender, completely beguiled him.

He was reminded again of Maggie playing for them—and Ellie looked every inch a comparable lady. Suppressing again the stab of anger at her father for stealing from her any chance of being recognised as one, he focused on simply enjoying the performance.

All those nights, listening to buxom girls belting out bawdy tunes, when I could have come home to something like this.

Wistful envy stirred again for what Giles had—a lovely woman to play for him like this, uplifting his spirits, inciting his desires. If Ellie were his, he could place his hands on her shoulders as the piece drew to a close, brush the wisps of hair from her neck and lean down to kiss her.

Caught up in the music and the moment, before he realised what he intended, he'd done just that.

The concerto ended abruptly in a jangle of discordant notes. Cursing under his breath, he straightened and jerked his hands away, his heart thudding with regret—and arousal.

'You may definitely *not* do that,' she said in a strangled voice.

He blew out a gusty sigh. 'I know, I know. Sorry! It's just—I was imagining, not a parlour with my Virtuous Virgin playing for a roomful of guests, but being in my own drawing room with my wife. After coming home, disgruntled from a day arguing with stubborn opponents, I'd be relaxing with a brandy, while she played a beautiful melody like that, soothing away the irritation and anger.'

She looked over her shoulder at him, her eyes wistful. 'That's exactly what you should have. A wife to revive, soothe and refresh you.'

'Fascinate and delight,' he added.

'That, too.'

He clasped his hands behind him to prevent himself from reaching for her. Maybe it was the music, lingering in his brain and his senses, but he felt even more powerfully drawn to her. Something more complex had layered itself over the ever-simmering desire that kept him always on the knife's edge of arousal, something more intimate, a connection that had no need of touch. Almost a...linking of souls, that communicated an affection and comfort and understanding too powerful for words. He'd never experienced anything like it, and found it as compelling as physical passion.

How he longed for them both!

'Thank you,' he said at last. 'For giving me a vision of what marriage might be with greater clarity than I've ever had before. If this sense of peace and belonging is what Giles and Davie and Ben experienced, I now understand why they felt driven to marry their ladies.'

'I'm sure it is,' she replied softly. 'I hope you find it, too. I know you will.'

With someone other than you? But he must get past that desire, he knew, anger breaking the music's spell. Ellie was out of bounds, impossible to claim as mistress, unsuitable to be his wife. He must learn what he needed from her and break off these lessons, before the conflict between what he wanted and could not have brought him to the breaking point, to some rash action that would destroy them both.

As if aware of his distress, she pushed away from the piano. 'Enough of that. Sophie should arrive soon. If you linger a little longer, it would be good practice for you to meet and talk with her.'

In his current unsettled state, he wasn't in the least interested in making polite chat with the sort of Virtuous Virgin who must replace Ellie in his life. But Ellie delighted in her sister, and would probably be hurt if he snubbed her. 'I suppose I can spare the time,' he said, trying not to sound ungrateful.

Ever perceptive, she picked up on his aggrieved tone and gave him an amused glance. 'She's quite lovely and accomplished, you'll remember. I don't think speaking with her will be a burden.'

Feeling his face redden, he nodded. 'Sorry. I'm sure it won't be.'

Needing to put some space between them, he strolled to the bookcases that lined the walls of the salon. 'It appears Lady Sayleford is quite a reader—or some ancestor was.'

'Yes, it's an impressive collection,' Ellie agreed, walking to a shelf a safe distance away. 'I've missed having a library. Not that my father was a reader, but his grandfather was. Fortunately, not realising how valuable some of the volumes were, Papa never thought to sell them when the estate fell on hard times. Great-Grandfather possessed all the classics, many in original Greek and Latin.'

'I suppose literature is another safe topic of conversation, if my questions are confined to the poetry of Wordsworth, Southey and Robert Burns?'

'Yes, although I'd start with a discreet enquiry to discover whether or not the young lady is a reader. Not all mamas consider a knowledge of literature appropriate for a gently bred girl. Your questions could expose an ignorance that might embarrass her.'

'Yet another rule.' Christopher heaved an exaggerated sigh. 'No questions that might reveal an embarrassing ignorance. What subjects might I enquire about which even a narrow-minded mama would consider appropriate?'

Ellie looked over from her perusal of the shelves, her eyes sparkling in amusement at his exasperation. 'You can safely ask her preferences in sketching, watercolours, and musical perform—oh, my! I'd not expect to find *this* in Lady Sayleford's library!' she exclaimed, looking down at the book she'd just pulled from the shelf, a blush suffusing her face.

Unable to resist discovering what had caused it, Christopher paced to her side—and saw the volume in question was Ovid's *Ars Amatoria*. 'It *is* in the original Latin,' he noted. 'Lady Sayleford—or more likely, her late husband—probably believed no one who might be offended would be able to read it anyway.'

'You mean, no respectable ladies would be able to read it. On the other hand, it sounds just like Lady Sayleford to have deposited such a volume in her drawing room. How she might smile, knowing that the assembled arbiters of the *ton* would be shocked out of their chemises, if they but understood what it was.'

'*You* understood it,' he realised suddenly. 'Did your father possess a collection of…scandalous writings?'

'No, but Summerville did. I'm not sure he could read Latin—he generally preferred the crude illustrated volumes he kept in a locked cabinet. I discovered the Ovid when he'd gone off hunting for a week, and I was looking for something to occupy myself. I used it to review my Latin, until I bought some Sophocles and Euripides as more suitable material. Still, good for naughty Lady Sayleford, if shelving the volume here *was* her idea.'

Christopher couldn't help imagining Ellie perusing the descriptions of lovemaking so graphically detailed at the end of the third volume. What would please her most? Ah, that he had the chance to experiment! That was a study to which he would enthusiastically devote weeks, months, years.

He came back from that thought to discover her gaze on his face. From her expression, he knew she must be imagining, as he was, reading the elegant poetry aloud to each other and then acting out the instructions, combining erotic and erudite into one delicious lesson of pleasure.

'You must have studied the arts of seduction in Books One and Two,' she murmured. 'You arouse with just a glance.'

He stepped closer, drawing his thumb across the plump softness of her lower lip. She moaned, parting her lips, and sucked his thumb into her mouth. Hard, aching, he stroked in and out along that wet surface, all the ferocity of his desire for the deeper, longer strokes he'd prefer confined to those small movements.

They were both gasping by the time he withdrew his thumb. He wasn't sure what idiocy they might have committed had the butler not opened the door to announce, 'Miss Wanstead has arrived. Shall I have her join you here?'

Avoiding his gaze, Ellie stepped away. 'Yes, please.' As the butler withdrew, she pushed the volume back into place with shaking hands. 'I can only hope Sophie's later governesses were not as learned as mine.'

'Before your sister arrives, have you decided on the next lesson?' *If, given their lapse in conduct today, there would be a next lesson?* But he must see her again!

To his relief, she replied, 'I called on your

mother and asked her to assemble the loveliest and most seductive matrons she knows. There will always be bored or neglected wives around to tempt you. If you hope to make your marriage a success, you will have to train yourself to resist them.'

'Ignore lovely and seductive ladies who tempt you,' he said wryly. 'A rule I definitely need more practice to perfect.'

'Will you be able to visit Lady Vraux tomorrow afternoon?'

He nodded, relief filling his chest at the knowledge that he would see her again soon. 'My afternoon is free.'

'Good. So, you may greet Sophie, exchange some innocuous remark about London or the weather, and take your leave.'

'Do I greet her...like this?' Craving one last touch, he seized her hand and brushed his lips across the ungloved fingers, setting off tremors he felt to his boots.

Only when she gently pulled free did he realise he'd held on far longer than courtesy permitted. 'It would be wiser not to,' she replied, her voice unsteady. 'Some mamas might find the gesture too...personal.'

Ah, how correct they would be. He'd shared intimacies with a score of talented, seductive women trained to draw out every pleasure. He never would have believed he could be this shaken by such a simple, limited touch. Or respect a lady as fiercely as he desired her.

'Very well. No kissing of hands. No discussion of literature without first ascertaining whether the young lady enjoys it. Make polite conversation only about her views on London, sketching, painting, music and needlework. Turn her music pages but absolutely do not touch her. Do I have it all aright?'

'I think you've mastered the lesson for today. Ah, Sophie, how lovely to see you!' Ellie exclaimed, turning to the smartly dressed young lady rushing into the room.

'My darling Tess!' her sister exclaimed, enveloping her in a fierce hug.

'Sophie, you'll remember Mr Lattimar, an associate of Lady Lyndlington's husband, and my…friend. Mr Lattimar, my sister, Miss Wanstead.'

She made him a curtsy. 'I'm always happy to greet one of Tess's supporters.'

'Your servant, Miss Wanstead,' Christopher said, bowing. 'But you've come for a good long chat with your sister, not to exchange politenesses with me, so I'll take myself off. Miss Wanstead, Miss Parmenter.'

Bowing again, Christopher left them in the Blue Salon. And strolled out to summon a hackney, still chuckling at the notion of Lady Sayleford hiding her scandalous book in plain sight.

His mirth subsided at the sober realisation that, after his lack of control in the parlour today, he'd probably not get another chance to listen to Ellie play the pianoforte. Regret and bittersweet yearning coursed through him. Whatever the spell she'd cast over him with her music, he wanted more of it.

Could he find that with someone else?

Recalling Ben's advice made it even more difficult to stifle his growing doubt that pursuing a Virtuous Virgin was truly the road to lasting happiness. But how else was he to find a woman of unimpeachable honour to become the mother of his children?

What if he couldn't find a respectable virgin to whom he felt he could remain faithful for life? Should he just abandon the notion of marriage, and return to his former life? Follow his mother's advice, and pursue Ellie for his mistress?

The brief flare of euphoria engendered by the idea of making Ellie *his* fizzled out at once. Hell and damnation, Ellie neither wanted to fill that role again, nor could he insult the lady he knew she was by asking her to. Neither his reformed self, nor his former self, would ever be able to claim her.

Black rage, with an edge of despair, revived at the thought. With difficulty, he once again suppressed it.

He couldn't go back, he could only move forward. A Virtuous Virgin *had* to be the answer. No matter how much desire and inclination tried to lead him down a different path.

Chapter Fourteen

Early that evening, Ellie walked from her solitary dinner to the wing chair in her sitting room, setting a glass of wine on the table beside her.

How strange that only a few months ago, after Summerville's death, she'd rejoiced at having this place all to herself, freed from anyone with the power to tell her what to do and when. Now, it seemed to echo with aloneness.

Perhaps it was seeing Sophie again, the joy of catching up on and hearing of a life wrapped in the warmth of a family's love, that made her feel the silence so keenly.

She'd better get used to it. She and Sophie would continue to meet at Lady Sayleford's, and she might even receive an invitation to dine at her aunt's house, but associating too often with her sister wouldn't be good for Sophie's chances of contracting an advantageous marriage. Once

Sophie did marry, her husband might well want her to break all connection with her disgraced sister. The rest of her family had already made it clear they didn't wish for any closer contact.

So there would be no warm family life in her future. No playing pianoforte in the soft glow of a fire, as she used to for Sophie. As she had for Christopher.

Ah, Christopher. If she were truly honest, yearning for him was more responsible than anything else for her present melancholy.

Perhaps playing for him had been a mistake.

She was supposed to be cutting him out of her heart and her life, not drifting into nostalgically thinking of *him* as family.

Even worse for her ability to keep her resolve was the fact that, the more time she spent with him, the stronger grew the desire he seemed to inspire just by breathing. When he'd kissed the back of her neck as she played, sending ripples of shock and pleasure throughout her body, she'd felt an unprecedented need to have him caress her, from her bared shoulders down over her bodice.

But that had been just the beginning. Later, when they'd teased each other with veiled references to Ovid? Oh, my! She'd been mildly amazed when she'd read the poet that long-ago winter. But to imagine Christopher doing those things to her, doing them with her, aroused not the incredulity or distaste she'd previously felt, but a...feverish excitement.

She was beginning to believe the other courtesans hadn't been exaggerating when they boasted of the delights of pleasuring. She quivered within with a strange, heated urgency at the thought of intimacy with Christopher—and she *craved* it.

She shook her head in aggravation. Rather than making progress in surmounting her desires, it seemed she stood in ever greater danger of succumbing to them.

Fortunately, she'd had the happy idea of conducting the next lesson at Felicia's, in the company of the most naughty, seductive matrons her friend knew. Though the ostensible reason for the lesson was to teach Christopher to ignore the allure of other women, he was only a man; he couldn't help being attracted by beauty. It would be useful for *her* to see him tempted by other women, see other women try to beguile him.

As his wife would. As his wife must. His caresses and his devotion were meant for that lady, whoever she might be. Never for her.

How much more could she teach him? He seemed to have absorbed the basic concepts of proper conversation, deferential treatment and the absolute necessity of maintaining a physical distance. Once he created an initial, favourable impression on cautious matrons of the *ton*, some charming, well-read, enthusiastic girl who hadn't had her life blighted and her innocence ripped from her would beguile him, marry him, and delight him for the rest of his days.

Perhaps she would play Beethoven piano sonatas for him without error.

With a huff of frustration, Ellie walked to the desk and retrieved her list of Christopher's faults. Most serious of them, the one that ought to put an end to all these futile imaginings, remained number four: *He doesn't think I'm good enough—to be his wife.*

Tonight, as she struggled to contain her desires, a rare burst of anger escaped. Seizing the pen, she underlined that sentence over and over, pressing down with such force that the nib cut through the paper.

The unusual fit of rage vanished as quickly as it had arisen, leaving dull emptiness in its wake. Ellie put the list away and drifted back to the sofa.

Were it not so late, she would pay a visit to Dean Street. Seeing Artis's bright face, the excitement in the eyes of the other girls as they did their lessons or practised their stitching, would lift her spirits. Remind her of what her life's work was meant to be.

Resolutely, she chose a book from the shelf and set her mind to reading it.

The next afternoon, Ellie presented herself at Lady Vraux's home at the appointed hour, curious to see whom her friend had summoned. As vehemently as his mama opposed Christopher's desire to wed, she knew Felicia would have chosen ladies she felt most likely to break her son's resolve.

Halting inside the sitting room door, she found the salon empty but for her hostess. 'Good afternoon, Felicia. How lovely you look! But—did I mistake the time?'

Christopher's mother came over to give her a hug. 'No, you didn't mistake it. I asked you to arrive a little early, so we might have a chance to talk before Christopher's "tempters" arrive.'

Ellie chuckled at her friend's choice of descriptive. 'Who did you invite to play that role?'

'Alice Fairchild—old Lord Malmonsey's wife. She's always had an eye for Christopher, and is quite beautiful enough to distract him. Jane Dalrymple—the *on-dit* says she's been scorching the sheets with a succession of young lovers since her husband died. And Elizabeth Falconer. She and Jane have always competed in everything, and with her husband enamoured of his latest mistress, Lizzie is trying to beguile the most appealing young men before Jane can entice them. It should be amusing to watch them at work.'

'You believe Christopher can be distracted from his resolve?' Ellie asked curiously.

'I'm nearly certain of it. At least, I hope so.'

Ellie hesitated before replying carefully, 'I know you have no affection for wedlock, but truly, taking a wife would be useful in advancing his Parliamentary career.'

'Not if it leads to a lifetime of regret.' His mother frowned. 'My son possesses a passionate nature—as do I, I'm afraid. I grant he may have grown tired of sowing wild oats and be ready to settle down with one woman. But to choose a wife in such a dispassionate manner? I cannot believe he could make a success of such a marriage. No, to quell his wandering tendencies and remain happy, Christopher must be completely, madly in love with the woman he makes his wife. No career is worth personal misery. And being imprisoned in marriage to a partner you cannot love is misery.'

Saddened for her friend, who knew that bitter truth from her own experience, Ellie clasped her hand in wordless sympathy. 'Christopher is too intelligent to rush into marriage, or choose a wife for whom he doesn't feel genuine affection.'

Lady Vraux squeezed Ellie's fingers before releasing them. 'Let us hope not. Now, what of you? I've heard glowing reports about your worthy project, but I still cannot believe the school alone will be enough to keep you content. Are you still set on living like a nun? You could have Christopher, you know, if you but crooked a finger.'

Avoiding responding to that for fear of what her face might betray, Ellie said, 'You found fulfilment in raising your children. Why shouldn't I, even though they are not my children by blood?'

'I had masculine...*attention* as well,' Lady Vraux said, giving Ellie a wicked look.

Her thoughts flew back to Christopher, kissing her neck, caressing her lips with his finger. To her chagrin, she felt her face heat.

Naturally, her perceptive friend noticed. 'Ah, not quite so dismissive of that now, are you?'

There seemed no point denying what her blush had already betrayed. 'No, not as much. Though I still think I can exist quite comfortably without it. I...might consider a relationship at some point—but not without marriage. Which rather limits my prospects, since no gentleman would marry me now,' she said, adding a smile to take some of the sting out of that fact. 'Except perhaps an earnest, reforming cleric, with an interest in helping me run the school.'

Lady Vraux made a face. 'He'd doubtless look down on you, as men always do when a woman's behaviour fails to meet *their* standards. Hypocrites! And he'd be more likely to try to take over your school than help you run it.'

Nodding agreement to the truth of that, Ellie said, 'I could always consider a man of business. Or a printer or a lawyer. Either of those would at least be educated and literate.'

'An ambitious, enterprising young lawyer of talent, ability—and seductive charm—might be just the thing!' Lady Vraux agreed. 'Like Christopher's friend Davie.'

'What's this about Davie?'

The sound of Christopher's voice jolted Ellie out of the conversation. As if pulled by an invisible magnet, her gaze swung over to meet his, and every sense stirred in anticipation.

She was dimly aware of Lady Vraux looking from her son to Ellie and back, a little smile playing about her lips. 'We were just discussing who might be right for Ellie,' his mother replied. 'Not your friend Davie, of course, but someone of similar background. I'd still rule out that reforming cleric, Ellie, but a clever solicitor or barrister, perhaps even one of Christopher's fellow MPs, might well do. If he's a reformer, he'd probably be excited at the notion of helping poor girls to a better life. What do you think, Christopher? Should it be a politician for Ellie?'

'A politician to do what?' Christopher asked. 'Join Lady Sayleford as one of the school's directors?'

'No, silly,' Lady Vraux replied, waving an impatient hand. 'A politician to *marry* her. Since she refuses to entertain the idea of taking another protector. Such a waste of beauty it would be, were Ellie to remain celibate the rest of her life! A man like your friend Davie wouldn't care a jot about Society's disapproval. Enterprising, intelligent, fair enough to consider Ellie for her own merits, a man like that might be just right for her.'

A look of almost…consternation on his face, Christopher made no immediate reply. As for Ellie, the idea of finding companionship and affection with someone other than Christopher, some day in the misty future, was one thing. She felt no more enthusiastic than Christopher looked at the prospect of embracing such a relationship any time soon.

Though she should consider it, she realised. If she truly didn't wish to live alone the rest of her life, she should consider it carefully.

And she would, she promised herself. Later. *When she no longer had the delight of Christopher's company.*

Before she could steer Lady Vraux's thoughts in another direction, Christopher said, 'With your friends about to arrive, shall we delay that conversation for another time? Who have you invited to this gathering, Mama? If I know who I'll be facing, I can better arm myself to resist.' He looked over at Ellie. 'And win my teacher's approval.'

After Lady Vraux revealed the names, Christopher laughed. 'I'm surprised you got Alice Fairchild here. Didn't you ruffle her feathers recently by stealing one of her admirers? Henderson, wasn't it?'

His mother shrugged. 'I admit, she can be tiresome, always thinking I'm vying with her for masculine attention. I'm not her rival, nor have I ever been.'

When Christopher lifted a sceptical eyebrow, she continued, 'To be a rival, one must *wish* to compete, and I don't. I am simply—myself. If that interests a gentleman, he seeks me out, and if the attraction is mutual, a relationship may develop. But I never *invite* adulation.'

She didn't need to, Ellie thought. Her beauty, wit and allure drew men to her. As Christopher's charm, good looks and intelligence would draw the attention of these rival matrons. And soon, the attention of an eligible bride—who would claim him and carry him away for good.

'So how did you inveigle Alice to come?' Christopher asked, pulling her from those reflections.

'Told her you would be present,' Lady Vraux said with an arch look. 'She's always had a *tendre* for you, even before she married Malmonsey—as surely you know.'

'Since—up until now—I've carefully avoided unmarried maidens, I did not know. Although she has been rather flirtatious on the few occasions I've encountered her since her marriage,' he admitted.

'I told her you'd just ended your most recent liaison, and were feeling restless, so I invited several of the most charming ladies of the *ton* to entertain you.'

Christopher groaned. 'So I'm to play a man on the prowl? That's the role I'm trying to abandon!'

'No, hear me out. You're to focus your attention on Ellie. Believing you are trying to win her as your next *chère amie*, they will each try to entice you to favour them instead.'

'Ah, giving me practice in resisting their charms. Try what they may, being able to focus on Ellie will make resisting them easy,' he said, turning to give Ellie the full force of his most intimate smile.

Her mouth dried, sensation spiralled in her stomach, and she stopped breathing for so long, she felt dizzy. If he had held open his arms, she would have walked right in.

She felt her face heat as she forced herself to look away. She was supposed to be accustoming herself to watching him entice other women— not falling victim to his charm herself. She could only hope Felicia's seductive matrons were experts at their art, and Christopher as susceptible as his mother believed.

A knock at the door brought the butler, who ushered in the ladies. Although all three had attended some of the more rakish entertainments at which she'd been present, she wasn't on intimate terms with any of them.

Ellie had to admit they were all dazzling.

First to walk in was Lady Malmonsey. Tall, with masses of black hair intricately arranged beneath an enormous bonnet, she wore a fashionable gown whose wide, lace-trimmed shoulders were cut low enough to display a tempting expanse of pale skin, while the belt at the skirt emphasised her narrow waist. Although she made her curtsy to Lady Vraux, her large green eyes immediately sought and lingered on Christopher.

Behind her came Elizabeth Falconer, an exquisite blonde with a sultry mouth and huge deep blue eyes, her assets also displayed in a gown cut lower at the bodice than was usual for day wear. Bringing up the rear was Jane Dalrymple, a redhead whose flame-coloured tresses were rumoured to reflect her fiery character in the bedchamber.

If Christopher could resist this trio, his eventual wife would believe him a saint.

He turned from Ellie to bow to them, as the ladies exchanged curtsies.

'Welcome,' Lady Vraux said. 'I'm so pleased you could all join me. Billings, will you bring tea? I believe you all know my son, Christopher, and my friend, Ellie Parmenter.'

As the guests added their chorus of greetings, Ellie watched Alice Fairchild measure with a narrowed gaze exactly how close she stood to Christopher. 'Nice to see you, Miss Parmenter—or shall we call you "Summerville's Sweetheart"?'

Since the question was patently rhetorical, while Ellie gritted her teeth at that reminder of a time she tried hard to forget, the Countess walked over to link her arm with Christopher's. 'So good to see you, too, Christopher. And available, I understand?' she added in a murmur.

'Always available to compliment a beautiful lady,' he replied, artfully removing her arm from his by taking her hand to kiss. 'So to be in the presence of so many is...dazzling.' He stepped away from the Countess to gesture around the room.

Mrs Dalrymple sidled up next, making sure she positioned herself to give Christopher a good view of her décolletage. 'So nice to see you again, Mr Lattimar. Though I'm sure you are doing great work in Parliament, it's very selfish of you to spend all your time there, leaving us poor females bereft of your company. One hardly ever sees you at a rout or a ball. Promise me that will change.'

'With such charming partners to dance with, I shall certainly have to give that idea some consideration.'

Mrs Falconer approached him, too. 'Come, Mr Lattimar, won't you take a seat beside me on the sofa? We can become better acquainted, and I can pour for you when the tea arrives.' She held out her arm.

Though he took it, once he'd steered her to the sofa, he detached himself. 'Since it's clearly impossible to choose a partner from among so many beauties, I must return to my first love,' he said, and seated himself beside his mother.

Ellie followed them and, exchanging a rueful look with Lady Vraux, chose an armchair beside the hearth, a safe distance from the struggle.

For struggle it was, each lady vying with the other to engage Christopher in conversation, and after the tea arrived, to pour him a cup or offer him refreshments. Mistresses of seduction they all were, too, for as they went about these commonplace tasks, an entirely different conversation was going on, spoken in gliding touches of his hand when offering a tea cup, a finger drawn slowly across parted lips to remove an errant crumb, and provocative glances from sultry eyes. If she had any desire to become a more proficient courtesan, Ellie thought, she need only study the moves of these 'respectable' matrons.

But while he bantered with them, accepted tea and biscuits, Ellie noted he withdrew his hand from those caressing fingers and looked away from both parted lips and heated glances. Sometimes to speak to his mother, but often, to give her a smile or a wink.

The show went on a little longer, the matrons seeming determined not to desist until they'd received a more encouraging response. But to their ever more blatant movements and suggestions Christopher remained remarkably impervious, even when the outrageous Countess, who managed to manoeuvre herself so that his hand, after returning his tea cup to its saucer, grazed her bared shoulder, returned to his polite apology a look of such naked invitation, a libertine might have blushed.

Eventually, the tea was finished and even Mrs Dalrymple could find no excuse to linger. Looking somewhat aggrieved, the trio thanked their hostess and departed, the Countess lingering on the threshold to glare at Lady Vraux. 'For a man who's supposed to be available, he looks rather *taken*,' she announced, with a darkling look in Ellie's direction before flouncing off.

'Oh, dear, has our lesson ended up making you enemies?' Ellie asked, feeling a bit guilty after the angry Countess departed.

'Not any more so than they were already.' Lady Vraux gave her tinkling laugh. 'In their ceaseless battle to subjugate every desirable man they meet, they've always viewed every other woman as the enemy.' Turning to Christopher, she added, 'I would rather worry that they may cast slurs on your manhood, after you remained remarkably unresponsive to every one of their lures.'

'Ellie would say that would be an excellent

outcome. If they spread the word that I'm incapable of being seduced, I may improve my chances of winning a wife.'

'Better that message be spread after you're wed, not before. I doubt even your Virtuous Virgin wishes to marry a husband who can't... satisfy.'

'Mama, you'll make me blush,' Christopher protested, reddening in truth.

'I agree, it was well done,' Ellie said. 'The ladies offered you every encouragement, but you managed to resist all of it.'

'Easy enough, when one has eyes only for one woman,' he murmured, his caressing gaze capturing hers.

The words sent a jolt of anticipation and delight through her before she realised it was essential she redirect their meaning. 'Which you will have, once you've met your wife.'

The sparkle in his eyes died. 'Yes,' he agreed with a sigh. 'For my wife.'

'Amusing as it was to hostess this little tête-à-tête, I must rest if I am to be ready for the Carrington ball tonight,' Lady Vraux said, rising. 'So good to see you both again.'

'Thank you for putting up with my little scheme,' Ellie said. 'I hope Christopher found it useful.'

'Useful indeed,' he agreed with a look she couldn't interpret.

With a kiss to his mother, Christopher walked Ellie out. 'So, I passed your test?'

'Brilliantly!'

'Can I see you home?'

Visions of tempting proximity in a closed carriage flashed into her head, generating a wave of arousal. If she rode to Hans Place with him, she didn't think she could resist kissing him—and more.

'Better not,' she said, hardly able to get the refusal past her lips as she battled the urging of her needy senses.

He didn't look surprised. 'You're probably right,' he agreed, looking as regretful as she felt. 'What have you planned for me next?'

Suppressing a strong if illogical disappointment that he'd given in so readily, she made herself look forward, as he had done. 'After today, I think you are ready for the ultimate test. I'm to ride with Sophie and several of her friends in Hyde Park tomorrow. Why don't you join us?'

His eyes widened with dismay. 'You wouldn't leave me alone with them, would you?'

She had to suppress a chuckle at his panicked tone. 'It's not as if you'd be facing Genghis

Khan's ravaging hordes! Just several innocent misses. But, no, I wouldn't abandon you to them.'

'I'd prefer Genghis Khan's ravaging hordes,' he muttered. 'At least I'd know how to handle them. But if you promise not to desert me, I'll chance it. Besides, if you ride anywhere near as well as you play the pianoforte, I would love to see it.'

'As for that, I'm equally out of practice,' she admitted. 'I promise to try not to fall out of the saddle.'

'Another slice of your old life you preferred not to bring forward?'

She glanced up quickly, though by now, she shouldn't be surprised by his perception. 'Yes. But more than that. Even though I knew if I rode early, I probably wouldn't encounter anyone from the *ton*, I still didn't want to risk being seen…in my new role. Especially at first, I almost never went out of doors. By the time I'd… accepted my changed status, I'd adjusted to no longer riding.'

Something like anger rippled briefly across his face. 'You should begin again.'

'Perhaps I will. I always loved riding. Though I'm not sure a sedate trot through the park will be the same as galloping *ventre-à-terre* across the meadows at Wanstead Manor.'

'Make it early enough, and you can gallop in Hyde Park. I'll show you.'

How she would like to ride with him! Share with someone who cared about her another lost delight of the past. A safe one to share, too, since they'd be separated from each other on their respective mounts, with no possibility of succumbing to the temptations offered by a closed carriage.

Since she had to resist all the other things she'd like to do with him, why not allow herself this one?

'I'd like that,' she said, capitulating. 'I'll set the time early, and send you a note.'

A smile of genuine delight lit his face. How easily she could lose herself, gazing into those turquoise eyes! As she stared raptly, the twinkle changed to something deeper, desire writ there as clearly as she felt it spiral through her.

With a start, she realised she was leaning towards him, lifting her lips to his, and pulled back abruptly even as he took a step away.

Merciful Heavens, if she was so beguiled she was almost kissing him in his mother's front hall, she'd better only meet him on horseback.

'I'll get you a hackney,' he said, giving her a sketch of a bow. 'Until tomorrow, then.'

Putting her hand to her chest to calm her stampeding heartbeat, Ellie watched as he walked down the steps and set off towards the hackney stand. Resisting the urge to call him back.

He'd done a better job at his task this afternoon than she had at hers, she thought ruefully. She'd been proud at how cleverly he navigated the treacherous path of three beauties. And he had played well the part his mother had assigned, frequently glancing over and smiling at her, subtly telegraphing that his interest was fixed elsewhere. Felicia's three temptresses had doubtless left feeling sure he intended to claim her as his next mistress.

If only that were possible.

Easy enough to resist others, when one only has eyes for one woman.

You could have Christopher, if you but lifted a finger.

Her fingers curled in her gloves as she resisted the urge to make their play-acting this afternoon real. But the emotions and desires heightened by that little scene didn't alter the unchangeable facts of their respective positions.

Desolation slicing towards pain stabbed at her heart, bringing tears in its wake.

With a fortifying anger, she brushed them away and walked down the steps to the arriving hackney. Yes, she would meet him tomorrow, introduce him to the girls, and observe his behaviour. The excursion might well provide the proof she needed that he was ready to launch himself into Society.

If her infatuation could not be squelched, better to get him out of her life as soon as possible.

Chapter Fifteen

The next day, in the early morning chill, Ellie rode her borrowed mount through the gates of Hyde Park. She'd felt unsteady at first, but the transit through the streets to the park at a sedate trot had given her time to adjust to the new mount and to being in the saddle again. She felt sure now she would not disgrace herself by taking a tumble in front of Christopher and the girls.

Testing that resolve, she directed the mare down the first pathway and signalled her to a canter. And then she saw Christopher.

She pulled up, feeling again that involuntary jolt to her senses and leap of joy in her heart, sharper, stronger than ever. And for once, for this morning, she would not try to suppress it. This might well be their last lesson, and she meant to enjoy every moment with him. Freeing herself of constraint, she let a radiant smile emerge as he trotted up.

He gave her a smile just as joyous before he bowed to her from horseback. 'You look magnificent astride, just as I'd imagined.'

'Thank you, kind sir,' she replied, her foolish heart exulting at his admiration. 'Though the thanks should go to your mama. When I asked to borrow a habit, she insisted on lending me her mare as well. What a sweet goer she is, so much finer than any hack I could have rented.'

'Ah, yes, I thought I recognised the horse. Mama's taste in habits and mounts has always been excellent. Shall we have that gallop, before the Mongolian Hordes arrive?'

A trot was one thing, but a gallop? Not sure she was yet up to that, Ellie said, 'I'm feeling more secure than when I started, but I'm not sure I dare yet attempt a gallop.'

He turned the full force of his eyes on her, holding her immobile. 'Sometimes one simply must dare.'

Oh, how she wished she could!

His gelding stirred, and he had to look away to control him. 'We'll start with a trot, and increase the paces gradually. You'll be fine, you'll see.'

If she could not dare what she truly wanted,

she could at least do this. 'Very well, I'll give it a try. But you must promise not to laugh if I fall!'

'I promise to pick you up again, and no laughing,' he said, tracing a cross pattern over his heart.

It would almost be worth falling, to have a perfectly acceptable excuse to be in his arms, Ellie thought as she signalled her mount to begin.

But as they directed their mounts through their paces on a long circuit of the park, Ellie found herself signalling the mare to a gallop as her love of speed re-emerged.

The startled look on Christopher's face as her horse surged past his spurred her competitive spirit. A joyous laugh emerging, she leaned low over her mount, urging her ever faster. Her heartbeat accelerating to match the pounding hoofbeats, she exulted in the wind buffeting her face, snatching at her hat, trying to tear her hair from its pins as the little mare flew along the pathway.

They were still neck and neck as they neared the park gates. Laughing from sheer exhilaration, Ellie pulled up her mount. 'Oh, thank you!' she cried. 'That was marvellous! I'd forgotten how marvellous it could be.'

'You were fabulous,' he replied, the fire in his eyes and the urgency of his expression proving he'd been as stirred by the gallop as she was. His excitement calling to her, she had the strongest urge to run to him, throw herself into his arms and kiss him in gratitude for returning this part of her life to her.

Fortunately, she had enough sense to remain mounted. Before she could settle her disordered senses, a group of riders entering through the park gates caught her eye.

As Christopher made to dismount, she waved a hand to stay him. 'Don't get down. I believe I see the girls.'

He made such a sour face, she had to laugh. 'After that wonderful gallop, I'm not pleased to be joined by the infantry.'

'You'll find them delightful,' she said, a sinking feeling draining away her exuberance even as she hoped it would prove true. 'You must be on your best behaviour, though. Promise?'

He gave an exaggerated sigh. 'Very well, I promise.'

Sophie and two other young ladies rode up, followed by their grooms. 'Tess,' her sister cried. 'What a fetching habit! And I love the mare! What a delight to be able to ride together again. But I'm forgetting my manners. Miss Parmenter, may I introduce two of my friends, Lady Audrey Thornby and Miss Higgins. Girls, may I present my sister, Miss Parmenter, and her friend and eminent reform Member of Parliament, Mr Lattimar.'

After nods and bows, Sophie said, 'I saw you galloping as we rode in. What fun! Once your horses are rested, shall we all have a gallop?'

Dismay registered on the women's faces. Fearing those two ladies might not be skilled enough to handle a gallop, but be unwilling to admit it, Ellie was searching for a way to refuse when Christopher said, 'I'm afraid the park will soon be too crowded for that to be wise, Miss Wanstead. We don't want to run down any nurse-maids or their charges. Another time, perhaps.'

'You are an associate of Lord Lyndlington, are you not, Mr Lattimar?' Lady Audrey asked, riding up closer to Christopher.

'I have that honour, Lady Audrey. Are you acquainted with the Viscount?'

'My brother knows him from his club. And my father is acquainted with Lady Lyndlington's father, Lord Witlow.'

'Your father must attend the Lords while you are in town. There are important votes coming up.'

'Yes, I understand that the Reform Bill passed the Commons and has been sent on to the Lords. I'm ashamed to confess I know almost nothing about it. Won't you tell us more?'

If the girl were trying to pique Christopher's interest, it was good strategy. Well born, attractive, and probably well dowered, if she were genuinely interested in politics, Lady Audrey might make a good match for him, Ellie thought—the sinking feeling intensifying.

Somewhat to her relief, Christopher replied, 'That's a weighty matter for so bright a morning. Would you object if we postpone the discussion for a later date? Surrounded by such loveliness, all I can think about is how pleasant it will be to ride with all of you. Being in Parliament, I spend most of the year in London. Are you ladies newcomers? I should appreciate hearing your impressions of our capital city.'

A gentle set-down to the questioner, she thought approvingly, and an even better ploy to involve all the young ladies in the conversation—which might have excluded the rest, had the topic remained politics.

As the party set off at a walk, encouraged by Christopher's leading questions, the girls in turn discussed their first London experiences. He laughed at Lady Audrey's confession that for the first week, she'd had difficulty sleeping for the noise, seconded Miss Higgins's enthusiasm for the theatre, and recommended to Sophie some lending libraries she might visit to supplement the selections available at Hatchard's.

Watching him alternate between the girls and come up with just the right questions to tease out the speaker's interests and lead her to talk about them, Ellie could understand why he was such an effective member of the reform team. In a situation that required compromise, it must be advantageous to have a colleague who prompted the opposition to speak and listened carefully to their opinions.

He was proving himself skilful enough this morning that she wasn't required to intervene at all, even Sophie focusing on Christopher as he artfully directed the conversation.

Despite his supposed trepidation, he looked totally at ease— and she didn't think it was because he knew she was there to provide an assistance that was proving so unnecessary. The attention the girls had accorded him at first for his good looks was changing, she could tell, to admiration for his engaging manner and clever conversation.

With a deep ache in her heart, she watched him kick his horse to a trot, the girls following eagerly as he bantered with them, conveying just the right mix of teasing familiarity and courteous deference. Any suspicious mama watching him would see, not a rogue who might endanger her daughter, but a thoughtful, articulate and courteous gentleman who would make a perfectly proper suitor.

She steeled herself to face the fact that he had no need of further lessons.

Fighting off a wave of desolation, she reminded herself that she'd suspected today's outing would prove exactly that. That terminating their arrangement at once would be better. She had kept her pledge to him without losing her self-respect, and was certain he could enter the polite world, ready to defuse any suspicions about his character. Ready to charm cautious matrons and Virtuous Virgins alike, and find the lady destined to be his bride.

Though she was gratified that their experiment had been a success for him, for her it had been a disaster. Rather than discover faults that would allow her to master her feelings for him, being with him so often had deepened her affection, making her long for his continued presence. As for passion…what had been only a suspicion of the sweetness and power it could wield had grown, over the course of their interludes, into a compulsion for intimacy that forced her to resort to meeting him on horseback to resist its mesmerising spell.

It was time for her to shut him out of her life, before her heart shredded any further or her control over those desires collapsed.

Arming her heart and mind to the necessity of ending it, she rode up to meet the group, which had pulled up before the Park gates.

'A true delight to meet all of you ladies, but the morning is advancing, and I must turn you back into the care of your grooms,' Christopher was saying.

'What a lovely ride, Mr Lattimar! I'm so glad you were able to accompany us,' Miss Higgins cried. 'I hope to see you again soon.'

'The date hasn't been set yet for the ball my sponsor will be holding for me, but I will see that you are sent a card,' Lady Audrey said. 'You mustn't try to steal a march on us, Miss Wanstead,' she continued, looking at over at Sophie, 'just because he is a friend of your sister's.'

Even Sophie gave Christopher a flirtatious look before replying, 'In love and war, every girl must look out for herself. Do you not agree, Mr Lattimar?'

'So the saying goes,' he said with a smile. 'I hope I'll have the pleasure of seeing all of you again.'

'Tess, I'll be meeting you at Lady Saylebrook's later, yes?' At her nod, Sophie turned back to her companions. In a chatter of girlish voices, trailed by their grooms, they rode out of the park. As Christopher stared after them thoughtfully, the even more depressing thought struck her that Sophie might be perfect for him.

That possibility should strangle her yearning at once. She didn't even want to imagine meeting him in future—as Sophie's husband.

As she tried to rid her mind of that awful image, Christopher rode over to her.

'I think that went off rather well,' he said, looking relieved. 'You were right—they weren't *too* terrifying. Though I'd still prefer Genghis Khan's hordes.'

'You handled them beautifully, showing respect, a little deference, and a great deal of skill in drawing out thoughts and opinions. You certainly impressed them. It's not often that a gentleman makes more than a cursory effort to ask a young lady's opinion, or listens to it so attentively. Most men spend their time favouring a girl with their own.'

'Sound like dead bores,' Christopher said.

Despite the ache in her heart, she chuckled, as she knew he meant her to. 'In any event, I think this excursion proves you've mastered all the lessons you need.'

The smile on his face abruptly faded. 'Surely

you don't mean to end them! There must be some finer points of etiquette I still need to work on.'

The distress on his face so closely echoed the ache in her heart, she couldn't make herself utter the words that would terminate their association. Silently chiding herself for her weakness, she temporised, 'At the moment, I can't think of any. But I will reflect further on the matter.'

That reassurance restored his smile. 'Even if I know most of the rules, I could use more practice, to build my confidence. As it was, I rode the circuit in a state of wary caution, like an impostor worried at any moment he might be found out.'

'You're not an impostor! You truly are the courteous, intelligent, engaging gentleman they all saw here today. And you are ready to meet them on their own turf, at the balls and drawing rooms of the *ton*.'

Where he could not help but be a success. *You ought to send him away now and begin moving on*, she urged herself silently.

While she agonised, he said, 'Can I escort you back home?'

Temptation beckoned. They were on horse-back, which would forestall any contact. But after the horses were led away…

She might not have the strength to break

with him completely, but she could summon up enough resolve to be prudent. 'Thank you, but that's not necessary. After I return the habit and the horse, I must visit the school. I owe the girls a story today.'

He grimaced, but thankfully didn't press her. 'As much as you enjoy riding, you should borrow both more often. I'm sure Mama wouldn't mind.'

'I wouldn't want to impose. Best not to become accustomed to riding again, since keeping a horse of my own would be much too expensive.'

For an awkward moment, they sat regarding each other, neither of them ready to bid goodbye, but having nothing further to say that could delay their parting. For a few more moments, Ellie let her gaze rove over his handsome face, admiring the fine figure he made astride, losing herself in those mesmerising turquoise eyes.

He seemed equally content just to gaze at her.

Finally, pulling herself free of his spell with an effort, she said, 'Thank you for accompanying me today. I think it provided useful experience.'

He nodded. 'It did. Thank you for including me. I feel somewhat easier about the project ahead now.'

That's what *she* should do—concentrate on

the project ahead. His being marriage to that Virtuous Virgin, while hers led to the school. 'I'm glad. Good day to you, then.'

Before she could ride off, he waved a hand. 'Wait a moment! When will I see you again?'

Instead of the 'never' she still could not voice, she found herself saying, 'I'm not sure. I'll send you a note.'

Exasperated that she had passed up two perfect opportunities to declare their association over, she kicked the mare to a trot and rode out of the park, conscious of his following gaze.

Resisting the strong urge to look back, she did instead what she must—ride away from him.

Chapter Sixteen

Several hours later, habit and horse returned and dressed back in her own gown, Elle returned to Dean Street. But her musing over which of the tales from the *Arabian Nights* she would read to the girls halted the moment she entered the workroom.

Instead of students seated at the tables working on stitchery or studying lessons, she found two of the girls wrapped in each other's arms, weeping, Mrs Sanders trying to soothe them, while Lucy argued with a white-faced Artis.

Sweeping past an anxious Jenson, she cried, 'What's wrong? What's happened?'

'It's Artis, miss,' Lucy said, turning towards her. 'She says she's going to leave us. You must convince her to stay!'

Surprised that Artis, who'd seemed so excited and grateful for her new opportunities, suddenly wanted to go away, she said, 'We can't make her stay against her will, Lucy. But—won't you come to the office and tell me what is troubling you, Artis?'

Refusing to meet her eyes, Artis nodded. 'Aye, I owe you that. Won't make no difference though, Lucy. I'm still agoin'.'

The dejected slump of the girl's shoulders and her obvious sorrow mystified Ellic further. Alarm building, she realised the intelligent, enterprising girl had already carved a place in her affections. She'd be as distressed as Artis appeared if the girl truly wanted to leave them.

With the imminent departure of Christopher, she didn't feel up to dealing with yet another loss.

Closing the office door, she gestured Artis to a seat. 'What is wrong, Artis? Have someone done something to distress you?'

'It's Gentleman Bob, miss,' the girl said, pleating her skirt with nervous fingers. 'He knows where I am, and he'll be coming to fetch me, I know it.'

'But he doesn't control this area, which is why you came to this part of the city to begin with. What makes you think he knows where you are?'

'That day I took you and the toff to the Tottenham market, I seen one of his boys. There weren't no reason for Keppy to be hangin' about there, exceptin' the Gentleman sent him, even if this isn't his usual lay. You remember how I led you away all sudden-like, in and out of them side lanes? I thought I lost Keppy, and I knew he hadn't followed us back. I been more careful than ever, any time I went out to run errands for Mrs S., but comin' back yesterday, I seen Keppy again—not two streets from this house. The Gentleman musta had Keppy drop a coin here and there among the merchants, so's he could figure out where I was staying. Gentleman always used to boast to us that he never let loose of what was his, not while it lived. So I gotta move on, miss, some place outside London, prob'ly.'

'You don't need to run off! Jensen is here to protect us. I don't believe even Gentleman Bob would be bold enough to kidnap someone from within a locked house! You must simply remain safely inside until this Keppy gives up.'

'Mr Jensen's got a fiercesome uppercut, but it's more than that,' Artis said with a sigh before continuing, 'I'm a sight better looking now than when you took me in, but compared to me, Sally is an angel, and Lucy's a real beauty. If Keppy hangs about long enough, lookin' to capture me, he'll find out there are other pretty girls here, all of 'em havin' no more than one man and Mrs

Sanders to protect 'em. Considerin' how much the Gentleman could earn off 'em in one of his schools, he'd want the lot, and he'd send more than just one boy to get 'em. I can't put all of 'em in danger, miss! I gotta lead Keppy away afore he discovers the other girls.'

Ellic paused, considering. Initially she'd been inclined to discount Artis's alarm—they were well away from the rookeries here, and Jensen was quite capable of handling one adolescent thief. But she knew enough of the flesh markets to realise Artis was right, both in her estimate of the other girls' value and their vulnerability. They'd be a prize worth the risk of capturing for someone like Gentleman Bob, for if he managed to make off with them, he'd not have to worry about irate families trying to retrieve them or powerful fathers sending the law after him.

She certainly didn't want Gentleman Bob learning anything more about her school. But neither was she prepared to send Artis off on her own, the sacrificial lamb giving herself up for the welfare of the group.

'You are right, you must leave, and visibly enough to draw Keppy away. But I won't have you going off alone to some other town, to be discovered by Keppy or fall into the hands of another Gentleman Bob—or even just to go back to thieving. We'll find another way to keep you safe and still protect the other girls. Gather your things while I talk with Jenson. And don't despair! I don't let loose of what's mine, either!'

Looking a little reassured, Artis went off to the dormitory and Ellie walked back to the workroom to beckon to Jensen—who'd been standing guard by the window, a frown on his face. With a nod, he followed her back.

'What can we do, miss? I'd protect all these lasses to the death, but there's only one of me. Gentleman Bob's a pretty powerful name in Seven Dials. There's lots of ruffians he could finger to help him snatch 'em.'

'I'm sure there are, and Artis is correct, we must move her and lure Keppy away before the Gentleman enlarges his plan beyond capturing just one girl. Even once we do, though, I'd like to have some extra protection for the girls, until we are sure the danger is past. Do you have some friends you could recruit?'

The big man nodded. 'Have a couple mates who owe me favours. Once I've explained the situation, I'm betting there are several who would come help me watch day and night for a spell.'

'Good. Assure them I will pay them.'

The big man grinned. 'They'll come for certain, then!'

'Can you find some this very afternoon?

Jensen nodded. 'Shouldn't take me long to turn up a couple. I'll have them tell their mates I could use a few more, that the toff I works for has friends what needs extra watchmen for a spell.'

'Excellent. Go at once! I'll keep the doors and windows locked until you return.'

'What of Artis, miss? You're not jest sending her away, are you?'

'We'll do for Artis what we did for your sweetheart. Find her a place where no Gentleman Bob dares venture.'

Satisfied, the watchman nodded. 'I'll be off, then.'

Ellie followed him out, locking the door behind him. Looking over to Mrs Sanders and the frightened girls, she said, 'No need to worry. We shall be safe enough here until Jensen returns with some friends. But it would be a good precaution to bolt the kitchen door and coal chute, Mrs Sanders. Girls, would you help me close and latch the shutters?'

They were busy about that task when Artis returned to the workroom, her few belongings tied up in a bundle. Walking over to Ellie, she held out the book Christopher had bought for her.

'Best give you this, miss. Won't be nowheres safe to keep it where I be going. And, if you please, I'd like to ask Mrs S. for my old duds back. I'll travel safer if'n I'm dressed as a lad.'

Accepting the book, Ellie motioned for the girl to follow her back to the office. As soon as Ellie closed the door, Artis said, 'Shall I get into those duds here, miss? The sooner I'm gone, the better. I do thank you for everything you done, and I'm so s-sorry...' Her voice breaking, the girl went silent, her brave front at odds with the despair in her eyes.

Setting her book on the desk, Ellie walked over and pulled her into her arms, holding her close while Artis shook with silent sobs. She recovered herself in a moment, pulling away. 'Sorry, miss.'

'No apologies necessary.' Ellie picked the book back up and returned it with ceremony. 'You will definitely have a place to keep this where you are going.'

'No, miss, you don't understand—'

'Really, Artis, you can't believe I would truly send you away to deal with this alone? As soon as Jensen returns, I'll take you to a place where you'll be better protected.'

Artis shook her head sadly. 'You try to help me, he'll figure a way to hurt you, too, and I couldn't stand that. Ain't no place in Lunnon beyond the Gentleman's reach.'

'Not even the house of a marquess?'

Artis's eyes widened. 'Cor, miss, is your nob a marquess? And him not at all high in the instep! I shoudda been m'lording him!'

'No, not Mr Lattimar. But one of the sponsors of this school is a marquess, and he would take it very ill that some rookery rogue was threatening my students.'

'A marquess,' Artis marvelled. 'That's almost like a king, ain't it? But…would such a person concern himself with the likes of me?'

'He'd want to make sure you are safe. We'll go first to see his daughter, Lady Lyndlington—whose husband is a viscount. She'll know the best place for you to stay. I doubt even a devil like the Gentleman would dare test the power of a marquess.'

'I spec' not,' Artis said.

'As soon as Jensen returns, I'll have him summon us a hackney, and we'll go straight to Lady Lyndlington's. Although I hope Keppy will follow us, I doubt one boy would be bold enough to try to intercept us in broad daylight in front of a viscount's town house.'

'Will I...never see you no more, after this?' Artis asked, a catch in her voice.

'Of course you'll see me! I consider you one of my most promising students! We'll settle the details later, but you will either return to the school, if we deem it safe, or continue your education in whatever household Lady Lyndlington places you.'

Artis jumped up to give Ellie a hug. 'Thank you, miss! Ain't nobody cared nothing for me since Ma died! If there's anything I kin do for you...'

Ellie hugged her back. 'Promise to study hard, so you may some day attain a position that will make me proud. I know you can do it.'

Ellie smiled at Artis, heartened to see her spirit rekindled, and gratified that she could be the reason for it. *Caring for girls like these is a worthy life's work that will atone for any loss*, she told herself firmly...until the image of Christopher's handsome face focused in her mind.

While she tried to convince herself the school would compensate her for even that, there was a rap at the door. ''Tis me, Jensen,' a voice called.

Ellie hurried to the front door, unlatching it to admit Jensen and two companions as broad and heavily muscled as he was.

'Come in, gentlemen! And welcome.'

'This be Smith and Thomas, miss,' Jensen said. 'Both handy with their fives, and up to any rig.'

'I'll trust you to keep everyone safe, then. Jensen, will you call us a hackney? Artis will be going with me.'

Nodding, her henchman walked back out, one of his compatriots latching the door behind him, while Ellie gathered up her things. A few minutes later, Jensen returned, scratching at the door to inform them the hackney stood outside.

'I checked it out, and the driver too,' he said as she stepped out the front door, Artis close by her side.

'Thank you, Jensen. Take good care of my girls.'

'Guard 'em like me own daughters,' Jensen assured her as he helped them both into the vehicle. After scanning the street, he called to the driver, 'You can spring 'em now!'

As the hackney set off at a brisk pace, Artis tapped her arm. 'What will this Lady Lyndlington do with me, miss?'

'She will decide whose household might have a place suitable for you, where you will be safe.

Don't worry; I'll make sure she takes good care of you.'

The girl nodded. 'I knows I can trust you.'

The mid-afternoon streets were crowded, the carriages of the fashionable adding to the throngs of vendors' carts, barrows and market wagons and slowing their transit. Ellie was still distracted, mulling over what might be the best placement to recommend to Lady Maggie for Artis, when the vehicle halted in front of the Lyndlington's town house.

As she descended the step, her charge having scrambled down before her, a man leapt out from behind several stopped vehicles—and grabbed Artis.

Screaming, the girl twisted in his grasp, but a boy came up to assist the man, trying to grab the arm she was flailing at her attacker. Wishing she had a parasol or anything that would serve as a weapon, Ellie shouted, 'Let her go at once!'

Several passers-by slowed to gaze at the altercation, but none halted to intervene. 'You, there!' Ellie shouted at two boys dressed in shop assistant's smocks. 'Knock at Number Four and ask for help! A guinea for the one who gets there first!'

The boys raced away, and Ellie launched herself towards Artis, who was steadily losing ground as she was pulled backwards across the street. Targeting the boy, she slammed her fist into the arm holding Artis. Yelping with pain and surprise, the boy let go.

'You stay outta this,' the man snarled, back-handing her with his free arm.

Reeling from the blow, Ellie careened backward, catching her balance at the last moment. Steadying herself, she prepared to take on the boy again, despite the pain in her head and her stinging cheek.

Before she could launch herself, shouts from behind her announced the welcome arrival of Lady Maggie's staff. 'Free those ladies at once!' the butler bellowed as he ran up, trailed by two stout footmen.

Once the assailants realised they'd be taking on, not just one woman and a girl, but several full-grown males, both man and boy released Artis and took to their heels. The footmen gave chase, but weaving in and out among vehicles, horsemen and pedestrians on the congested street, the attackers soon disappeared.

'Artis, are you all right?' Ellie asked, pulling the girl to her.

'I be fine, miss, but, oh, your cheek's bleeding! Rigger caught you a good 'un. He musta joined Keppy in watchin' the house, and what with the carriage movin' so slow they was able to follow us. I should never have let you come with me!'

'Miss Parmenter, you *are* injured!' the butler said, looking aghast at her face. 'Let me help you in! Young miss, can you walk unassisted?'

'Aye, sir,' Artis said. 'You take care of Miss Parmenter.'

Wrapping an arm around her protectively, the butler led Ellie to the town house. 'Ruffians, attacking honest citizens right here in Upper Brook Street? Lord Lyndlington will be furious! The magistrate shall hear of this.'

Dismissing the butler's suggestion that he help her to a guest bedchamber to lie down, Ellie said, 'A cold cloth for the cut on my cheek will be sufficient, thank you. I would like to speak with your mistress at once.'

'I'll fetch her straight away,' he promised, assisting her up the entry stairs and depositing her carefully on the sofa in the reception room. 'I'll have the housekeeper prepare a posset.'

'No posset, please, but I should be glad of some tea.'

'Certainly, miss.'

With the ringing in her ears making her dizzy,

Ellie was glad to sit still and wait for the room to stop spinning. Kneeling on the floor beside the sofa, Artis watched her anxiously. 'You sure you be all right, miss? Might be wise to lie your bones down fer a spell, like that gentl'mun tole you.'

Despite her discomfort, Ellie had to chuckle. 'That "gentleman" is Lady Lyndlington's butler, Artis. He is in general charge of the household and the male servants, as the housekeeper has charge of the females.'

'Cor, he be dressed as fine as a lord,' the girl observed. Gazing around her with awe at the elegant salon, she said, 'Ye think I might get to work in a fine house like this one?'

Before she could answer, Lady Maggie came rushing in. 'Good Heavens, Ellie!' she cried, her eyes widening at the sight of what Ellie could feel must be a purpling bruise at her jaw and a swelling cheek. 'When Dawkins said you'd been attacked on the street, I could scarcely believe it! Come, you must lie down and let me bring you a compress for that!'

Ellie started to shake her head—and stopped immediately, as the pain and dizziness intensified. 'Dawkins has already sent to the housekeeper for a compress, and the tea I'd especially like.'

'You must at least remain the afternoon and rest! And you, too, miss. You are one of Miss Parmenter's students? What a frightening experience for you both!'

'Lady Lyndlington, may I present Miss Artis Gorden?' Ellie said. As the girl curtsied, she continued, 'Yes, Artis is one of my students. If fact, it was on her behalf that we came today. Because that attack was not random.'

'Not random?' Lady Maggie repeated, frowning.

'No,' Ellie said grimly. 'Thank heaven we decided to bring Artis here today. That outlaw might soon have been able to threaten the entire school. But please, sit, and let me explain.'

Over tea—and extra sandwiches the housekeeper sent along with the cold compress, fully appreciated by the always starving Artis—Ellie described the girl's background, ending with the threat that had led Ellie to bring her to Maggie.

'Of course I will help you!' Maggie declared, an angry glint in her eye. 'The audacity of that villain, thinking he could attack you before my very door!'

'With all the hubbub on the street, I expect they thought they could grab Artis without anyone stopping them. Though having the hackney halt on a Mayfair street must have given them pause. I doubt they had any notion when they started following us from a modest house on Dean Street that reinforcements from a viscount's establishment would be on hand at our destination.'

'Can you help me, my lady?' Artis asked.

'I certainly can,' Maggie replied stoutly. 'We shall find you a family to live with where you will be entirely safe. What would you like to do?'

Gesturing to the room around her, Artis said, 'I'd like to take care of a place like this. Miss Parmenter been telling me if I learn good, I might be a housekeeper some day.'

'You certainly might,' Ellie said. 'You are bright, good at numbers and dealing with people, and quite wonderful at obtaining bargains!'

'You shall stay here until we can convey you to a safe position elsewhere,' Maggie said, going to ring the bell pull. 'I'll have my housekeeper get you settled.'

Artis bobbed another curtsy. 'Thank you awfully, your ladyship. And you, Miss. Don't want to think what mighta happened, if'n I hadn't met you that day in Green Park.'

Ellie didn't want to think either, with her head aching more than she cared to admit. 'I'm glad we met, too, Artis. I know you'll have a bright future.'

After the butler bore the girl off, Maggie bent a penetrating look on her. 'Don't try to persuade me you have recovered, Ellie. The afternoon's nearly gone. Why don't you stay the night?'

'No, I must get back and check on the school—especially after this attack on Artis!'

'Naturally, you'll want to make sure the other girls are secure. I certainly hope you got Artis away before this Gentleman Bob creature discovered Dean Street houses other young females! Still, the extra protection you've arranged should be enough to discourage him from trying to abduct them.'

'I hope so. And I do thank you for taking Artis in. Now, I really must—'

'Please, don't go yet!' Maggie said, staying her with a hand to her arm. 'Drink the rest of your tea, and keep the cold compress on a while longer, if I can't persuade you to lie down. We can send a footman to check on the school. Stay through dinner, at least. By the looks of that cheek, you took a nasty blow.'

In truth, she'd be relieved to rest until her head stopped throbbing. 'Very well, I'll stay. But just for dinner—and only if you promise to continue whatever you were doing before my unexpected visit. I would appreciate having someone check on the girls.'

'I'll have Dawkins dispatch a stout footman at once,' Maggie promised, going over to tug at the bell pull. 'Would you like more tea? A pillow for your back? A powder for that headache?'

'I wouldn't refuse a headache powder,' Ellie admitted. 'But you mustn't stay here and fuss over me.'

The door opened a moment later—revealing not the butler, but a frowning Giles. 'What's this I hear about an attack on Ellie Parmenter on our very doorstep?'

'Giles!' Maggie cried, her face lighting up as she rose and went into her husband's arms. 'I wasn't expecting you so early.'

'Dawkins sent a footman to the Quill and Gavel to tell me what happened. Christopher's paying our shot, and will be here momentarily.' Turning towards her, he said, 'Ellie, are you all right?'

As she began assuring Lord Lyndlington that she was just fine, the door opened again and Christopher rushed in, anxiety on his face.

'Hell and the devil!' he swore, stopping short, his expression blackening as he took in her bruised and battered face. And then he was at her side, halting beside the sofa. 'My dear Ellie, who did this to you? I'll throttle the blackguard!'

Her fortitude and composure shaken more than she'd like to admit by the attack, Ellie didn't even try to resist as he seated himself beside her and drew her into his arms. It was more than worth the throbbing pain to have an excuse to lay her head on his chest, feel the glorious warmth of his arms around her, his protective strength comforting her.

What a joy it would be to have his care and comfort for ever! Knowing that blessing would never be hers, despite the presence of a curious Giles and suspicious Maggie, she snuggled deeper into his embrace.

Chapter Seventeen

Nearly speechless with shock, distress and outrage, Christopher cradled Ellie close. He'd been alarmed when a footman from Maggie's house interrupted their meeting to inform Giles a guest had been attacked, then horrified to discover it was Ellie. One look at his face was all it had taken to convince Giles he wouldn't be left behind while his friend went to check on the incident.

He thought he'd been prepared for whatever he would find at Upper Brook Street. But seeing Ellie with her gown dishevelled, her face cut and bruised, he'd felt as if he'd taken punch to the chest. There'd been no conscious decision—he'd simply gone to her, gathered her in his arms as if by right, laying his cheek against her head as she burrowed into his embrace. Drinking in the warmth of her, letting the steady beat of her heart reassure him she would be all right.

Anger came next, that someone would have the audacity to attack her—and here in Mayfair! Whoever it was, Christopher would track the perpetrators down and see to their punishment personally.

Only Giles's blatantly speculative look forced him to finally, reluctantly release her. He steadied her as she sat back up, asking again, 'What happened? Who did this to you?'

'It's a long story,' she said grimly. 'I've already explained the whole to Maggie.'

'But we don't know,' Giles said. 'Please explain again.'

In a few terse sentences, she described to Giles taking in the girl who'd tried to rob Christopher outside the Gloucester Coffee House, their trip to the Tottenham Court Road market, the girl spotting a former thieving associate tracking her near Dean Street, and the girl's fear, which Ellie shared, that the crime boss might target not just Artis, but her other students, too, should he find out about them. Thinking a transit in a public vehicle across the city in daylight would not be dangerous, she had brought Artis here for Maggie to find her a refuge.

'We ought to do something about Gentleman Bob,' Christopher said when she'd finished. 'Running thieves and bordellos in Seven Dials is one thing, but abducting citizens on the streets of Mayfair cannot be tolerated!'

Ellie shook her head. 'Satisfying as it would be to take him down, such men are very clever. Although Artis knows quite well that he was behind the attack, there is no way we could prove that in a court of law.'

'Would you be able to identify the man who struck you?' Giles asked.

'Possibly. Artis knew him by name, as well as the boy who'd been sent to spy on her. I'm sure she could identify them both. But what good would it do to transport them? The Gentleman will just replace them. There's an endless supply of ragged boys and desperate men in Seven Dials.'

'Regrettably, I'm afraid you're right,' Giles agreed. 'While I will certainly alert the magistrate, I doubt those men will venture here again. The Gentleman Bobs of the world know better than to tweak the tail of the tiger by sending their minions into aristocratic neighbourhoods.'

'So we just…give up on any pursuit?' Christopher said, still intent on retaliating for the attack on Ellie. 'That goes against every instinct!'

'I don't think there's much we can do to punish those responsible for this, but now that we are forewarned, we can make sure no one else is harmed,' Ellie said. 'And guarantee the Gentleman can't get to Artis.'

'She should be safe enough now,' Giles said. 'Once his minions report back that she was taken into the home of a viscount, he'll know it's not worth the trouble that would rain down on his head, should he try to snatch her here.'

'I just hope Keppy hasn't yet discovered the other girls at the school,' Ellie said, her face anxious.

'Why don't you have Jensen and his friends keep watch around the school for the next several weeks?' Giles suggested. 'Should they discover anyone hanging about, they can haul the miscreants in and let them know the school is supported by several prominent members of the aristocracy. Warn them that, should anything happen to any of the students, the perpetrators would be pursued with as much tenacity and zeal as if the attack had taken place in Mayfair. I'm sure your sponsors would be happy to fund any protective measures you find necessary.'

'Yes, I suppose I could do that,' Ellie said, looking more reassured. 'Now that all is secure here, you gentlemen can get back to work. I'm sorry this incident interrupted your meeting.'

'Once the fight in the Lords winds up to full force, we'll have nothing but meetings, strategy sessions, and discussions, so I think we can call a halt for today. You'll stay for dinner, Christopher?' Turning to Ellie, he said, 'Please stay, too, Ellie. Not to be less than gallant, but you are looking rather pale. Why don't you rest before we dine?'

'I've been urging her to do just that,' Maggie said.

'I really would like to check on the school,' Ellie said, starting to rise—and then sinking back on to the sofa, her pale face going even paler.

Checking the strong urge to gather her in his arms again, Christopher said, 'Are you feeling ill? Let me carry you to a chamber!'

'Ellie, you must lie down! You are obviously still unwell,' Maggie said.

'Yes, you must rest,' Giles urged. 'If the footman isn't back with his report soon, Christopher and I will go personally to check on the school.'

'Very well, I'll stay. But I don't want to lie down. If it won't be too much trouble, Lady Maggie, I'd rather remain here on the sofa.'

'Wherever you are most comfortable,' Maggie said.

Loath to leave Ellie, but knowing it wouldn't be wise to remain alone with her in the salon,

Christopher was hesitating when, giving him a speaking look, Giles said, 'Why don't we finish our discussion in my study, Christopher, and let Ellie rest?'

It was the prudent choice—even though everything within him resisted it. Reluctantly, he nodded. 'Very well. If you need anything at all, you'll let us know, won't you, Ellie?'

The sad gaze she focused on his face sent a pang to his heart. 'I'm sure there is nothing you can do for me, but thank you, Christopher.'

Stripped of any excuse to linger, he followed Giles from the room. Though his heart had settled back into normal rhythm, he was still shaken by the violence of his reaction when he'd learned of the attack on Ellie. The depth of his distress at the idea of her being hurt, the urgency of his need to reassure himself she was well, the strength of his desire to hold and comfort her.

He'd thought over the course of their lessons that he was making progress in leaving past desires behind and moving forward to embrace a new life. Ellie wasn't his to comfort and protect. And she never could be.

He knew now that he'd been deluding himself about putting her behind him. The shock of finding her injured made him realise he wanted to be with and help her, *wanted* her, more urgently than ever.

How he was going to sort out that tangle, he had no idea.

Ellie seemed much recovered by dinner, though Christopher was still consumed with the desire to pummel someone every time she angled her head and he caught a glimpse of the vivid bruise on her swollen cheek.

He hated that he wouldn't be able to get his hands on the men who'd hurt her, and vowed to himself he'd do whatever was necessary to better protect her in future.

Christopher was gratified to discover an opportunity to fulfil that pledge later that very evening. Despite the reassuring report the footman had brought back from Dean Street, at the conclusion of dinner, Ellie insisted she would never be able to sleep until she'd seen for herself that her girls were safe.

'We couldn't possibly allow you to return to the school alone,' Christopher objected. 'If you simply must go tonight, let me escort you.'

'Yes, you must have an escort,' Giles agreed. 'And take our carriage. With footmen outriders and a crest on the door, it's much less likely anyone would be foolish enough to try to attack you.'

'I would feel safer in your carriage,' Ellie admitted. Although the dubious glance she slid *him* said she didn't think riding in a closed vehicle together was at all safe.

'I'll ride outside on the box, to help keep watch,' he said. Her relieved look and little nod told him she appreciated his discretion.

Though discretion was hardly what he preferred, he thought, blowing out a frustrated breath. After the attack today, he didn't want her out of his sight.

A short while later, the carriage arrived, Giles and Maggie saw them out, and the footman helped Ellie into the vehicle. 'If anything concerns you, knock on the panel, and we'll stop at once,' he instructed before climbing up beside the coachman.

The transit to Dean Street completed without incident, Christopher instructed the groom to walk the horses while he ushered Ellie inside. To their mutual relief, the matron reported all the girls were sleeping, and there had been no further incidents. Consultation with Jensen revealed he'd stationed two of his compatriots at the street corners, one outside the girls' dormitory upstairs, one near the service entrance in the cellar, while he himself kept watch at the front door which, like all the others, remained locked, the windows shuttered and latched.

After thanking him again, Ellie turned to Christopher. 'I appreciate you letting me allay my concern. I'm ready to go home now.'

'Not so sure going to your house is a good idea, miss,' Jensen cautioned. 'You crossed Gentleman Bob before, over my Annie. Now you've crossed him again with Artis. You said the lass told you them what attacked you was Keppy and Rigger? Rigger is one of the Gentleman's right-hand men. He'll have made it his business to know who you are, and he'll know you ain't got no man to protect you at Hans Place. Better you stay here, or with your friend Lady Lyndlington. Ain't nobody going to attack a viscount's house.'

Alarmed—and irritated that he'd not thought of that obvious danger before—Christopher said, 'Jensen's right, Ellie. You ought not to spend the night at home. At least not until you can arrange for protection at your house, as you have for the school.'

Ellie sighed. 'I suppose you're both right. But I'm not prepared to spend the night away from home—I'll need to get some things. And I do hate to inconvenience Lady Lyndlington.'

'You wouldn't be, and you know it,' Christopher argued. 'Let me accompany you to Hans Place and stand guard while you collect your things, then see you safely back to Maggie's.'

'Very well, you may come with me to Hans Place. Jensen, if I deem it too late to go to Lady Lyndlington's by the time I finish my preparations, expect me to return to the school.'

'Any time, miss. I'll be on watch.'

After checking carefully up and down the street, Christopher ushered Ellie back into the Lyndlington carriage, then climbed up on the box and gave the coachman her direction on Hans Place.

Once the coach halted before her house, Christopher hopped down and inspected the street to ensure all was safe before handing Ellie out again. Standing protectively close, he ushered her up the stairs and into the hall. While she went up with her maid to gather her things, he informed her manservant about the attack and the need for her to stay somewhere else until they could hire additional staff to protect the house.

Despite her assurances that she was fine, Christopher thought she looked utterly weary by the time she came back downstairs, the maid hovering protectively. He went over to offer her his arm, and to his relief, she took it.

'Sure you won't be needing me, mistress?' the girl asked. 'Ought to put another poultice on that cut tonight.'

'Thank you, Mary, but I can tend to it. I should be back tomorrow, Tarleton, though I'm not sure what time.'

'We'll watch for you, mistress,' the maid said.

'Goodnight to you, then,' Ellie said and, leaning on Christopher's arm, walked out.

'I don't know that I can afford to hire additional staff,' she said as helped her to the carriage. 'Perhaps I ought to stay at the school until the danger is past.'

'Stay with Maggie,' he advised. 'It would be better for you and the girls. If the Gentleman does try to target you, and you shelter at the school, he may find out about the girls after all, putting them back in danger. And if he's trying to target you, there's no place you'd be safer than with Maggie—or Lady Sayleford.'

'As if I would present myself uninvited at the home of a countess!'

'You need only tell her that in admitting you, she was confounding one of London's most infamous crime bosses. I think she'd relish the opportunity.'

'You're probably right,' Ellie admitted with a smile. 'Though I do hate to impose on anyone.'

Before he could assure her once again that Maggie would not think of her stay as an imposition, the clock on the nearby church tower struck the hour.

Pausing on the carriage step, she said, 'What time was that?'

'Midnight.'

She made a face. 'Regrettably then, I shall have to stay at the school. I can't invade Lady Maggie's this late—and before you assure me again she wouldn't mind, you must remember, she is increasing. She could scarcely keep her eyes open through dinner! You know if I return to her house, she will insist on dragging herself out of bed to see me settled. No, I can make do with a cot at the school.'

'Even if in so doing, you will be putting the girls in danger?' he countered.

'Damnation,' she muttered, the unusual oath surprising him. 'I don't want to do that, either.'

The solution occurred to him in a flash. He just had to convince her of it—and steel himself to make it work.

'Overnight at my place in Mount Street, then. No, hear me out!' he said, holding up a hand to forestall her immediate refusal. 'I agree, under ordinary circumstances, bringing you to my rooms would be extremely ill advised. But after the extraordinary events of today, I think it's the wisest choice. I'll have my servants prepare you a room, while I keep watch in my study—on the ground floor, a full flight down from the bedchambers. Lock your door. Tired as you are—' he allowed himself one brief caress of her uninjured cheek '— you'll be asleep the minute your head touches the pillow, so no chance to be overcome by temptation. In the morning, we'll whisk you away before you, in your renewed state of health and vigour, can ravish me.'

She smiled a little, as he'd wanted her to. 'Very well. Since I want neither to trouble Lady Maggie nor to endanger my girls, I suppose Mount Street is the best choice—for tonight.'

'Let's get you safely there, then.' He handed her into the vehicle and climbed up to the box, giving the coachman the address.

He wouldn't need much stimulation to stay on watch tonight. Knowing that her loveliness reposed just steps away from him, in the privacy of his own home, he didn't think he'd be able to sleep.

And he'd need all the resolve he could muster to keep from breaking his promise to get her safely out of his house without trying to seduce her.

The image of her bruised cheek rose in his

mind, damping down lust as it revived his anger and his determination to protect her. He'd do anything to keep her safe—even if having to resist the temptation to visit her in his bed nearly killed him.

Chapter Eighteen

As Christopher had predicted, Ellie was so exhausted that by the time his sleepy maidservant had been roused to assist her, she'd fallen into bed and asleep without a single thought about how risky it was to spend the night at his home.

Some sixth sense roused her in the pre-dawn stillness. At first, foggy with fatigue, she had no idea where she was. Then memory clicked in and she came fully awake in an instant.

She was in Christopher's house—in his own bedchamber. But not in danger—for she was alone, while he kept watch in his study on the floor below. Relieved of the need to withstand temptation, she suddenly realised she'd just been handed a unique opportunity to take an intimate glimpse into his life. Seized with curiosity, she lit a candle and edged out of bed, eager to inspect the room.

The chamber was neat, its furnishings comfortable rather than elegant. A chair and table sat near the hearth, the polished wood and soft leather burnished by the glowing embers of last night's fire. A decanter of wine stood on a sideboard, along with an assortment of papers she supposed must be draft bills. A tall bookcase held an eclectic assortment of volumes, from poetry and history to classic works in the original Latin and Greek.

It was the room of a scholar, an intellectual, but also, she thought, returning to sit on the bed, the room of a man who appreciated good wine and fine linen sheets—which held the scent of his shaving soap.

Could she sneak an equally revealing glimpse at the man himself? Although he said he'd keep watch, he had to have been almost as weary as she was. Surely he'd fallen asleep in his study. It would be several hours before any servants were about. If she were to tiptoe downstairs and peek into the room, she might indulge herself by gazing at him openly, for as long as she wished.

When would she ever have such an opportunity again?

Dismissing the protest of conscience that doing so was even more an invasion of his privacy than snooping about his chamber, she tossed a dressing gown over her nightgown and, abandoning slippers to ensure a silent transit, took her candle and crept down the stairs.

Though in her weary state last night she'd scarcely noticed the arrangement of the rooms, she was pretty sure the one behind the stairs would be his study, the front room reserved for receiving guests. Heart beating rapidly at her daring, she made her way down the hallway to the door.

Which, thankfully, was ajar, saving her from the danger of squeaky hinges. Slipping inside, she saw, in the glimmer of light from the fireplace embers, Christopher lounging in the chair behind his desk, his left cheek resting against the hand he'd wrapped over the chair arm. Asleep.

For a time she watched the gentle rise and fall of his chest. Then, emboldened by the depth of his slumber—and too far away to see him with the clarity she wanted in the dim light—she tiptoed closer, placing her candle on the table by the hearth and gradually drawing nearer and nearer, until she halted right beside him.

She smiled, tenderness warming her as she took in the shadow of stubble on his cheeks, the tousled hair tumbling over his forehead. He'd shed his waistcoat and cravat, which left his shirt lying open so that she could see bare skin from his throat down to the top of his chest.

Even in repose, he radiated strength, confidence—and a powerful masculinity. Struck anew by the force of it, she hungered to touch him, to run a finger down that bared throat and under his shirt to explore the muscles of his chest. That would surely wake him, though—but might she comb her fingers through that tousled hair, or very gently touch his cheek?

While intellect warned she ought to beat a hasty retreat while he still slumbered, her senses clamoured for more than filling her eyes with him. Just one touch, her needy senses begged. One brief caress of the man she loved and could never have.

After vacillating between the wise decision to flee and the temptation to seize this chance and savour the feel of his skin, she slowly raised one finger—and touched his cheek.

His hand grabbed hers, his body going instantly alert as he awoke with a start. Jumping at the sudden movement, she shrank back, pulling at her captive hand.

As recognition registered in his eyes, he released her. 'Ellie? What are you doing here? Is everything all right?'

'Yes, everything's fine! All still and quiet.'

'What woke you, then?'

'I'm not sure. Some sense of being in a strange room?' *The need to see you.* But she couldn't tell him that.

'You're safe here, and it's several hours yet before dawn. Go back to bed...' his voice trailed off as he scanned her, from her unbound hair, to the unfastened robe that revealed her nightgown beneath, to her bare feet '...before you catch a chill,' he finished, his voice husky.

Though his words urged her away, his gaze held her captive, burning hotter as he slowly scanned her again. She felt his glance like a caress, from the lingering inspection of her feet, up legs barely concealed beneath the fine linen of her nightgown, to her breasts, where it lingered, growing hotter still. She could feel her body warming, melting, as a spiralling heat began to build at her centre while, as he continued to stare at them, her nipples tightened.

Gazing still, as if he could not tear his eyes away, he opened his lips to speak, but no sound emerged. His hands on the chair arm tightened, his arms going rigid—as if he were fighting to keep himself from reaching for her.

He wanted her, she knew, a certainty confirmed by a quick glance at the hard ridge outlined by the straining trouser flap.

And she wanted him, all the desire that had built steadily over the days of their association peaking in a demand that she take now what she'd been trying to resist. Seize this one chance to love him completely before she must let him go for ever. That voice shouted louder than the demands for caution.

For the first time in her life, passion was what *she* wanted.

'Come upstairs with me,' she whispered, holding her hand out to him.

He dragged in a ragged breath. 'Are you sure? I won't be able to make myself stop at a goodnight kiss.'

'I'm sure. And I don't want to stop at kisses, either. I want to experience all of it. With you.'

At that, he leapt up and gathered her into his arms, his touch still incredibly gentle. He pulled her close, one hand cupping her bottom to hold her against the hardness in his breeches while with the other, he tipped up her chin and kissed her.

Softly. Tenderly. The passionate hunger so evident beneath his fierce control making the kiss all the sweeter.

He could have seized her, forced her, ravaged her. All he did was give. Her heart melted even as her body heated.

'Are you sure?' he whispered again against

her lips. 'I didn't bring you here for this, sweeting, I swear it.'

'I know.' She took his hand and moved it to her breast. 'But I'm bringing you here for this.'

'Then you shall have it all, everything you desire.'

With that, he picked her up and carried her up the stairs.

And then he lay her on the bed, her head on the pillows, and leaned over to kiss her. It was a gentle, leisurely exploration as he traced the outline of her lips with his tongue, then nuzzled and nibbled her bottom lip.

As his tongue beguiled, one hand caressed her breast, massaging from the outer fullness to pull at the peaked nipple, sending sparks through her body with each stroke, while pinwheels of sensation rolled through her, set off by the movements of his mouth, his fingers.

Driven by some irresistible urgency, she opened her mouth to him, setting off another blaze of liquid heat as he stroked hers with his, suckled it. Another, as his fingers found the opening in her night rail and slipped under to caress the naked skin of her breast, the puckered hardness of her nipple.

And then he stopped and pulled away. She gave a garbled mutter of protest.

'Tell me what you like, what you want,' he said, gazing at her intently.

Frantic that he'd ceased caressing, she shook her head. 'I don't know! Touch me. Show me what you think I'll like. Just—don't stop now!'

Chuckling, he gave her a quick, hard kiss. 'If you think of anything, tell me. If you don't like anything, stop me. This is for you, my darling. All for you.'

'I want it to be for you, too!'

He laughed again. 'Never worry, my sweet. It most definitely will be for me, too. First, I want to undress you. May I?'

She bobbed her head. 'Of course.'

He pulled her to a sitting position and slipped the robe from her shoulders. Then, while he bent and kissed her, using his lips and tongue to suckle and caress, his fingers worked to free the little buttons of her night rail. Parting the garment, he slid it down to reveal one shoulder, an expanse of neck and back, and moved his fingers there, kissing her still as he massaged and caressed the column of her neck, her collarbone, the rounds of her shoulders and the peak of a shoulder blade, his fingers dipping down in front to almost but not quite touch her breast.

Then, gently pushing her back down on the bed, he kissed the bared skin his fingers had just caressed while he moved his hands lower, to slide over the outline of each rib, down the narrow of waist and out the flare of hip.

Her skin seemed on fire where his lips touched it, ready to ignite where his hands caressed, and each new flame of discovery heightened the throbbing urgency that was building deep within her, driving her towards...something.

Then he moved his mouth down over her breast, taking linen and all into his mouth, licking and sucking at the nipple. The sensation so much more intense than the provocative touch of his fingers, she felt her body buck, a bolt of sensation at her centre making her instinctively raise her hips towards him.

Though she didn't understand why she'd done it, he seemed to, for he moved one hand to meet her thrust, sliding his hand down to cup her. With his thumb, he caressed her there, rubbing the linen nightgown between her nether lips.

She wanted more, closer, his touch freed from the barrier of cloth. She reached down, tugging the night rail upward.

'Impatient darling,' he murmured with a chuckle. 'I was getting there.'

But he helped her, pulling the night rail up, under her bottom, over her shoulders, so she lay naked and exposed to him. Vulnerable—but for the first time, she didn't *feel* vulnerable, just consumed by a need only he could satisfy.

Though she had no doubt of the strength of his desire, he did nothing for a long moment but inspect her with his heated gaze. 'How beautiful you are,' he whispered as he lay her back against the pillows.

For the first time, she rejoiced in possessing a beauty that provoked desire. 'Hurry!' she said, not sure what she needed, only certain she must have it, and *now*.

He kissed her again, taking her mouth this time with an urgency that was no longer sweet or gentle. She kissed him back just as fiercely, arching her body into his exploring hands as he caressed every surface he could reach, hair, neck, shoulders, belly, hips, thighs. Then brought both hands back to her breasts, massaging and tugging the nipples in time to the rasp and pull of his tongue against hers.

The urgency was almost overwhelming now, peaking somewhere in the centre of her, near where his thumb had teased. Thought, intention, scattered like leaves caught up in a gale, leaving only sensation and instinctive motion, as she grabbed for his hand and guided it there.

With a murmured assent, he cupped her again, at the same time releasing her lips and moving his mouth to her breast. She gasped, the heat and wetness of his tongue suckling her nipple so much more intense without the linen barrier. As he pulled and suckled harder, he slipped a hand between her legs, caressing her upper thighs. Instinctively she parted them, offering access to the most intimate part of her, crying out when his exploring fingers touched where she seemed so hot and inexplicably wet.

Sensation built and built as, suckling her nipple, he slid a finger across her throbbing nub, then into her wet passage.

Her breath coming in gasps, she writhed against him, pushing towards some pinnacle she didn't understand. Until her body released the tension in a spiral of pleasure so intense it rocketed to every corner of her body in wave after wave of blinding delight.

For long moments afterwards she lay limp, spent—and amazed, hardly aware of where she was until she realised Christopher reclined on one elbow above her, watching her, one leg wrapped over her naked body. 'Breathe,' he whispered, smiling down at her.

'That was... I don't even have words for how wonderful that was.'

'That was how it should be every time, sweeting.'

'*Every time?*' she repeated wonderingly. 'And one's heart manages to keep on beating?'

He laughed. 'One hopes so. If not...what a way to leave this life!'

She'd floated down from the peak far enough now to be more aware of him—and the fact that he had not been satisfied. 'But it wasn't that for you.'

'Not yet,' he allowed. 'It can be. But only if you want that.'

'More than ever. I want you buried in me so deeply, I cannot tell where you end and I begin.'

He smiled. 'I'd be very happy to oblige. But how?'

'How?' she echoed. 'I don't understand.'

Still smiling, he said, 'There are many ways to delight, sweeting.'

She deliberately didn't want to compare him, this night, with anything she'd previously experienced—but she was at a loss. 'I only know...one.'

'Start by undressing me—if you want to.'

Undressing and tasting and teasing each limb she unveiled, as he had? Thinking that a marvellous idea, she tugged at his shirt until he obligingly lifted his arms and let her pull it over his head.

Ah, what powerful shoulders he had, what

a wonderful muscled chest! She couldn't wait to run the pads of her fingers lightly over that marvellous expanse of masculinity. He closed his eyes and sucked in a breath as her thumbs descended to rub his flat nipples.

'Tell me what you like, what you want,' she said, echoing his query back to him.

'Anything, everything you do. Just don't stop touching me.'

Following the pattern he'd set, after exploring with her fingers, she started sampling him with her mouth, delighting in the salty tang of his skin, the spicy scent of his soap. While he held himself rigid, she moved her hands lower still, to the edge of his straining trouser front and below, barely but not quite touching his hard length, driving him to cry out when she sucked one nipple between her lips and bit down.

Sweat sheened his shoulders, his forehead when she looked up at him. 'You appear overheated. It must be an excess of clothing.'

'You may rectify that fault any time you please.'

And she did, easing open the buttons of his trouser flap and pulling the garment down, freeing his erection. For a moment, she halted, staring in awe and a little trepidation.

'Are you sure I can…accommodate that?'

'It is all for your pleasure.'

A jolt of sensation sparked within her, just thinking about sheathing that magnificent length within her. She'd meant to pull off his trousers and peel off his socks, but his hard length fascinated her.

She simply must touch it. Taste it.

And so she did, slowly, taking his measure first with her fingers, then her tongue, marvelling at the satin texture. But as she began to lick and suck, he stopped her. 'Just a warning. Continue that, and I will reach my peak without you. As indescribably wonderful as you would make that, I'd rather you accompanied me.'

By now fully aroused again, she wanted that too—both of them joined, finding ecstasy together.

Freeing him, she knelt down to strip off the rest of his garments, then clambered up on the bed. But when she went to lie down, once again he stayed her.

Sliding up to recline against the pillows, he lifted her to straddle him, positioning one leg on either side of his, his erection jutting up between them. Guiding her up on to her knees, he motioned her forward, until the tip of his erection rubbed against the warm, wet centre between her legs.

'Take me this way,' he whispered. 'As much, as little as you like. As quickly or slowly as you like. You won't be trapped under my weight, so you can move freely—however you wish.' Then, guiding himself just to the opening of her passage, he pulled her down to kiss him, stroking her tongue with his.

Instinctively understanding, she pushed down, bringing his hardness within her. Instead of the harsh, burning pressure she expected, all was smooth, sensual glide of satin skin against skin.

She couldn't get enough of the novel sensation— his length stretching and filling her, but gliding freely, as she directed, striking sparks of pleasure with each stroke. Though she tried to experiment with short, slow movements, within moments her hips, of their own accord, thrust harder, taking him deeper, every increased inch of possession driving her further along the path towards the peak she now knew and strove for, until she'd sheathed the whole of him.

And then she couldn't stop moving, frantic for the explosion of sensation ignited by each advance and retreat. Her hands knotting on his shoulders, she drove into him as he cupped her bottom, pulling her closer. An instant later, she lost herself in another glorious fireball of sensation, his cry echoing her own.

As the last sparks drifted down, she found herself lying on his chest, his heart beating a thunderous rhythm against her cheek. Peace, and a joy purer than anything she'd ever known settled over her. With a little sigh, she snuggled her head against his shoulder and drifted to sleep.

Dawn light woke Ellie. Still drowsy, she opened her eyes to discover with delight that Christopher lay beside her, deeply asleep. After stretching with the languid satisfaction of a well-pleasured body, she spent a moment indulging in the sheer wonder of gazing upon his face, revelling in the warmth of his body beside her. Ah, that she could wake this way every day for the rest of her life!

With that thought, full consciousness returned and with it, the shock of realising just what she'd done.

Perhaps, deep in her bones, she'd known from the moment she agreed to come to his home that she would not leave until she had finally done this.

She'd wanted to experience pleasure, and ah, she had—the sensations this caring and tender lover drew from her more intense and overwhelming than she could have dreamed possible.

But worse than that, the physical closeness merged into and magnified the spiritual bond that drew her to him, to the point where it seemed unthinkable to leave him. She *belonged* here with him, sharing his days, his bed, his thoughts, his goals, his desires.

There would be only one way she could do that. Would becoming his *chère amie* really be such a bad thing? With no reputation to lose, she'd be no worse off when they finally parted than she was right now. And while they were together, she would have all this—intense pleasure and soul-deep joy.

Then she recoiled, sliding away from him, aghast at where her thoughts had taken her. Could her resolve to never become another man's mistress really have been shaken this completely?

She'd been right to be wary of giving in to passion. She knew now just how dangerous and irresistible it could be, for now that she'd tasted it in full, she was ravenous for more.

She'd already broken her word to offer him only assistance to reach his goals, not temptation. And she knew without a shadow of a doubt that after their tempestuous, glorious coupling, Christopher's resolve to move forward and find the wife he needed would be compromised, too.

When he woke, he would be no more eager to see her leave than she was to go. He would ruin his future by offering her *carte blanche*.

Did she really believe, now that she'd experienced the all-consuming joy of intimacy with him, she'd be able to resist accepting his offer if he exerted even the smallest amount of persuasion? One sweet kiss? Another mind-searing round of lovemaking?

If she stayed here until he woke, they would both be lost, their noble ideals tarnished and their plans for the future in ashes.

She must go, now. And not see him again.

Fighting the resistance of both body and spirit, she eased herself from the bed, careful not to wake him. Angrily swiping away the tears of the regret, anguish and pain that had already started gnawing at her, she gathered her clothing and slipped into the hallway, haphazardly doing up her gown.

Surprising the cook and the maid at work on breakfast, she enlisted their help to finish dressing and sent a footman to find her a hackney, forbidding any of the staff to rouse the master who, she said, had remained on guard all through the night, and needed his rest now.

A short while later, the footman returned to announce her hackney waited outside. Wrapping herself in her cloak, forcing down the sorrow and anguish, she whispered an almost silent, 'Goodbye, my love…' as she passed the stairs and walked out.

Chapter Nineteen

Slowly ascending from the depths of sleep, a supremely satisfied Christopher stirred, then opened one eye. Startled to see the room bright with a sunlight that showed the day far more advanced than he'd expected, he jerked to alertness. His smile as he recalled the delights of the previous night dimmed only as he noted the bed beside him was empty, the space warmed by a wicked, willing Ellie now cold.

A quick glance around the chamber confirmed that her clothing was missing. Given the lateness of hour, he wasn't surprised she'd gone, but he did wish she'd awakened him to say goodbye.

Though if she had…he would doubtless have persuaded her to linger, he thought, his grin returning.

He regretted being such a slug-a-bed, but

wasn't surprised he'd slept so late. He couldn't have had more than an hour's rest before Ellie woke him. And given the satisfaction and deep content of their lovemaking, he wasn't surprised he'd slept so soundly.

He really had intended to remain chastely in the study, seeing her this morning only to speedily convey her back to Maggie's. But when she appeared before him, looking like desire incarnate, and held out her hand...could any man breathing have resisted her? Refused her, after she assured him not once but twice that having him make love to her was all that she desired, when it had been all he'd desired for years?

He'd *known* that loving her would be glorious, and reality had more than confirmed his instincts. But, though it had been some time since he broke with his last mistress, what he felt now was more than just the hum of well-satisfied body. He was...happy, replete with a delight and contentment that penetrated to the very core of his being, as if warm honey had dripped into his bones. The warmth and sweetness and delight that was Ellie.

Joy and an excitement beyond anything he could remember bubbled up, and he laughed out loud.

He couldn't wait to see her, to make love to

her again. After what they'd shared last night, surely she would realise, as he did now, that they belonged together. On some instinctive level, he'd known it for a long time, which was why he'd pushed to continue his lessons and dragged his heels about moving on to court a proper lady. How could he honourably offer himself to another woman, when his heart and his senses were filled with Ellie?

But how to make being together happen?

He frowned, his euphoria dimming a little. It still smacked too much of insult to offer *carte blanche* to a woman whom he knew should— but now never would—be a respectable member of the *ton*. Would it be possible to add a discreet intimacy to their friendship, become lovers without making any public acknowledgement of their association and keep it hidden from the world?

But such a relationship would almost certainly, eventually, be discovered. And living discreetly separate would not allow the day-to-day intimacy he craved. He wanted more than Ellie in his bed, he wanted her sitting at his table and in his library, riding in the park, visiting in the countryside—everywhere, all the time.

He sighed. Nothing very discreet about that.

And no matter how he looked at it, the stark fact remained that abandoning his goal of respectable matrimony would hinder his political career.

Very well, but the impediment was surmountable, surely. Although nothing short of legitimate marriage would allow him to complete his circle of friends by taking a wife he could be seen with anywhere, he was reasonably sure the Hellions would receive them, if only in private.

A niggle of doubt shook him. He knew his friends and their wives liked Ellie, had accepted her and dined with her—as a former courtesan. Would they continue to welcome her if he involved her in another illegitimate relationship?

The sort of relationship she'd vowed never to enter again? Could he retain any sense of honour if he urged her back into a role that had filled her with shame and regret? The last thing he wanted was to hurt her.

He couldn't marry her. But how could he give her up?

The sense of delight with which he'd awakened now dissipated by realising how difficult a dilemma he faced, Christopher jumped out of bed and hurriedly dressed. He'd call on Ellie, talk over the situation with her. Surely they could come up with a solution that would allow them to be together without causing her more pain.

While he stood before the mirror, knotting

his cravat, a knock sounded at the door, followed by the entrance of his valet, Marsden. 'Sorry, sir!' the man said, checking as he saw his master almost fully dressed. 'I would have come up at once to assist you, had I known you were awake.'

'Why did you let me sleep so late?'

'Miss Parmenter instructed us not to rouse you, since you had kept watch most of the night.'

'When did she leave?'

'Just after daybreak. Rollins got her a hackney.'

'Did anyone accompany her?'

'No, sir, she said that since no one knew she'd been staying here, she would be safe enough travelling alone.'

Frowning as he recalled that she'd been attacked in broad daylight, Christopher hoped so. Would she have gone home? Or to the school? They really needed to finalise the matter of additional watchmen to protect her.

'I brought up the post, sir. Would you like breakfast now?'

'Just coffee. I shall be going out almost immediately.'

Accepting the stack, Christopher thumbed through them, setting aside one that was obviously an invitation. The last one had only his name inscribed, in a flowing feminine hand. Ellie's.

He broke the seal and eagerly scanned the lines.

Dear Christopher,
I think we can both agree that my work is done, and you are now equipped to begin your search for a suitable wife. I wish you all the best in finding the right lady to brighten your days and offer you the assistance you need to reach the highest levels of your career.

Thinking it best to end for good any temptation to delay that task, I will bid you goodbye and good luck.
Your friend, Ellie

PS So you might commence without delay, I've sent along an invitation to a reception this afternoon at the home of my Aunt Marion, which will be attended by my sister Sophie and other eligible maidens.

Marsden brought the coffee and set the tray on the table beside him, but Christopher scarcely noticed. He read Ellie's note over several more times before finally, incredulous, disbelieving, he had to acknowledge that she had just walked out of his life.

With no acknowledgement of the night they'd shared. With barely any indication of warmth at all—just a tepid, 'your friend'. Without offering him even the courtesy of saying farewell to his face.

Numb disbelief thawed into a piercing pain as the joy within shattered into jagged shards that stabbed deep into his chest. He'd been transported—energised—consumed with need for her. And she had…left him without a word?

For a moment, he felt like that little boy again, holding out the treasure he prized above all others to the father whose love he'd been so desperate to win—while the man passed him by without a glance.

Bile rose in his throat, and for a moment, he thought he'd be sick.

But as he subdued the nausea, a furious anger boiled up. How could she just *dismiss* him, like a servant whose work didn't suit? How could she walk away without acknowledging the bond between them, the passion they'd shared, the joy they gave each other? How could she coolly say goodbye as if what had happened last night was as ordinary as afternoon tea, and as soon forgotten? When he'd been touched by bliss as never before?

Damn her, then, and damn her lessons. She wanted him to move forward and court another woman? Well, he'd happily oblige. Hadn't that been his aim all along? He'd find a wife so skilful and virtuous she would shatter all his doubts about remaining faithful, filling him with confidence that he could dote on her all his life. A woman of such unimpeachable virtue that she would never cause their children a moment's embarrassment.

Feeding his fury to mask the anguish beneath, he took Ellie's note and threw it in the fire. Then returned to the table, scanned the invitation, and went to ring the bell pull.

It appeared he'd have that breakfast after all. And then have Marsden dress him in something suitable for impressing a bevy of Virtuous Virgins.

That afternoon, Christopher presented himself at the town house of the Countess of Enfield, where the afternoon reception Ellie had bid him attend was already in progress. He should be grateful for this chance to mingle with other people, since he'd had little luck focusing his mind on work. In the hours since he'd read Ellie's note, he'd tried to study the report Giles had sent, but found his attention distracted by the need to periodically rekindle his anger to keep at bay the black depression beneath.

Time to master that for good, and move forward.

After greeting Lady Enfield, who met him with stiff civility, he moved into the room, where he soon realised he knew very few of the attendees—not surprising, since he almost never appeared at Society functions. Bypassing most of the gentlemen, who all appeared younger than he was, he walked over to Lord Bronfield, an ally of Maggie's father—and recent widower, he recalled. Who, if he were attending this gathering, must be trolling for another bride.

'Lattimar!' the baron said, his eyes widening in surprise. 'Good to see you! If unexpected. Can't recall you ever taking part in an affair that wasn't political. What brings you here?'

'The same reason that brings you, I would expect,' Christopher replied, snagging a glass from a passing waiter.

'*You're* looking to marry?' the baron said in disbelief. 'The ladies of the demi-monde must be weeping!'

Ignoring that, Christopher said, 'I have on the authority of my friends that marriage is a most desirable estate. Which it must be, if you are angling to enter it again. Already have several heirs, don't you?'

'I do. But your friends are correct. There's a companionship and warmth in marriage that one finds nowhere else. With the right lady, of course. I thought to live without it, after I lost my dear Emma two years ago, but I find I yearn to have that closeness again.'

'I hope you'll find that right lady, then.'

'You, too, Lattimar. Anyone who's caught your eye?'

'I must confess, this is my first reception, and I know practically no one.'

'Ah, well, let me rectify that! Come along.'

Like a lamb to the slaughter, Christopher couldn't help thinking as the baron led him where a large knot of guests stood conversing. 'Ladies, let me present my colleague in Parliament, Mr Christopher Lattimar. Christopher, it's my pleasure to make known to you Lady Elaine Wyminster, Lady Quinley, her daughter, Miss Quinley, Lord Warner, and Mr Whittiker.'

After bows, curtsies, and greetings, Christopher turned to lady standing nearest him. 'Miss Quinley, are you newly come to London?'

Miss Quinley, a slender blonde with pale blue eyes, looked down hastily when he focused on her, her face flushing. 'Yes,' she said belatedly.

'How have you found it?' When she moistened her lips without coming up with a reply, he prompted, 'Interesting? Noisy? Frightening?'

Casting a desperate look at her mother, who gave her an encouraging nod, she said, 'Interesting. But noisy.'

'Do you prefer life in the country?'

With another panicked glance at her mother, she said, 'I...like the country. Of course, London is...nice, too.'

A very shy girl probably won't look at you at all, will say little and defer to her mother. Which might be a sign she's not right for you.

A bittersweet smile tugged at his lips as Ellie's advice echoed in his ears, before he was distracted by Lady Elaine's tinkling laugh. 'Mr Lattimar, spare poor Miss Quinley! My friend is the most gentle creature imaginable, but quite dreads drawing-room conversation.'

That maiden's relieved smile at the interruption told Christopher Lady Elaine did care about the girl and wasn't merely trying to steal away his attention.

'You are part of the Reform movement, Mr Lattimar?' Lady Elaine was saying. 'My late husband wasn't political. Perhaps you could tell me more?'

She took his arm, the touch surprising Christopher until he recalled Ellie saying that a widow had more latitude in behaviour than an innocent miss. Since a quick glance around showed no raised eyebrows, he figured the widow's gesture must be permissible.

Though he felt the strongest desire to remove her hand.

He suppressed it as she led him a little apart, pulling away once she'd halted in a vacant alcove. 'Now we can talk without shouting. For I do wish to catch every…intimate…word.' She gave him a flirtatious glance from under her long lashes.

Though he felt no immediate connection to her, the male in him noticed how close she stood, the alluring tilt of her head, the flicker of tongue moistening her lips.

He looked up to find her watching him inspect her—a knowing smile on her face. And he felt, for the first time in his life, almost… *irritated* to be the subject of a woman's amorous overtures.

Before he could think of a way to escape her attentions, a young gentleman hurried up. 'Lady Elaine!' he cried, giving Christopher a hostile glance. 'Here's the wine you asked me to procure.'

'Mr Armbruster, how kind,' she said, bestowing on the young man a smile so dazzling that he froze in mid-step. She plucked the glass from him, in the process giving his hand a lingering caress that rendered him red-faced and speechless.

Lady Elaine's behaviour brought to mind that of the naughty matrons his mother had invited to 'distract' him. A memory that called up Ellie's voice.

A lady who seems intent on attaching every gentleman around her, as if believing she must always be the focus of attention, would make a taxing wife.

As Lady Elaine turned her seductive smile back on him, he had to agree. This wench must have led Lord Wyminster a merry dance, and he had no desire to follow in the late baron's footsteps.

'Why, Mr Lattimar, I had no idea you'd be here today!'

Happy for the interruption, Christopher turned to find the girls from the park walking over.

'Ladies, a pleasure to see you again. Lady Elaine, you are acquainted with Lady Audrey Thornton and Miss Higgins? And Mr— Armbruster, wasn't it?'

As they all nodded, Lady Elaine gave the

younger girls a brief smile. 'Hello, girls,' she said. 'Mr Lattimar was telling us about politics. Not much to interest you, I'm afraid.'

Though Miss Higgins appeared cowed, Lady Audrey met the older beauty's stare with a level glance that said she was not at all intimidated. 'You are mistaken, Lady Elaine. In fact, Mr Lattimar promised me a fuller discussion of his political views when we last rode together. Did you not?'

'I did indeed,' he confirmed, to Lady Elaine's obvious annoyance.

'Won't you let me steal you away? Sophie wanted to hear about your work, too, and she's still assisting her aunt as hostess. She'd be so disappointed to miss the discussion. You'll excuse us, Lady Elaine, Mr Armbruster?'

Christopher had to chuckle as she bore him away. 'Neatly done, Lady Audrey,' he murmured as they walked off, the matron's affronted gaze following them. 'Though you may have made yourself an enemy there.'

His escort shrugged. 'Lady Elaine knows nothing about politics. She just wanted to monopolise the attention of the handsome newcomer.'

'Audrey!' Miss Higgins exclaimed in an undertone, flushing. 'She'll hear you.'

'I probably shouldn't have said that,' Lady Audrey admitted. But you *are* new to these gatherings, and I'd be lying if I didn't admit we all find you handsome.'

'Audrey!' Miss Higgins exclaimed again, her flush deepening.

'Don't worry, Mary. You're not offended, are you, Mr Lattimar? Sophie says her sister thinks you the most admirable and understanding of gentlemen.'

Ellie said he was admirable and understanding? Then why? As he struggled to suppress the pain that stabbed anew, it was several moments before he realised the girls were gazing at him, still awaiting an answer. 'No, I'm not offended,' he said, dragging himself back to the present. 'As a politician, I appreciate plain speaking. One reaches the heart of the argument—and discovers the possibilities for compromise—much faster that way.'

Could they not do that, if he were just able to see Ellie again?

His already unsettled senses startled again when, after rounding a group of guests, he saw Sophie, the instinctive leap of delight followed by the bitter disappointment that the girl who resembled her so closely wasn't Ellie.

Then, angry at being once again pulled from

the present by the woman who'd abandoned him, he resolved to dismiss her from his thoughts and concentrate his full attention on the ladies before him.

Greeting Sophie politely, he engaged for half an hour in a discussion of the progress of the reform bill that both she and Lady Audrey seemed to want.

If he gazed at Sophie through lowered eyes, he could even for a moment imagine it was Ellie beside him, debating the politics he loved. But when he looked with eyes wide open, he knew that lovely, intelligent and interesting as Sophie was, she was only a pale reflection of Ellie, her character young and not fully formed. She lacked the depth, the sense of calm confidence, the unique spirit of her sister.

Their hostess came to reclaim Sophie, and with an exchange of bows and curtsies, the girls walked off with her. An aching sadness filled him as he watched them, wondering if he'd ever feel like himself again.

In stark contrast to his normal behaviour, this afternoon he'd recoiled from flirtatious overtures to which he would usually have responded, been unable to summon up enough empathy to encourage the ingénue lacking in confidence, and had to push himself to converse with two young ladies who seemed to possess all the attributes he thought he was seeking.

Except for one. Neither one was Ellie.

Disinclined to any further gestures of politeness, he abandoned his original intention of remaining to talk with the girls again, instead seeking out the Countess to take his leave. A few minutes later, he halted on the street, gazing back at the Countess's town house.

Angry, bitter, scoured by loss. Unable to make himself move forward to do what he must.

The realisation swept through him with the force of a high wind, carrying away frustration and resistance. Why was he trying to deceive himself? It was Ellie he really wanted.

He would cease this minute trying to talk himself into doing what everything within him fought against—settling for a woman who could never be more than an inadequate substitute. It would be agony for him and unfair to the lady, when his heart and soul hungered for Ellie. Just as, throughout this gathering, memories of Ellie and her ghostly voice in his ear had held more of his attention than the conversation of the actual guests.

For the first time since the devastation of reading her note this morning, Christopher felt a surge of excitement and a renewal of purpose.

Having finally admitted that he wanted Ellie and no other, now he needed to find her—and convince her they belonged together.

Chapter Twenty

As he set off for the nearest hackney stand, Christopher still didn't know how he could reconcile their nearly impossible situation. But he would fight as long as it took to win Ellie over.

He instructed the driver to carry him to Dean Street, reasoning that, despite the risk to the girls, she might have felt compelled to check that all was well with the school.

But as he impatiently waited through the transit, an even more obvious truth struck him, so clear and simple, he wondered it had taken him so long to realise it.

He'd fight to keep Ellie, just as he'd been fighting for ten years to make the government of England more equitable. To see that it responded to the wishes and needs of all its citizens, not just the wealthy few who had controlled power for centuries. So that all hard-working men—

and eventually women—would have a voice in determining their destiny.

Then why was he letting the choice of his heart be dictated by the strictures of the same small, closed group into which he had been born, but with whom he'd scarcely associated since his entry into Parliament? Dismissing the idea of marrying Ellie without really considering it, because Society dictated she was unfit to be his wife? Letting himself be subtly prejudiced against her, acquiescing in the *ton*'s opinion that she wasn't *worthy* to be his wife.

When, in the depths of his heart, he knew there was no one *more* worthy to fill his life, his heart and his bed than the woman he now acknowledged he loved, fully and completely.

Society would ostracise them—but since he'd almost never attended Society functions, that would scarcely bother him. The guests at the political dinners that did matter to him—like Lord Witlow's 'discussion evenings'—came from all backgrounds and walks of life, and Ellie had already been welcomed there.

He had a brief moment of hesitation when he considered how marrying a former courtesan might affect their children. But unlike his mother, who had continued her scandalous life all through the years he was growing up, Ellie's situation before they wed would be overwritten by years of faithful marriage and effective work as a political wife long before their children grew old enough to understand any gossip about her. They need only ignore the whispers—and besides, a little adversity made one stronger. It had him, hadn't it?

Dismissing that doubt, he moved to a more troubling one: would the Hellions approve his decision? He *thought* so—Davie and Faith had also defied Society to marry. But hurtful as it would be to forfeit their friendship, if it came to a choice between winning Ellie and losing the Hellions, he had to choose Ellie.

He hoped it wouldn't come to that. But first he had to find, and persuade, Ellie—who had been indoctrinated from birth as thoroughly as he had to believe herself no longer worthy of his hand—that he thought her not just equal, but superior, to any Virtuous Virgin he might ever meet. And that marriage was the only answer for them both.

Arriving at Dean Street, after instructing the driver to wait, Christopher bounded up the stairs and knocked on the door. Then returned to the carriage a moment later, after Jensen assured him they hadn't seen Ellie since they stopped by the previous evening.

Surely she wouldn't have been reckless enough to return to her unprotected house? Still, worry gnawed at him as he gave the driver that direction and hopped back into the coach, consumed with urgency to see her.

What exactly had she said when she wrote him goodbye? He wished now he hadn't burned her note. There'd been something about his being prepared and her job being done. He knew she'd not mentioned anything about their night together, or the warmth, laughter and enjoyment of their lessons, an omission which had struck him on the raw.

But the more he considered it, the more he realised that, given the character of the woman he loved, the very coldness of the language indicated not a *lack* of feeling, but rather a need to conceal it.

As the carriage bowled along, he recalled she'd written something else about ending for good any temptation to delay his quest, a phrase he'd skimmed over the moment his eyes saw the 'goodbye' penned at the ending.

End the temptation for good? What could she have meant by that?

A few minutes later, the jarvey pulled up at Hans Place, but his stop here was equally brief. His relief at having her staff confirm she'd not returned home was offset by a deepening worry over where in fact she had gone.

Given her previous protests about not wishing to intrude, he hadn't thought she would go to Maggie's without his escort—but that must be where she'd sheltered. Where else could she go?

Returning once more to the carriage, he had the driver set off for Upper Brook Street. Dismissing the jarvey, he paced the parlour to which Dawkins showed him while he waited for Maggie.

Trying to mask his urgency under a veneer of courtesy, he speeded to the door the moment she entered. 'Hello, Christopher! What an unexpected pleasure.'

But the veneer mustn't have been very convincing, for after a single glance at his face, her smile faded. 'What is it? What's happened?'

'Nothing, I'm sure,' he replied against the nagging apprehension in his gut. 'I just wanted to stop by and see how Ellie is doing.'

'Ellie? She's not here, Christopher. Didn't you escort her to the school last night?'

So sure was he that she must be with Maggie, he had no glib answer prepared to explain her whereabouts the previous evening. When he hesitated, not sure whether or not to reveal the truth, Maggie said sharply, 'You did escort her to the school, didn't you? Surely you didn't send her home alone!'

'No, of course not. I wouldn't let her go to the school—or home—without protection. But after we arrived there, Jensen pointed out it might put the girls in danger if she were to remain at the school, should the ones who attacked her trace her there. We determined it would be safer for her to overnight...elsewhere.'

'Elsewhere?'

'I intended to bring her back here after she'd gone home to collect her things. But by that time, it was late, and in your delicate condition, she didn't want to disturb you. So...I took her back to Mount Street.'

Maggie gave him a penetrating look. 'Where she spent the night. After which somehow you've managed to misplace her?'

He felt his face flush. 'She left before I woke. I had...some matters to take care of, and intended to seek her out this afternoon,' he improvised. 'I thought she'd go to the school. But she isn't there, she hasn't been home—and you say you've not seen her either.'

'After being attacked yesterday, she's been travelling about since this morning without any protection? Christopher, how could you have permitted it?'

Maggie couldn't excoriate him any more harshly than he did himself. How *could* he have failed to check on her, despite his hurt and dismay? Even if he believed she didn't want to see him again, he should have made sure she was safe before haring off to that reception in a self-righteous rage. 'I agree, it was thoughtless and inexcusable, so you may save your wrath. I'll keep looking. It just occurred to me that she might have gone to my mother.'

'Or to Aunt Lilly. If you'll wait a few moments, I'll call the carriage for us and get my wrap.'

'Should you be bouncing about in a carriage now?' he asked, with a gesture towards her thickening body.

'Better that then waiting here, not knowing. I'll be fine. And if I'm not, you deserve having me get sick all over you for not taking better care of Ellie.'

After increasing their anxiety when their first stop revealed Ellie had not called on Lady Sayleford, both felt vastly relieved when their consultation with Christopher's mother confirmed that Ellie had, in fact, visited her earlier that afternoon.

'She was most upset—for which you are almost surely responsible,' his mother said to Christopher after seeing a queasy Maggie to a chair and sending for chamomile tea. 'No, she didn't tell me what you did. But I know it's your fault.'

Two sets of feminine eyes looked at him accusingly. Though he didn't want to confess the whole, he was honest enough to take responsibility for the debacle. 'Yes, I'm sure it's my fault.'

'I knew it!' Lady Vraux sputtered. 'When I told her I feared she might do something desperate, she replied, only half-jokingly, that to preserve her sanity, she might have to turn her back on everything she'd vowed. Now what, I ask you, did she mean by that?'

Christopher was about to protest that he had no idea when the most unpalatable suspicion struck him. Tempted beyond bearing to accept the offer of *carte blanche* he would surely have made, had she still been in his bed when he woke, certain that beguiling him into renouncing marriage would ruin his career, and still in need of protection from the villains threatening her, there was one other place she might go.

Where, after turning her back on her solemn vow never to become a kept woman again, she would be swept beyond the reach of the villains—and beyond his.

'There is somewhere else she might have gone. But by heaven, if she did refuge there, it won't be for long. Mama, will you see Maggie returns safely home after she's rested? I must leave at once.'

Anguished, almost beyond control with rage, jealousy and dismay at the idea of her with another man and remorse that his own stupidity might have forced her to it, he ran down the stairs and out to the hackney stand, telling the driver to spring 'em to Brook Street—and the home of Lord Mountgarcy.

Short as the transit was, he had ample time to reflect on what it would mean if Ellie had indeed given herself to another man. Before taking so agonising a step, she would have closed her heart to any chance of a future between them. Once she was known as Mountgarcy's mistress, she would feel certain Christopher would never look to her again.

He would marry her anyway, and damn the consequences. But to have a better chance of convincing her that wedding him *was* possible, he needed to find her before any potential understanding with the Viscount became known.

She might not agree to see him. To protect her from him and the Gentleman, she might even have had Mountgarcy take her out of Lon-

don. The Viscount would lose no time returning
to crow about his conquest, Christopher knew.
With no idea where to find Ellie, he might truly
lose her for good.

He thought he'd been devastated when he read
her note. The idea of losing her for ever was so
horrifying, it stripped him bare to the soul.

His work, his projects in Parliament, his
friendships—everything fell away when he considered a life without Ellie. Without her, nothing
else held meaning. Whatever it took, he must
find her and woo his way back into her heart.

Any other outcome was unthinkable.

At Brook Street he met with frustration again,
for the Viscount's minions denied that any lady
had visited the house and insisted his lordship
was not at home. But when he advanced upon the
butler, the urge to strangle doubtless reflected in
his eyes, the man revealed that his master had
gone to spend the evening at Brooks's.

Once again, he went careening in a hackney, this time back to St. James's Street and
into Brooks's, where he demanded to see Lord
Mountgarcy. Directed to the card room, he found
his quarry playing whist.

'Mountgarcy, I must speak with you at once.'

The Viscount looked up with his usual languid air. Though he didn't seem surprised to

see him, Christopher could not discern from his voice or manner whether or not the man knew why he'd sought him out.

'Good evening to you, too, Lattimar. Can this urgent matter wait until I've finished this hand?'

Though he wanted to snap back a negative, no sense rousing more curiosity than his precipitous entrance had already generated. He gave the Viscount a short nod.

A few minutes later, adding the winnings to the stack in front of him, the Viscount rose. 'Keep the chair for me. It's been lucky this evening.'

He followed Christopher into the deserted reading room. 'So, what is it that has you invading Brooks's with this air of desperation?'

'Has Ellie Parmenter come to you?' he asked, too anxious for polite preliminaries.

'Ellie come to me?' Mountgarcy repeated, the surprise on his face too genuine to doubt. 'I only wish!' He narrowed his gaze on Christopher. 'Surely you've not misplaced the elegant Miss Parmenter.'

Christopher studied him, wanting to be sure. 'You are telling the truth, aren't you?'

'Why would I lie? Had the divine Ellie sought me out, I'd be boasting of that good fortune to everyone. Especially you.'

Which was doubtless correct. The Viscount gave him a mocking smile Christopher itched to punch off his face. 'Does this sudden wrath indicate a quarrel? Perhaps there is an opportunity here.'

'Don't even consider it. Ellie belongs with me, and I intend to marry her.'

'Marry her?' the Viscount echoed, the mockery shocked off his face. 'Your mind must truly be disordered to contemplate such an outrage. You'd be ruined! And never be allowed to set foot in this club again.'

'Then I wouldn't ever have to speak with you again, would I? Good evening.' With that, Christopher turned on his heel and walked out.

As relieved as he was that she had not fled to Mountgarcy, his worry over Ellie's welfare intensified. She must be safe, he told himself, trying to ratchet down the fear. His mother had seen her in mid-afternoon. Of all the places she might have gone after that, Maggie's was the most logical. He'd return there first.

Calling back the hackney, he endured the short drive with mounting impatience. He was rushing up the entry stairs at Upper Brook Street when Giles came out to meet him.

'Relax, Christopher! We have Ellie safe. You

and Maggie must have just missed her at your mother's.'

Christopher took a deep breath, relief making him light-headed. 'Praise Heaven!'

'You look like you could stand a brandy. Shall we?'

'I'd love one, but later. First, I need to see Ellie.'

Giles gave him a troubled look. 'I'll…ask if she'll see you, but she seemed very upset. It might be wiser to wait.'

'I need to see her *now*,' Christopher said flatly, just as Maggie walked into the hallway.

'Oh, you do, do you?' she said, fire in her eyes. 'Really, Christopher, haven't you hurt her enough? And before you ask, no, she didn't tell me what happened. But you admitted she'd spent the night in your rooms. Given the fact that one could light a taper from the sparks in the air when you two are together, it doesn't take a logician to deduce what happened. You wretch! Couldn't you have taken her somewhere else—anywhere else? You know she never wanted to become…*that* again—not even for you! I never thought I'd have to say this to any of my husband's friends, but I must ask you to leave.'

'You can throw me out, but one way or another,

I will see her, Maggie,' Christopher said, holding his ground. 'And I am going to marry her.'

Shock registered on both Giles and Maggie's faces. 'Marry her!' Giles exclaimed.

'Yes. I hope you won't oppose me, but if you do, so be it. I *will* see Ellie, and I intend to do whatever it takes to convince her to marry me.'

To his consternation, Maggie burst into tears— then came over and hugged him. Patting her back awkwardly, he said, 'Does this excess of sentiment mean you approve?'

'Oh, yes! And also that I'm increasing, which seems to make me fall victim to the most extreme emotions. Society won't receive either of you, but what do any of us care about that? Ellie's endured so much, and I've come to love her so dearly! Marrying her will make her a part of our circle for ever. I couldn't be happier about it!'

Heartened, Christopher looked over to find Giles grinning at him. 'Never did believe the greatest rakehell among us would be content to wed some mealy-mouthed virgin.'

'You sound like Mama.' Enormously pleased that his friends approved of his plans for Ellie, Christopher handed Maggie over to her husband. 'Now, it just remains to convince the lady.'

'Which will be no mean task,' Maggie told him tartly. 'She's wounded and despairing and loves you so much, she will insist she cannot do anything that will harm you. Don't expect her to yield easily!'

Christopher grinned. 'I'm sure she will not. But yield she will, in the end.'

To forestall any chance of her refusing to see him, Christopher slipped quietly into the sitting room where Ellie had taken refuge, an open book on her lap. The weary droop of her shoulders and the misery reflected in her far-away gaze stabbed at his heart, sending the opening speech he'd intended right out of his head. Instead, he went over and gathered her in his arms.

'Ellie, I'm so sorry for all the distress I've caused you.'

'Christopher!' she cried, starting in surprise—and then clinging to him. For a few precious minutes, he revelled in the warmth and scent and delight of her, his heart turning over at what he'd almost lost. All too soon, doubtless remembering her intention to break with him, she pulled away.

Regretfully, he let her go, vowing that before long, she would be back in his arms—this time for good.

'I…didn't expect to see you again,' she said, looking away as she struggled for composure. 'I thought I'd said all that was needed in my note.

After…what we shared, I knew I wouldn't have the strength to refuse you. I'm so sorry I tempted you into breaking both our vows. And that I took the coward's way out, and sent you away with a note, rather than face to face.'

'Your note said enough to terrify me. I thought… I thought I'd hurt you so badly, and tempted you so cruelly, that you'd gone to Mountgarcy.'

'I did consider it,' she admitted. 'But after I left your mother's, I realised that if I was to retain any self-respect, I had to face this on my own.'

'You don't need to face anything alone, my love. I admit, your leaving me with only a note enraged me, but that turned out to be useful. It made me angry enough to attend Lady Enfield's reception. Just one session of trying to make myself agreeable to eligible maidens was enough for me to finally realise I don't belong with any of them. To open my eyes to what I've been too stupidly blind to see—that I've come to love and cherish you, and cannot imagine spending my life with anyone else.'

She shook her head, tears starting again as she held out a hand, as if to ward him off. 'I can't, Christopher. If you care for me at all, please, *please*, don't entreat me further.'

'Just one more thing. Having you depart so abruptly shocked me into realising how much I've let myself be constrained by Society's evaluation of your character.'

She gave him a sad smile. 'You don't think I'm good enough—to be a wife. Which I completely under—'

'No!' he interrupted. 'I wronged you by doing that. When I thought deeply about it, I realised I don't believe in Society's rules. With all you have suffered and triumphed over, you are worthy of the highest honour and greatest dignity. I apologise for taking so long to fully comprehend that, but I do now, with all my heart.'

With that, he dropped to one knee. 'Ellie Parmenter, née Miss Tess Wanstead, will you do me the honour of becoming my wife?'

Her eyes widened in shock. 'Wh-what did you say?'

He grinned, amused, but with his heart overflowing with tenderness at her patent disbelief. 'My dearest Ellie, I asked you to marry me. Don't you feel it, too, my darling? The absolute truth that we belong together, now, for ever?'

A cascade of emotions passed over her expressive face—shock, disbelief, incredulity, then a trickle of tears as the reality of his proposal sank in.

'Say "yes", my darling,' he urged, 'and make me the happiest man in England.'

Then he saw what he'd braced himself to fight—dismay, caution, and a brief flash of anguish before she submerged all emotion beneath a polite mask.

'Marry you!' she exclaimed. 'Oh, my! That's not at all what I expected!'

'I know,' he admitted. 'Had you still been in my bed when I woke this morning, to my deepest shame, I might have made you the sort of offer you *were* expecting. But I've come to my senses now. I'm making you the only offer you deserve—an honourable one.'

'I would rather say you've *lost* your senses! Marry *me*? Whatever can you be thinking? Granted, we shared a…a magnificent night together, but with a woman like me, that hardly requires marriage! Such a union would spell disaster for your future, and for mine.'

'Not at all. I'd hardly be the first politician to marry a woman not received by Society. Fox did so, and had a highly successful career. Society's opinion carries no weight in the world of politics, which is the only world I care about. That, and being happy—which will only be possible if you agree to spend your life with me.'

She pulled her trembling hands free, refusing to meet his gaze. 'I suppose I might be willing to—to risk marriage, if I truly loved you. I don't wish to be unkind, but…I'm afraid I don't. Oh, I count you as a very dear friend, a superb lover, but I have my own needs and my goals for the school, while you have yours in Parliament. You need a wife who can assist you with those, as I never could. Whereas I… I would need the freedom to move on to another man, once the passion between us cooled. So, though I thank you for the honour of your offer, I must refuse.'

He might have been cast down by her denial of loving him—except for the bit about moving on to another man. Which was so unbelievable, so completely a contradiction of everything she had vowed for the future, he knew she must be lying. And why would she do that, unless she was trying to be noble, refusing the man she loved because she believed marrying him would destroy his career?

She'd stated that conviction many times. It would take some time to dissuade her of it.

'You're sure you won't reconsider?'

'Absolutely not. I hope we can remain… casual friends, but I'm afraid I can't offer anything more.'

She sat with her head bowed now, refusing to meet his gaze. Her body drooped, fatigue in every line, while her clenched hands told him she was hanging on to composure by a thread.

Compassion filled him. Though he would prefer to argue further, take her in his arms and force her here and now to recognise the bond between them, he knew such an action would bring her anguish rather than comfort. She'd been attacked, fled into the night, seduced him, sent him away for his own good, and then been blindsided by a marriage proposal all within the space of a few hours. He wanted to woo and win her, not cudgel her into submission when she was distraught and exhausted.

He wouldn't harangue her any more.

Today.

'Very well, if that is your final answer, I won't take up any more of your time. Goodbye, Ellie.'

Tears came to her eyes again as she nodded quickly. She raised her head to fasten her gaze on his face, looking so hungry, desperate and despairing, he had to fight again not to embrace her. 'Goodbye, Christopher,' she whispered.

Discouraged, but by no means defeated, Christopher left her. As he'd learned in Parliament, when heated emotions preclude any chance for compromise, there is no point in berating the opposition further. Better to retreat, find another approach, and try again later.

But if Ellie thought he'd given up at the first check, she didn't know anything about the man who'd battled Tory recalcitrants for the last ten years.

Chapter Twenty-One

Despairingly certain she had done her work well, and that Christopher was lost to her for ever, a listless Ellie reclined on the sofa in Maggie's sitting room the following morning, attempting to read the paper. She'd scanned the same article three times when, after a knock, Dawkins entered.

Scolding herself for the hope that had flared within, she was trying to compose herself when the man, a rare smile on his lips, walked over to her. 'This came for you, Miss Parmenter,' he said, holding out a wrapped package.

A package with a single hothouse white rose tied on top. Opening it, Ellie found a volume of Shakespeare's love poems, bound in beautiful leather with gilt lettering that would have excited Artis's envy. Inside was a note—from Christopher, addressed to 'My dear Miss

Wanstead', telling her he intended to call upon her later.

A white rose—symbol of beauty and purity. A classic book, with devotion its theme. Perfectly acceptable gifts, laden with double meanings, for a gentleman intent on wooing a respectable maiden.

Amusement warred with anguish. It appeared he hadn't taken her refusal as final. Though it must be. Even if it were true that marrying her would not ruin his political career, such a union would hardly be as advantageous for him as wedding a respectable maiden with a large dowry and important family contacts.

Still, she wasn't sure how well she'd be able to maintain a façade of disinterest, were he to continue to press her—when she wanted him and loved him so desperately.

If he did call, she would tell Dawkins not to admit him.

Decision made, she leaned forward in her chair, cradling the soft leather volume in her lap as she inhaled the sweet scent of the rose— sweet as the love that filled her, and as soon to be lost for ever.

Morning turned to afternoon with no inter-ruption, Giles being away from home at a meeting, Maggie feeling unwell and keeping to her bed. After taking a light nuncheon on a tray in the sitting room, Ellie walked to the library and browsed the shelves, looking for something to take her mind off the constant wonder over whether Christopher would in fact seek her out.

Dawkins already knew to deny her, if he did appear. Would that refusal be enough to discourage him for good?

She hoped so, for with every new entreaty, her resolve to resist him weakened. Even now, she had to shut her mind to the insidious voices murmuring that he knew the political world better than she did, and if he felt marrying her wouldn't ruin his political future, she should believe him. Smash down the euphoria that kept trying to rise up at the notion that he did in fact think her good enough to become his wife. For if she truly believed marrying him would not cause him harm…

But he *was* a politician, and would present the argument most likely to convince the opposition, she argued back, pushing away the temptation to capitulate.

Were Maggie not so ill, she might have asked her opinion. But after the maid told her Maggie could scarcely lift her head without being overcome by nausea, she didn't want to intrude.

With an exasperated sigh, she grabbed a volume at random and turned to take it back to the sitting room. Then gasped, to find Christopher standing on the library's threshold.

'I... I told Dawkins to send you away.'

'He tried to. I ignored him. And since I have about ten stone and twenty years on him, he eventually gave way.'

Not asking her permission, he advanced into the room. Attired, she couldn't help notice, in immaculate day wear, as if he'd just stepped from the pages of a gentleman's magazine, that thick gold hair she longed to run her fingers through carefully brushed back, and those eyes—ah, those eyes that always sent a ripple of longing through her focused on her with such yearning, she could hardly breathe.

Without noticing how she got there, she found herself seated. 'Though I appreciate the gifts, they were really unnecessary. You don't need any more practice. As I said in my note, you've quite mastered the art of courtship.'

'Quite obviously I haven't, if the maiden I wish to court refused to receive me. I need a good deal more practice to win the heart of the lady I love above all else. Above career, if it came to that—but it won't. Above friends and family, should it come to that—but it won't. For they already love you, almost as much as I do. And they would rejoice, if you would do me the honour of accepting my hand.'

Finding it harder and harder to resist, she said, 'You can't know your friends would accept it.'

'But I can. I told Giles and Maggie last night that I intended to marry you. They were both delighted. Maggie even kissed me. And if Giles approves, as focused as he is on getting our Reform Bill through the Lords, you can be assured he doesn't think marrying you will impair my effectiveness in Parliament.'

The hope she'd been ferociously squelching rebounded, fighting her attempt to control it. 'You…you are sure?'

'I am. Now it just remains to convince the lady that I cannot live without her.' Before she could think what to reply, he paced over, pulled her up into his arms, and kissed her.

There was nothing tender or tentative in it, but an all-out assault on her senses intended to beguile, ravish and reduce her to complete surrender. Helpless before it and the onslaught of her own desire, she opened to him, welcoming the sweep of his tongue as he claimed her mouth, kissing her deeply, intensely, in a way that said she belonged to him alone. She revelled in it, kissing back just as fervently, already aching for his touch in every part of her body.

When finally they broke the kiss, they were both dizzy and breathless. His arm about her, he eased her down on the sofa and sat beside her, then kissed her again. This time, his touch was so gentle and cherishing, she almost wept with tenderness of it.

'You see,' he whispered, 'there is only one Virtuous Virgin for me. But as a former rake, I will need a great deal of practice to learn to properly cherish her. A lifetime's work, probably. I know you care about me, despite what you claimed. Will you give me that lifetime to earn your love, my sweet?'

'Oh, Christopher, I've loved you since the night you found me at that masquerade ball. Much as I've tried to fight against it, everything we've shared since has only deepened the emotion. Besides, I did promise to teach you everything,' she added, still having trouble comprehending the marvellous truth that they would be able to share their love openly after all. Such happiness began filling her, she felt one body could not contain it all. 'You know I never go back on my promises.'

'I'll take that as a yes,' he said, and claimed her mouth again.

Epilogue

On a fine August morning four months later, Christopher and his new wife joined the other Hadley's Hellions in the reception room at Giles and Maggie's town house, the friends bearing gifts to honour the christening of the Lyndlingtons' new daughter.

'How lovely she is,' Ellie murmured, looking over to where the proud papa stood by the hearth, cradling the baby on his shoulder.

Christopher put a hand protectively over Ellie's stomach, its slightly rounded form concealed beneath the full skirt of her gown. 'As beautiful as our child will be, my heart,' he whispered, kissing her ear. 'As beautiful as you've made my life. Why did I resist marriage for so long?'

'You were waiting for me,' she replied with a smile. 'But let's not announce our happy news yet. This day is for Giles, Maggie, and Liliana.'

'Isn't she perfect?' the proud papa declared, as they walked over to join the others. 'As beautiful as her mama.'

'And twice as loud,' Maggie said, slipping her hand in her husband's arm.

David Tanner Smith, his arm around his petite wife Faith, raised a glass of champagne. 'Can you believe it was almost eleven years ago to this day when, soon after Giles invited me to join your group at Oxford, we embraced the name "Hellions" and vowed to reform Parliament?'

'Indeed it was!' Ben Tawny said, his wife Alyssa at his side. 'So now the cycle is complete. The Reform Bill has passed through the Lords, even reprobate Christopher has found fulfilment in marriage with his lovely Ellie, and we have a new generation to carry on our work.'

'Giles has a *daughter*, Ben,' Christopher reminded.

'Which just means your work is not yet done,' Alyssa said. 'Until Maggie's daughter—'

'And her mother and all her aunties,' Maggie inserted.

'Win the right to aid in determining her country's future, just as the men of England now can,' Alyssa finished.

'Who could argue with that assessment?' Ellie asked, giving her husband a pointed look.

Laughing, Christopher held up his hands in a gesture of surrender. 'Certainly not me! Let us toast then, gentleman. To the Hellions—eleven years of friendship and achievement. To our wives, who have made us complete and our work worth accomplishing. And to the next generation of Hellion sons and daughters, who will carry on the work we've begun.'

'To the Hellions,' they said, raising their glasses.

'And to the best prize of all, my precious wife,' Christopher murmured, bending down to give Ellie a kiss.

* * * * *

If you enjoyed this story you won't want to miss the other three books in the HADLEY'S HELLIONS *quartet from Julia Justiss*

FORBIDDEN NIGHTS WITH THE VISCOUNT STOLEN ENCOUNTERS WITH THE DUCHESS CONVENIENT PROPOSAL TO THE LADY

MILLS & BOON®

&HISTORICAL

AWAKEN THE ROMANCE OF THE PAST

A sneak peek at next month's titles...

In stores from 5th October 2017:

- **Courting Danger with Mr Dyer** – Georgie Lee
- **His Mistletoe Wager** – Virginia Heath
- **An Innocent Maid for the Duke** – Ann Lethbridge
- **The Viking Warrior's Bride** – Harper St. George
- **Scandal and Miss Markham** – Janice Preston
- **Western Christmas Brides** – Lauri Robinson, Lynna Banning *and* Carol Arens

0917/04

MILLS & BOON®

EXCLUSIVE EXTRACT

Spy Bartholomew Dyer is forced to enlist the help of
Moira, Lady Rexford, who jilted him five years ago.
He's determined not to succumb to her charms *again*,
because Bart suspects it's not just their lives at risk—
it's their hearts…

Read on for a sneak preview of
COURTING DANGER WITH MR DYER

Bart longed to slide across the squabs and sit beside
Moira, to slip his hands around her waist and claim her
lips, but he remained where he was. If he could give
her all the things the far-off look in her eyes said she
wanted, he would, but he wasn't a man for marriage and
children. To take her into his arms would be to lead her
into a lie. Deception was too much a part of his life
already and he refused to deceive her. 'I'm sure you'll
find a man worthy of your heart.'

'I hope so, but sometimes it's difficult to imagine,
especially when I see all the other young ladies.' She
picked at the embroidery on her dress. 'I don't have
their daring, or their ability to flirt and make a spectacle
out of myself to catch a man's eye.'

'You may not make a spectacle of yourself, but you
certainly have their daring and a courage worthy of any
soldier on the battlefield.'

This brought a smile to her face, but it was one of
embarrassment. She tilted her head down and looked up

at him through her eyelashes, innocent and alluring all at the same time. 'Now I see why they only allow male judges on the bench. No female judge could withstand your flattery.'

'Perhaps, but a man is as easy to flatter as a woman, one just has to do it a little differently.'

She leaned forward, her green eyes sparkling with a wit he wished to see more of. 'And how does one flatter you, Bart?'

He leaned forward, resting his elbow on his thigh and bringing his face achingly close to hers. He could wipe the playful smirk off her lips with a kiss, taste again her sensual mouth and the heady excitement of desire he'd experienced with her five years ago. Except he was no longer young and thoughtless and neither was she. He'd experienced the consequences of forgetting himself with her once before. He had no desire to repeat the mistake again, no matter how tempting it might be. There was a great deal more at stake this time than his heart.

Don't miss
COURTING DANGER WITH MR DYER
By Georgie Lee

Available October 2017
www.millsandboon.co.uk